THE BEST OF US

USA TODAY BESTSELLING AUTHOR

KENNEDY FOX

I woulda walked through hell
To find another way

I woulda laid me down
If I knew that you would stay

I woulda crossed the stars
To keep you in my life

But now I'm falling hard
Without you here tonight

"Walked Through Hell"
-Anson Seabra

CHAPTER ONE

KENDALL

Day 1

I WHEEL my two large suitcases down the hallway and place them by the front door. I'm equally nervous and excited about spending today and tomorrow with my best friend's brother, Ryan. It's not a romantic getaway in any sense, but rather the complete opposite. Cami and Eli are planning to honeymoon at the cabin, and Ryan and I have been put in charge of getting it ready. He's on his way to pick me up now.

Not that I've ever admitted it out loud, but I've had a crush on him for as long as I can remember. Even if he's never been able to hold a conversation with me without pissing me off, there's always been an underlying attraction. Maybe this weekend will be different or at least that's what I hope, but Ryan openly despises me. I've dealt with him over the years because Cami's been my ride or die since we were in grade school.

Ryan treats me like a spoiled rich princess who has been given everything on a silver platter. While there's truth in it, there's more to me than my family's money or the way I look. I didn't choose my parents and didn't ask to receive such a significant inheritance from my grandparents. Regardless, he's dead set on judging me for things I have zero control over.

In a few weeks, Cami will marry Ryan's best friend, Eli. Because Eli wants to make it a honeymoon to remember, he asked me to help decorate and stock the cabin with all her favorite things before they arrive. Somehow, the two of them convinced Ryan to join me so I wouldn't have to do it alone. Considering he's a doctor with a packed schedule, I'm shocked he found time, but I'm also not complaining.

While trying to keep busy, I go through my list to make sure I got everything Eli requested—chocolate, extra Christmas decorations, sparkling water, and enough booze to last two weeks. I just hope it all fits in Ryan's Range Rover because I went overboard, but I'd do anything to make my best friend's honeymoon magical.

Just as I finish double-checking my list, my phone vibrates. I see a text from Ryan, and nervous energy soars through me.

Ryan: I'll be there in fifteen. Got stuck in some traffic.

I'm not sure what to think about him joining me. Maybe a night alone will allow me to prove that I'm more than a pretty face with money. Considering he's a St. James, he understands what it's like to be raised by an elite family, so he's not impressed by the glitz and glam. He's humble and wanted a different life, another reason he went to medical school.

Regardless of our differences, we're going to have to find a happy medium this weekend because he's the best man, and I'm the maid of honor. Over the next few weeks, we're going to spend time together, even if he's the definition of stubborn.

I'm almost tempted to drink a glass of wine before he gets here to calm me down but decide against it. Instead, I grab one of my favorite bottles of Merlot and set it next to my suitcases, then text Cami as I wait.

Kendall: Your brother's on his way.

Cami: OMG! Hopefully, you two don't murder each other in the cabin.

Kendall: As long as he's on his best behavior, I think we'll be perfectly fine.

Cami: If he's a dickhead, let me know, and I'll threaten his life.

I snort-laugh because Cami can be ferocious at times. As we're texting back and forth, I hear a vehicle outside, then a hard knock on the door.

Kendall: He's here. I'll let you know when we make it to the cabin.

Cami: Perfect! I hope the three-hour drive isn't too painful. Pee before you leave! Ryan hates stopping.

Kendall: Noted.

After tucking my phone in my back pocket, I swing the door open. Ryan's wearing a heavy jacket and slacks. His hair is messy in a way that makes me want to run my fingers through it.

"Kendall." The way he says my name in his gravelly tone has my panties nearly melting off. I have to force myself not to step closer because he smells so damn good.

Thankfully, confidence is one of my strengths, so I act as if his presence isn't a big deal. I smile and meet his honey-colored eyes. "Ryan. Nice to see you again. Oh, come in. I have everything stacked here that needs to go."

I step aside, giving him space to enter. He glances around, and his eyes widen at the pile. When I told Eli I was born to decorate and plan for this honeymoon, I meant it.

"You're not serious." He turns to me, eyebrows raised.

I play stupid, though I know what he's referring to. "Whatcha mean?"

He huffs like I've lost my damn mind. "Two oversized suitcases plus all of this? There's no way it's going to fit. How many clothes do you need for two days?"

I narrow my eyes at him, wondering if he's done with this conversation because I am.

"One suitcase only," he insists.

"Absolutely not. Both are coming with me," I argue. "This isn't up for discussion."

"This is ridiculous, Kendall. We're going up today and will be there tomorrow, and then we're leaving. We won't even be leaving the cabin, and I don't care what you wear."

"Don't flatter yourself. What I wear is not for *you*, but for me. I like to have plenty of options." I give him a shit-eating grin, trying not to let Ryan get under my skin, but he's already buried himself there. If he pisses me off before we leave, the drive across New York is going to be painful as hell.

"Options?" He rolls his eyes. It takes every bit of patience I have left not to tell him to quit being an asshole. He seems to be in a mood today, but it's not any different from any other time I've been around him.

I slip on my peacoat as he mumbles under his breath. Taking my time, I put on my gloves and matching knit hat. The temperatures have steadily dropped all week, and later today, it's supposed to start snowing again.

Impatiently, he taps his foot and watches me. I grab my suitcases and pull out the handles. "Coming?" I ask over my shoulder.

"I'll be shocked if all this shit fits," he repeats like I didn't hear his grumbles the first time.

All I can do is laugh. "I guess we'll see, won't we? Also, you

THE BEST OF US

can stop complaining now. Remember, this *shit* isn't for me. It's for *your* sister and best friend so suck it up, buttercup. We're making it special for *them*."

Ryan glares at me, then picks up one of the boxes of non-perishable foods and follows me. I made sure to buy enough non-perishables to last for two weeks. I also had fresh meat cut and sealed, then froze it. To make sure it doesn't defrost while we travel, I put it in an ice chest with dry ice. If he knows what's best, he'll make sure nothing's left behind.

When I step outside, the frigid air slaps me across the face. I guess I didn't realize how chilly it had gotten since earlier today when I finished shopping. Considering I hate being cold, it lights a fire under my ass to load the SUV as fast as possible. Ryan pops the hatch to the Range Rover, and after he sets the box down, he loads my suitcases.

"Holy shit," he mutters as he lifts them one after another.

"I packed my extra heavy dildos." I laugh, giving him a hard time. He doesn't say a word. I'll try my best to go easy on him, but he's making it difficult with his glares and groans.

After a few trips, all the food is loaded. At least three more boxes remain, plus the cooler with frozen meat. While we'll only be staying a few days, I bought food for us too so we wouldn't have to dip into Cami and Eli's stash. I made sure to get all my best friend's favorite snacks and more pasta choices than she can handle.

"You do know the cabin has a pantry full of items like this, right?" Ryan tells me as he stacks the final box on top of the others.

"And what's your point?" I glare at him.

He opens the top and pulls out a glass jar of marinara, Alfredo, then sees the vermicelli, angel hair, and spaghetti noodles. "The point is you probably didn't need to purchase all of this. How much can two people realistically eat in that amount of time?"

"And this is why they didn't ask you to go shopping," I snap.

"Damn. There's enough alcohol in here to open a bar." He studies me.

"All of it was *highly* requested. If you keep it up, I might have to open a bottle and drink it on the way there." I turn and walk back inside, not giving him the opportunity to respond.

I grab the strands of lights I want to wrap around the staircase along with the mistletoe for the entryways. Cami had conveniently mentioned a ten-foot Christmas tree and ornaments were stored in the basement, so I didn't buy one. By the time I'm done decorating the cabin, it will look like a winter wonderland escape. She's going to be so excited, and the thought makes me smile.

When the Range Rover is loaded, I notice a small duffel bag on the floorboard. Knowing that's all Ryan packed makes me snort. He's so damn efficient that he probably only brought one change of clothes for tomorrow. Meanwhile, I've got enough outfits to last me three weeks. I often allow my mood to decide my clothing choice, and I never know how I'm going to feel. So, options. It could be a legging type of day with running shoes or a pair of expensive slacks with heels. I never know.

After I make one last look around to make sure I didn't forget anything, I grab another bottle of wine because I'm going to need it, set the security alarm, then lock the door. Ryan's waiting inside the SUV, and once I climb in, I turn on the heated seat. A chill runs through me as he backs out of the driveway. His GPS is already set for Roxbury, and it says we should arrive around three.

Once we're out of my neighborhood, I suck in a deep breath when I realize I didn't bring any snacks with me. It's a total fail on my part.

I turn to Ryan, wearing a sweet smile. "Do you think we can stop and get some coffee before we leave civilization?" I'm already mentally making my order of a skinny mocha with extra whip cream and a pumpkin loaf just in case I get hungry. My mouth waters thinking about it.

"Absolutely not." Ryan doesn't even look at me.

"Wait, seriously?" My mouth falls open because I can't be without coffee, especially on a trip this long. Plus, it's cold as fuck outside, and a hot drink makes it all better.

"We're *not* stopping, Kendall," he says flatly without hesitation, and I realize he's not joking. If I had known he was going to be this much of an asshole, I would've just driven myself. I'm so frustrated I bite my tongue before I say something I regret. Trying to calm down, I force myself to stare out the window, but I can't stop dreaming about mochas and warm bread.

This might be the most painful three hours of my life.

When he turns on the radio, and I hear a bunch of doctors discussing medical procedures in full detail, I'm convinced I'm living in my own personal hell.

At times like this, I wished I carried a corkscrew in my purse, because if I had one, I'd open that wine I packed right now.

CHAPTER TWO

RYAN

KENDALL CAN WHINE all she wants, but she should've come fully prepared. One of my biggest pet peeves when traveling is stopping. If it takes thirty minutes, that's too much time wasted, and I just want to get to the cabin so I can get this weekend over with.

The *only* reason I agreed is because my best friend Eli asked me to join Kendall so she wouldn't be alone in the big house by herself. It was important to him, and I want my sister to be happy on her honeymoon, so I said yes. I should've known Kendall was going to go overboard with her shopping, but I tried to give her the benefit of the doubt.

After we're out of the city, Kendall reaches over and turns off the radio. I glance over at her, and she gives me a death glare. "I can't handle listening to this for the next two hours, so we're going to have to compromise."

I turn it back on. "Trust me when I say this *is* compromising."

She lets out a growl, and I wonder if she's going to knock the shit out of me by how angry she becomes. Reactions like this aren't new for me. Considering Kendall and Cami have been best friends for as long as I can remember, I'm used to her tantrums. They're each other's ride or die, and growing up, she was always around. If Cami wasn't at her house, Kendall was at ours, and they're still just as close.

Somehow Kendall was able to stay out of the eye of the paparazzi. Cami wasn't so lucky and basically had her teenage years documented in photos. It's another reason I was so adamant about breaking away from the glitz and glam of being a St. James. While I could've lived off my parents' money for the rest of my life, I'm wired differently than most who grew up in a family like mine.

An underlying current has always streamed between us, and it's why I've kept my distance. I never wanted to become a wedge between her and Cami's friendship, plus we're completely opposite. I want to be with someone who aspires to do more in life than look pretty. I need substance in a relationship, and she's too vain to understand that.

We ride in silence for the rest of the drive. Eventually, her breathing slows, and I glance over, noticing how peaceful she looks sleeping. The closer we get to Roxbury, the harder the snow starts to fall, and we drive into a whiteout. I change the radio to the local weather station to get an update.

"Massive snowfall happening in Upstate New York. If you're on the roads, be careful. We'll be right back after this message from our advertisers," the announcer says.

"Great," I mutter. I turn it off and focus on the road. I knew it would be snowing, but I thought we'd miss most of it. Kendall stirs, and her eyes flutter open. Immediately, she repositions herself in the seat, and her mouth falls open.

"How long has it been like this?" she asks, looking at me.

"About twenty minutes. It's progressively getting worse, but I'm not pulling over because I don't think we can wait it out. Want to look at a radar for me?"

She sarcastically laughs. "Uhh."

I hand her my phone and unlock it, then tell her which app to open. She does and shows me the screen once it's loaded. All I see is pink and blue, which means heavy snowfall. "Great."

"What? What does it mean?" The concern in her tone isn't lost on me.

"Basically, we need to take it slow so we make it there safely. Looks like it might be like this the rest of the way."

She sits up straighter and glances at the GPS. Worry washes across her face, but I stay calm. Her reaction is almost predictable because she doesn't typically leave her precious castle unless she absolutely has to. Kendall's the kind of woman who wouldn't risk breaking a nail or getting her designer shoes dirty.

"Trust me. I won't let anything happen to you. We're only an hour away, so I think it's best we continue instead of turning around."

"I agree. One hour this way is better than two hours the other with a storm chasing us back to the city." She keeps her eyes focused on the road even though it's barely visible.

"And this is the only time I have off before the wedding activities start, so it's kind of a now or never thing."

For the next half hour, I hold the steering wheel with white knuckles as I navigate down the winding one-lane roads. While driving conditions aren't ideal, I'm happy we left when we did, or we could've possibly had to pull over and wait it out. Not something I ever want to do because the conditions can turn very quickly, and the last thing I want is to be stranded in a car for hours.

When we're ten minutes away from the cabin, our phones alerts buzz.

"What's it say?" I ask.

Kendall unlocks her phone and reads it to me. "Basically, there's an arctic blast, and they're predicting a lot of snow. Roads are closing too."

When I finally turn into the driveway, relief floods through me because I was growing more concerned. I open the garage and pull in so we don't have to unload in this weather.

"I'm so happy we're here," she admits and gets out. The wind howls, and a shiver runs through me. It's much colder here than it was in the city.

"Guess we should start unpacking," I tell her as I unlock the cabin door and turn on the lights and heat.

When I walk back to her, she's wheeling her suitcases toward me.

"You get the heavy stuff," she snickers. "It's why you're here."

I pop an eyebrow at her but keep my thoughts to myself as she passes me, and damn, she smells so good. We make several trips until everything is unloaded. As we put the ridiculous amount of groceries she bought where they belong, I bump into her several times.

"Sorry," I say, grabbing her arm to keep her steady. For a moment, I think her breath hitches, but then she smiles.

"I got this," she tells me, brushing her body against mine before walking into the pantry again. "You weren't lying when you said there was a ton of food here, but I'm glad I grabbed what I did. Cami won't eat half of this," she explains.

I lean against the doorframe and watch her with my arms crossed over my chest.

Kendall points at the jars of caviar and oysters. "She'd rather starve than eat any of this."

"If she were hungry, she'd eat it. Anyone would." My parents always keep the house stocked with their favorite things, and since Cami loves visiting so much some of her staples are here too, but not enough to last for as long as she and Eli plan to stay.

"Hey, instead of standing around, do you think you can get the Christmas tree from the basement? Cami mentioned it being stored there."

I glare at her. "Do you have any idea how old that tree is? I wouldn't be surprised if it has dry rot."

"I don't care if it's covered in dust bunnies. We'll make it work, or you'll be going out in the snow and cutting me a fresh one. I'm not kidding." Kendall gives me a pointed look.

"Don't forget that I'm not one of your parents' workers that you can just boss around," I warn. "I'm here for my sister and best friend, that's it."

She lets out a sarcastic laugh. "Whatever you say, Ryan."

Kendall finishes stuffing the shelves, then goes back to the kitchen and packs the freezer and fridge. Though I don't want to go down to the basement, I do because the quicker we get everything set up, the faster we can leave. Instead of wasting any more time, I take the stairs to the lower floor two at a time.

Once I'm in the storage area of the basement, I click on the light switch and glance around. It's like a time capsule in here with old holiday decorations and old furniture. There's a thin layer of dust that I'll need to mention to my parents so their cleaning company can make sure they take care of this the next time they're out. The last time I was down here was over a decade ago.

After I find the gigantic tree, I search around for the old ornaments. When we were kids and Dad wanted to get away from the business, we'd escape to the cabin. Cami and I always loved it here because it was different from what we were used to. After Mom decided she wanted a newer, more updated place, we started visiting there more often, but Cami still comes as much as she can.

There're at least four giant plastic tubs full of ornaments, but considering I have no idea what Kendall has in mind, I only bring the tree because that's all she asked for. As soon as I set it down by the couch, Kendall walks in with her hair pulled up into a ponytail.

"Oh wow," she says after she unzips the tree bag. The lights flicker, and Kendall turns and meets my eyes. "Uhh."

Immediately, our phones buzz, and we both look at another weather alert.

WIND CHILL WARNING: VERY COLD AIR AND WIND WILL CREATE DANGEROUSLY LOW WINDCHILL VALUES EXPECTED OVER THE NEXT THREE DAYS ACROSS

WARNED AREA. PLEASE BE ADVISED OF ROAD CLOSURES DUE TO EXCESSIVE AMOUNTS OF SNOWFALL DUE TO THE ARCTIC BLAST. TEMPERATURES COULD PLUNGE FROM 10 TO -30 BY TOMORROW AND RECORD-BREAKING AMOUNTS OF SNOWFALL PREDICTED. TAKE PROPER PRECAUTIONS.

"Fuck," I mutter, then walk to the large windows in the living room and notice how bad it's gotten outside. The lights blip off, then come back on.

"Will we lose power?" Kendall asks.

"As long as the winds don't get any stronger, I think we'll be okay."

"We better be. I'm not prepared for a camping trip." Kendall continues scrolling through her phone.

"I can't imagine you camping, ever," I say.

She groans. "What's that supposed to mean?"

"You're just not the *type* of person to do outdoor things. I'm sure your version of camping is staying at the Four Seasons."

Her jaw clenches. "Sometimes you're such a dickhead."

"But am I wrong?" I push.

Kendall shakes her head and storms into the kitchen. I get my duffel and go upstairs to the room I typically stay in. Since Kendall is such a queen, she can have the master bedroom with the amazing bathroom. I'm fine in my peasant quarters.

When I enter my room, I try to remember the last time I was here. It's been a while, though Eli stayed in this room when he quarantined with Cami. When I think back to that time, it makes me sick. Watching so many people suffer fucked me up, and while a vaccine has finally been approved for mass distribution, what I saw during that time never left me. I've always loved my job, but I wasn't trained to deal with something of that nature. I lost a lot of patients as well as some colleagues, and I felt like I didn't sleep for weeks. Hell, months even.

I was numb for most of it just to get through the day.

After I've unpacked the small number of clothes I brought with me, I go back downstairs.

Kendall's sitting at the bar on her phone as she eats a salad. I open the packed fridge and look around.

"What can I eat in here?" I ask.

"You're smart, figure it out," she snaps, but I know a lot of these things aren't for us. Instead of asking again, I pull out some mayo and lunch meat. There's a loaf of bread on the counter, so I open it. I set a plate down on the bar, making the messiest looking sandwich ever, but it'll do the job. Kendall stares, silently judging my masterpiece of a meal, then goes back to her phone.

After I'm done eating, I rinse my plate and place it in the dishwasher, then go to the living room and check the amount of firewood we have. There's enough to last us a while, but considering we'll only be here a few days, I don't bother looking to see if there's more in the shed.

Plopping on the couch, I turn on the weather channel so I can get an update. I'm balanced on the edge of the couch watching how dangerous the conditions have become, and I'm worried it might linger. This storm needs to pass quickly so I can get back to the city. Kendall enters moments later, and from my peripheral, I can see her watching too. She lets out a long sigh.

Eventually, she sits, but she's on the opposite end of the large sectional couch. I know I've pissed her off, but she'll get over it. I won't suck up to her or stroke her ego like everyone else does. There's no way I'll be kissing the ground she walks on, and if she thought that'd happen, she's sadly mistaken.

After a few hours of watching TV, I yawn. I've been up since four because I went to the hospital and worked a few hours before I picked up Kendall. Eventually, she gets up and grabs her two suitcases, then struggles to get them up the stairs.

"You want some help?" I ask.

After she shoots me a glare from over her shoulder, she continues to lug her heavy ass luggage to the top floor.

"No," she barks.

"Master bedroom is yours," I yell, and when I hear the door slam, I know she heard me.

"Good night to you too," I mumble to myself, then turn off the TV and lights. Before going upstairs, I check the thermostat and set the heat higher because the outside temperature is still dropping. As I climb the stairs, I laugh knowing I can still get under her skin. The next few days are going to be interesting.

CHAPTER THREE

KENDALL

DAY 2

AFTER THE DAY I had yesterday, it feels nice to sleep in. As soon as I throw off the covers, I hear the wind howling against the cabin and see nothing but snow. The huge master suite overlooks the mountains, but right now, I can hardly see anything outside. It's a complete whiteout.

"Oh shit," I mutter, realizing there's no way we're leaving later today. Surrounded by trees and mountains with a long private driveway, the cabin is twenty miles away from Roxbury. It's the perfect getaway for a romantic honeymoon, but there's nothing romantic about being stuck here with Ryan. Instead, he acts as if it's his own personal hell.

It's definitely not normal to get this much snow this time of year. Usually this happens closer to Christmas and into January and February, but hardly ever mid-November. This rare arctic blast will probably keep me stuck here with Ryan longer than either of us intended.

After I throw on a sweater and slide on my slippers, I go downstairs for coffee. As soon as I enter the kitchen, I see Ryan at the table on his phone with his laptop.

"Dude, I think we're stranded here," Ryan says to whoever he's talking to, and he doesn't sound happy. He looks miserable too.

Great.

"No, the main road is snowed over. It's so bad they won't be able to get the plows out for a few days, and apparently, the news said they expect more snow to come. I had to take a few emergency vacation days from work. We got twenty inches so far, and it's still coming down. The wind is brutal, so it's just fucking blowing everywhere. Even if the roads were open, I wouldn't be able to see it."

Twenty inches? Jesus.

It's confirmation that we're not leaving anytime soon.

I grab a mug and pour myself some of the already brewed coffee. He's still chatting with who I assume is Eli or Cami.

After I grab some creamer from the fridge, I continue listening to his conversation.

Ryan releases a huff. "Thanks. I just wanted to let you two know so you don't get worried about us. Hopefully, we don't lose power. With my luck, an ice storm would make its way here too."

Lose power? Oh hell no. I can't be here without power. We'll just have to shovel our way out if that happens.

I sit at the breakfast bar with my coffee and scroll through my phone when I hear Ryan whisper, "Yeah, she's a fucking trip."

Wow. I haven't done anything, and he's already being rude as hell.

After he ends the call, he goes back to typing on his computer. His forehead wrinkles and face contorts, which makes me wonder if he's getting weather updates. If so, it's not looking good.

"Sounds like you're stuck with me for a bit longer," I say, hoping to break the awkward tension. "Won't be so bad. You'll get a few days off. Maybe take advantage of it and relax for once. Could also work on getting the stick out of your ass." I hold back a laugh knowing he'll probably ignore me for that last comment.

"Easy for you to say," he mutters. "Not everyone lives off their family's money. Some of us have jobs to do. I'm sure your biggest concern is getting to the nail salon on time every day."

"Really?" I snap my gaze toward him. "That's the best you got? How original." I roll my eyes though he's not looking at me. "For your information, I go every other week, and it's *far* from my biggest concern, asshole."

I hate that he thinks he knows me when he clearly doesn't. He's never even tried, yet he acts as though he has me figured out.

"Well, maybe if you had job aspirations and goals at your age, being stuck here would be a concern. It—"

"At my age?" I interrupt. "So because I'm twenty-four, I should have the rest of my life all planned out? And if I don't, I'm a slacker?"

He clears his throat, finally glancing at me. "I didn't say slacker, but that it might be hard for you to understand that I enjoy working. Being a doctor is who I am, and knowing I can't be at the hospital with my patients worries me. Not that you care."

"Don't put words in my mouth. I said to relax, which you're incapable of doing. Considering you can't do anything about being stuck here with a '*fucking trip*,' you might as well take advantage of the time off. But you know what?" I stand, grabbing my mug. There's no emotion in his face as I scowl at him. "Be miserable all you want. Alone."

I march toward the stairs and don't look back. He can sulk by himself. Just because I don't have an intense career doesn't mean I'm a worthless trust fund baby. If he'd bothered to ask or tried to get to know me, he'd learn there's a lot more to me than that. He's just like everyone else and has formed his opinions about me based on what he sees on the surface.

Once I'm in my room, I decide to take a bath in the jet tub while finishing my coffee. Cami always has it stocked with a variety of bath bombs, lavender oil, candles, and bubble baths. It's just what I need after Ryan ruined my morning.

I pair my phone with the Bluetooth speakers in the wall and

jam out to Halsey, who I have a major girl crush on. Her voice soothes me as I soak in the tub.

After a while, I decide to FaceTime my sister, Piper, to let her know I'll be here longer than expected. She's three years younger than me and a famous YouTube star. It's kinda funny because we're so opposite. I prefer to stay out of the limelight, and Piper lives for it. She's a perky, blond lifestyle vlogger and a natural extrovert. While I'd rather stay behind the camera, there are times when she's had me in her vlogs.

"Hey, what's up? I'm doing a live video on Instagram," she answers.

"Well, excuse me," I mock. "I just wanted to talk to my sister. So I'm stuck in Roxbury."

She looks into the other phone mounted on a tripod stand. Piper takes so many pictures and social media videos, she had to get a work phone so she could use her personal cell for calls and texts. "Okay, guys. I'll be back shortly for my 'get ready with me.' Love you!" Then she blows kisses before ending it.

"What's going on? You're stuck in Roxbury."

I snicker, shaking my head. "You're so extra." I give her my best kissy lips.

"Shut up." She flips her long hair and pouts. "Now tell me what happened."

"We got twenty inches of snow, and we're basically stuck here until they can plow the roads. It could be days, and Ryan isn't happy about it. Let me correct myself…" I clear my throat dramatically. "He's not happy about being stuck with *me*."

"Why would it take days?"

"We're on a private road, and it's on the outskirts of town, like in the mountain area. It's not a priority. Plus, Roxbury's population is like two thousand. They probably have one snowplow."

She chuckles. "True."

"And we're supposed to get more snow. When I looked out this morning, I could hardly see a thing. It's windy too."

"So yeah, you're definitely stuck there for a bit. Now tell me about Ryan being a jackass."

I snort because I've told her about Cami's brother a few times. She knows I think he's attractive, but his pissy attitude and dull personality ruin it for me. He's always been on the serious side, but since the pandemic started, he's changed a lot. Working in the ER at one of the largest hospitals in the city means he saw the worst of it.

"He called me a *fucking trip* when talking to Eli and Cami," I explain. "And he's just been super moody. I mentioned relaxing while he's here, and he blew up over it. Basically said I was a spoiled brat who had nothing to worry about."

"Wow…" She pops a piece of gum in her mouth and starts smacking her lips. "Sounds like he needs to get laid. Maybe you can help in that department." Piper waggles her brows.

"Yeah, that's not happening. He can't stand me. For whatever fucking reason."

"Sounds like this could be an opportunity to get him to like you. Show him the real Kendall Montgomery—inside and out." She shrugs, popping a bubble. "Both stranded in a mountain cabin surrounded by snow. Kinda sounds romantic to me."

I laugh, though not hating the idea. "Add in watching Hallmark movies by the fireplace and I'd be in."

"See? Worked for Cami."

"Yeah well, I'm not Cami. Eli was in love with her, so that's different. Ryan only sees me as his sister's annoying best friend. We're supposed to be decorating the cabin, but it looks like I'll be doing it alone since he's set on being an asshole."

"You have time to butter him up." Piper flashes a wink. "If you get my drift."

Rolling my eyes, I shake my head. "Yeah, I get your not so subtle hint."

"Mom's begging for grandchildren, and since I'm waiting till I'm forty, you'll have to take one for the team."

"I'm not getting knocked up just to make our mother happy!"

20

"Well, prepare for her to bombard you with 'your internal clock is ticking' reminders. I've been getting them for a year, and I'm only twenty-one!" Piper flashes an annoyed smile.

"Mom knows better, I guess. Probably thinks you'll be the first to have an oopsie pregnancy," I tease.

"Absolutely not!"

I take a drink of my coffee and realize it's starting to get cold, so I chug some more of it.

"Well, I better get back to my live stream so I can do my hair and makeup."

"Where are you going?" I ask, confused. "Did you get snow there too?"

"Yeah, but not as much as you. The roads should be cleared before noon." She flashes a shit-eating grin.

"Lucky." I groan.

We say our goodbyes after I promise to keep her updated. I need to text Cami next but decide to wait until after I'm out of the bath.

Once the water cools, I drain the tub and throw on a fluffy robe. My cup is empty, and I'll eventually have to go downstairs for food.

Kendall: Your brother's a jerk. Just thought I'd let you know.

Cami: What'd he do now?

Kendall: Snapped at me for no reason. So I told him off and walked away.

Cami: I'm sure he didn't mean to. He's under a lot of stress.

Kendall: That's no excuse to be rude. He made it very known how he feels about me, and it wasn't good.

Cami: I'm sorry. Just remember he's reserved and doesn't show emotion well. Just give him time to come around to the idea of being there with you. He'll open up.

I scoff.

Kendall: Doubt it, but I guess I'll try because I have no other choice. If I'm gonna be stuck here with nothing to do, I don't want to argue with him the whole time. But he needs to put in some effort too! It's not like I deserved his attitude. Well, I did say he had a stick up his ass...

Cami: Kendall!

Kendall: I was kidding! He can't take a joke?

Cami: I don't understand why you two fight. Probably because he likes you and is trying to push you away.

Kendall: HA! Now you're just being delirious.

Cami: You like him, or you wouldn't care what he thought.

Kendall: No. He's HOT. That doesn't mean I like him.

Cami: Whatever you say ;)

Kendall: This is your fault, ya know. You couldn't go to Hawaii for your honeymoon like a normal newlywed.

Cami: Nope :) The paps can find me too easily there anyway. I want pure privacy and romance. You two will have plenty of time to make it super special for us now!

Kendall: If he'll help. Right now, he's set on being miserable.

Cami: As I said, he'll come around.

Doubtful, but I guess time will tell, and it seems we'll have plenty of it. I just hope he doesn't think he can say mean things, then act like nothing's wrong like he used to do when I was a teenager.

CHAPTER FOUR

RYAN

Fuck.

I screwed up. Kendall overheard me talking to Eli, and I regret what I said. I was frustrated about the weather and not being able to work, but I shouldn't have taken it out on her. Especially since Kendall Montgomery is the poster child of happiness and has a genuine personality. She's never snapped at me like that before, and I hate admitting it turned me on a little.

As soon as Kendall walks away, I mentally slap myself. Those words hurt her, and that's the last thing I want to do. Once they left my mouth, I knew it was too late. Though she didn't think twice about putting me in my place and marching off. I thought about running after her, but I didn't want to risk her smacking me across the face.

I pour myself a cup of coffee and sit down with my laptop. Between checking the weather updates and work emails, I do some paperwork. I prefer being in the ER with my patients than trying to review results from afar. I love how fast a sixteen-hour shift flies by. I'm typically exhausted afterward but still struggle to fall asleep.

My life changed drastically two years ago when a pandemic

hit. It turned my life upside down, but it's still fresh in my brain. The things I witnessed still haunt my dreams. Hell, it haunts me when I'm awake too. Though the restrictions have lifted, I still take precautions since the vaccine is new.

Cami believes I have PTSD, and she might be right, but I'll deal with it on my own terms. Working and knowing I'm saving lives gets me through the dark days.

After a few hours, I get up to stretch my legs and look out the window. The wind howls as more snow falls. I can't see ten feet outside, and the weather channel says it won't clear up anytime soon.

I grab the loaf of bread and make myself a PB&J sandwich, then make another pot of coffee. I'm not used to doing nothing and find it hard to sit and relax. Luckily, I can read medical journals on my iPad and chat with my co-workers or my patients.

Once I've finished eating, I walk into the living room and stack more wood inside the fireplace before lighting it. Hopefully, Kendall comes down soon so I can apologize for being a dick. Maybe the smell of coffee and a fire will lure her.

Ten minutes later, I'm sitting at the table when Kendall enters. She doesn't look at me when she passes and goes straight to the fridge. She's wearing leggings and a baggy sweatshirt that hangs off her shoulder. Her dark, long hair is pulled up into one of those messy buns that looks really sexy. The Kendall Montgomery I know always has a full face of makeup, but she's bare-faced right now. Her natural pink lips and cheeks are hard not to notice. I love seeing her like this.

Awkward silence lingers in the air as she opens it and digs out food. I study her, wondering if this is how things will be between us the rest of our time here.

A few minutes pass, and neither of us speaks. I study the way she moves around the kitchen, momentarily fantasizing about bending her over the counter.

"What?" Kendall snaps, breaking me out of my trance. She

arches a brow, glaring at me. "Why are you watching me like a creep? What do you want?"

I clear my throat and stand, then walk toward her. "I'm sorry for what I said and how I acted earlier. I was out of line."

Kendall stares at me for a beat before shoving a piece of toast in her mouth. "Whatever." She shrugs before busying herself with cleaning the counter.

"Kendall," I plead. "Don't be stubborn. Either accept my apology or don't."

She furrows her brows. "Maybe you deserve to sweat it out. Maybe I will. Maybe I won't."

"Oh come on. I apologized. What else do you want?"

"I want you to get to know me instead of using the stereotypical crap you've heard against me."

I *know* her more than she realizes. While we've never hung out, she was with Cami so much that it was hard not to notice her. I learned a lot by observing even when I tried not to. She effortlessly crawled under my skin, and by the looks of it, she's still there.

"Alright," I say, taking a seat at the breakfast bar. She stands across from me and narrows her eyes. I continue, "I'm all ears."

"While you and the rest of the world think I'm a spoiled trust fund baby, I'm dedicating a lot of my time volunteering and giving back as much as I can. I know I'm privileged, but I'm not selfish like people assume. Aside from donating to charities and the homeless shelters in the city, I help struggling small businesses fundraise. I've hosted several events for free that were successful, which meant they didn't have to lay off their employees. I've helped with charity events that needed to fill tables too. What I do isn't for publicity, which is why you didn't know about it. I genuinely care about people and am not as self-centered as everyone makes me out to be. Before the lockdown, I served food at shelters every other weekend and on every major holiday. I've actually met a lot of people from all different walks of life and am learning what people struggle with the most. When I see people on the streets, I book hotel rooms so they can have a warm place to sleep for a few nights. Sure, I might not save lives, but I do what I can to make people's lives better."

"That's inspirational, Kendall," I say wholeheartedly. "I mean it."

"I don't do it for praise because it means more than that to me. I'm in the position to give, so I do my best."

I should've known Kendall was the type of person to donate her time and money. For the past decade, I was so focused on my career that I lost sight of who she is at her core.

"You should be proud. So many don't think twice about giving, and you're doing it regularly."

"I'm looking forward to serving them lunch on Thanksgiving since I couldn't last year because of the virus. My parents host a huge event at their home every year, and it gives me an excuse to skip." She shrugs modestly. "But really, I enjoy being at the shelter more. It's a no-judgment zone, and they're happy to just sit and chat with me."

I've treated thousands of people, including the homeless, and I know it's not easy for them. Over the years, I've seen my fair share of children and women who've escaped domestic abuse and need assistance to get back on their feet. Some great programs in the city focus on helping people get out of dangerous situations, and I'm sure they appreciate Kendall's efforts. The homeless communities were hit the hardest during the pandemic.

"Well I appreciate you sharing that with me," I tell her softly. "I'm sorry again. I mean it. I just hope you accept my apology since we're gonna be here for another few days."

The corner of her lips tilts up as if she's deciding. "I don't know. I kinda like having you by the balls."

My head falls back with laughter, something I haven't done in months.

"Alright, have it your way."

Before she can respond, my phone goes off. I glance down and see another weather warning.

"What's it say?" she asks as I unlock my cell.

"Shit," I mutter, reading over the words. "There's now a state of emergency in place due to the excess amounts of snowfall and ice caused by below zero temps and negative windchill. Another ten inches of snow is expected overnight."

"Jesus." She blows out a breath. "I can't remember ever seeing that much snow."

"More common in Upstate than in the city," I say. "And in these small mountain towns, it's common to be stranded for weeks waiting for roads to clear."

"*Weeks*?" she screeches.

"Yeah, I did some research this morning. It's been a while since they've experienced weather like this, but it happens."

"Of course it would be on the weekend we come up here." She sighs. "Oh well, I guess we'll just have to make the best of it. I mean, it could be worse. You could've been stuck with a crazy person." She flashes a wink, and I chuckle.

"Yeah, thank God." I snort. "Alright, we should prepare and get supplies together just in case we lose power." I tap my knuckles on the counter and stand. "Better to be ready instead of scrambling in the dark."

"Lose power?" Kendall's eyes widen in fear. "You said that on the phone, but doesn't the cabin have a generator?"

"Uh…" I scratch the back of my head. "A small one but I don't know if we have extra fuel. Even if we did, it'd only be enough to power the fridge for a day."

"Ugh, great." She brushes off her hands and wipes the counter, then puts her empty plate in the sink. "If it happens, how long do you think it'd be out?"

"It's hard to say," I tell her honestly. "It could be days until it's safe for crews to come out and fix the power lines, especially if the roads aren't clear."

"So what do we need to do?" she asks once she's done cleaning.

"Well, we'll need flashlights, extra batteries, candles, and matches. I think we have enough wood to last a while, but we'll have to sleep down here to stay warm if that happens. We should fill the tubs and sinks with water so we can flush."

"Wait…what? Hold up. What do you mean so we can flush?"

Kendall looks like she might have a panic attack. Her face goes pale, and she starts pacing.

I hold back a chuckle because I know she's freaking out, but it's a little funny. The girl has obviously never camped a day in her life and doesn't know how to be without electricity.

"If the power goes out, the well pump won't work, and you'll need to pour a bucket of water into the toilet so you can flush it."

"Great," she mutters, wrapping her arms around her waist. "What else? Will I have to hunt for our dinner and cook it over the fire too?"

My lips tilt up. "Not exactly but if the power's out long enough, we can't eat anything out of the fridge. If it's longer than a day, then nothing out of the freezer either."

"That leaves what…bread and crackers?"

"Well good thing you brought enough to feed an army for a month." I flash her a wink.

"Yeah, but if we can't use anything from the fridge, that really limits what we can make."

"Don't worry, we'll figure it out as we go. No stressing until we need to."

Kendall's visibly upset. I hate that I've scared her, but she needs to be prepared because losing power is a real possibility.

"Hey…" I step around the island and gently grip her arm. "It's gonna be fine. We're smart and can live without power for a couple of days if we have to."

She nods, and her brown eyes stare into mine as she holds onto every word I say. I love that she trusts me, and it makes me want to do everything I can not to let her down.

I release her, though we're still standing close. "Why don't you collect some extra blankets and pillows and put them in the living room so they're ready if we need them. I'll check the generator and start working on our backup water supply."

"Alright, and I'll fill the tubs and sinks upstairs, then search for candles."

"Sounds good." I flash her a smirk and a wink, hoping to ease her nerves.

After we separate to do our tasks, I grab my phone and send Eli a text update. I'm sure Kendall will tell Cami, but I want to make sure he knows I'll keep a close eye on her and not to worry about us since I'm sure Cami will be.

Just as I suspected, there's no fuel in the generator, and the extra gas can is empty. Honestly, I should've thought of it before we left.

I find some extra flashlights and batteries, fill the sinks downstairs, then grab the matches. When I make it back to the living room, I see Kendall and drop everything on the coffee table so we know where it is.

"Everything is taken care of upstairs," Kendall says.

"Great, thanks."

Taking a seat in the chair, I keep an eye on her and notice how anxious she is. "How about you pick something on TV to keep your mind off everything?"

Her bright smile returns, and it sends a rare shiver down my spine. "Okay."

We watch comedy shows for hours and eat dinner on the couch. The wind continues to gust, and more snow falls. Though I don't want to cause her anymore panic, we'll likely lose power tonight.

"Make sure you have an extra blanket," I tell her after we call it a night. "Oh and take a flashlight, just in case."

I hand one to her. "Thanks."

Kendall watches me, and I stare at her. Unspoken words sizzle between us, but neither of us knows what to say. We actually had a nice evening together, and I didn't hate most of the Hallmark crap she made me watch.

"No problem. I'm just going to clean up down here, then I'll be heading to bed myself."

"Okay. Good night, Ryan."

Her soft voice is like heaven.

"Sweet dreams, Kendall."

CHAPTER FIVE

KENDALL

DAY 3

I WAKE UP SHIVERING.

My hands are ice cold, and even though I put on socks before I crawled into bed last night, my feet are too. Wrapping the extra blankets around me, I get up to turn on the light. *Nothing.* We must've lost power overnight. Instead of freezing my ass off, I grab my flashlight and make my way to Ryan's room.

On the way there, the wind screams outside, and my anxiety gets the best of me. When I'm outside of his room, I lightly tap on the door and wait. He never answers, so I let myself in. Ryan's sleeping like the dead, and I almost feel guilty for waking him.

"Ryan," I whisper, not wanting to freak him out. I repeat myself a few times until he finally shifts awake.

"What's the matter?" He sits up, the blankets fall down, and I see he's shirtless. I catch a glimpse of his chiseled abs and force my eyes back to his.

"The power's out. Can you pretty please light a fire? I'm freezing my ass off."

"Fuck," he whispers, standing. His pajama pants hang

haphazardly on his hips, and I can't take my eyes off him as he moves across the room and grabs a sweater. The cold air brushes against my cheeks, and I think I see him shiver. Before going downstairs, he puts on some house shoes. I follow him and watch Ryan start the fire.

Walking over to the window, I look outside. Though it's still dark, the moonlight makes the snow shine bright. No telling how many inches fell last night. Once the wood crackles, I plop down in front of it on the floor, allowing the instant heat to warm me up. "Do we have a way to make coffee?"

Ryan, who's standing, looks down at me and laughs. "Don't think so. We'd need electricity for that."

"Just kill me," I groan.

"I think we're gonna have to be creative with what's in the pantry too," he admits.

Placing my head on my knees, I sigh. "I hope to God the power returns today."

Ryan's expression is unreadable as he sits down next to me. "I hope so too. I don't get a lot of time off, and waiting out a snowstorm with no electricity or the ability to cook isn't what I had in mind."

"I feel the same. Want some blanket?" I offer.

"Nah. I'm going to change into some warmer clothes, then check the weather report. Thanks, though."

I smile. "You're welcome. Will you grab my phone out of my room? It's on the nightstand."

He stands. "Sure. I'm turning mine off when I'm done, and you should probably do the same, just in case we need to call someone for help."

My eyes go wide. "Hopefully, we won't need help."

"We probably won't, but it's good to have contact with the outside world."

He has a point. I meet his eyes again. "I just hope the power comes on later. Trying to stay positive."

Ryan gives me a side grin, then climbs the stairs two at a time. I watch the flames lick up the fireplace, then let out a yawn. I'm still half-asleep and really wish I could have a big cup of steaming hot coffee. I grab a pillow from the couch and position myself comfortably in front of the fire and end up falling asleep.

When Ryan places more logs inside, I wake up disoriented.

"Hey, Sleeping Beauty." He chuckles and hands me my phone. He's wearing dark jeans, boots, and a knitted sweater. The mountain man vibe is fitting, considering he's typically dressed to the nines.

"Thanks. Why didn't you wake me up?"

"You were snoring and looked comfortable."

I gasp. "I was not!"

"Don't worry, you snore lightly just like a princess."

I snatch the pillow and throw it at him, but he catches it. "You forget who my sister is," he says, then throws it on the couch. Ryan moves to the kitchen, and I unlock my phone. It's nearly seven, so I group text Cami and Piper to update them on the current situation.

Kendall: My biggest fear has happened.

Piper: You're pregnant?

Kendall: No, asshole. We lost power. I don't know when it's coming back on or when we'll be able to leave.

A few minutes pass, and my phone buzzes.

Cami: And so it begins!

Kendall: Whatever. I hate this!

Cami: There's something magical about being locked in the cabin. You'll see.

I send an eye roll emoji because of all the stories she's told about falling madly in love at the cabin. There *is* something cozy about it, but I don't know if that's in the cards for Ryan and me. I wouldn't complain if it were, but I know how he feels about me, how he's always felt, and it's not in the least bit romantic.

Piper: I hope this happens. I need a love story to warm me up this winter.

Cami: Ha! I just don't want to hear any details about my brother.

Kendall: I'd spare you.

Piper: I want details. All the raunchy ones.

This has me snorting.

Kendall: My phone will probably die today or tomorrow.

Cami: Oh no! What will you do without it?

Piper: She'll go crazy. Poor Ryan.

Kendall: Damn right. But anyway, I'm starving. I need to figure out our breakfast situation. Please keep an eye on the weather, and if anything changes, let me know ASAP.

They tell me to keep them updated and to text if something happens. I take Ryan's advice and turn off my cell in the interim because I only have fifty percent left. Only a few more text conversations and social media updates and it'll be dead. Thankfully, I brought two suitcases of clothes and packed my drawing pad and pencils.

I get up and walk to the kitchen where Ryan's eating a Pop-

Tarts. It makes me smile because he gave me so much shit about the processed food I got Cami.

"Not so bad now, are they?" I ask, reaching over and opening a packet. I can't remember the last time I ate sugar like this, so it tastes amazing.

"It's *terrible*, but it's better than nothing," he tells me as he breaks off the edges and sets them down on a paper towel.

"You're not going to eat that?" I ask.

He shakes his head, so I reach over and pop the pieces in my mouth, then give him a smile. "Help yourself," he says, scooting the crust toward me.

"We can't waste food in our current condition, or we'll be eating caviar and oysters for breakfast," I say around a mouthful.

Ryan lets out a laugh, and it sounds so damn sweet. He's not his usual uptight self, which I like. I take this opportunity to chat because moments like this are so damn fleeting.

"How's work been going lately?" I ask, trying to make small talk.

"Fine," he answers.

"Just fine?" I push with a smile.

"Not really much to talk about other than it's my life and I can't imagine doing anything else." He finishes his Pop-Tarts and glances up at me.

"At least you still enjoy it. A lot of my parents' friends are burned out from working so many hours after what happened last year," I say.

He tenses.

"Can't relate. Also, I don't want to talk about this," he snaps, and I realize his wall has returned. It's a way he protects himself from being questioned. Anytime I've asked him about working, he's gotten super snippy with me. While I understand he doesn't like to talk about it since the pandemic, I thought maybe now that some time has passed, he would. Instead of pushing him, I turn on my phone and check the notifications I've missed.

As if Ryan realizes I'm shutting him out, he speaks up.

"I just acted like an asshole, didn't I?" he asks.

I nod. "Basically."

"I don't mean to. It's just a sensitive subject. I still have a lot of shit to work through," he admits.

"See, now that's what we call progress. That's all you had to say. And I understand, Ryan." I place my hand on top of his. "I'm not trying to make you uncomfortable."

He gives me a half-grin. "Thanks. Sometimes it's hard to talk about myself, and I don't want to relive any of last year."

"I get it. I don't like talking about myself either. It's hard."

"It's why I appreciate you sharing all that stuff with me yesterday. I was thinking about what you told me about helping nonprofits and businesses with events. Why don't you start a business doing that?" he asks, and I think about his questions.

"For me, it's not about the money," I remind him.

He laughs. "I know it's not, but you could start a business and donate whatever you make to helping the charities you're passionate about. You'd probably be able to give away millions."

I tilt my head at him, and see he's not joking. "I guess I never thought about that."

"It's just an idea. Then you could double help people."

A smile touches my lips as I think it over. I turn off my phone, not wanting to waste battery since I'm not on it. After I'm done eating, I slide off the stool and stretch. "Think I'm gonna change into real clothes," I mutter, realizing I'm still in my pajamas.

"Sounds good. I have some reading to do today, so I'm sure you'll see me around," he tells me with a cheeky grin.

As I go upstairs to put on warmer clothes, I smile. After our conversation, it seemed like the mood changed. Today it's almost as if Ryan sees me differently and I appreciate it more than he knows.

Before I return to the living room, I grab my drawing supplies and phone. Ryan's busy on one end of the couch reading on his iPad. He briefly looks at me with a smirk, then goes back to his book.

Giving him room, I sit on the opposite end and open my phone to text Cami.

Kendall: Your brother and I had a nice chat at breakfast.

Cami: Yeah? And you finally kissed?

Kendall: Omg, no. But his lips did look soft.

Cami: Just make a move on him and see what he does.

I steal a glance at Ryan over my phone and laugh.

Kendall: He'd probably deny me, and I'd be embarrassed as hell. Then I'd be stuck with him for eternity.

Cami: You never know until you try. What's your phone at now?

Kendall: 40%. I might make it until tomorrow, then I'll be completely cut off from the outside world. Have you heard anything else?

Cami: I did some research, and I think you might be there for a while. I just hope the power comes on sooner than later. It makes me worry about you two with no electricity or heat.

Swallowing hard, I grab the blanket hanging on the back of the couch and throw it over my legs.

Kendall: We'll be fine. I'm in good hands.

Cami: Mm-hmm. Really good doctor hands. Anyway, put your phone on low battery mode and stop using it. I want to be texted if you two bang it out.

I bite my lip and sink deeper into the couch.

Kendall: Okay! Good idea. Bye!

After I turn the screen brightness down, I click on low power mode so it uses less juice. I try to get an update on the power situation, and the city website says it could be at least a week. No matter what I do, I know my phone won't last that long. I let out a calm breath and turn it off.

A few magazines litter the coffee table, and I flip through them until I find a *Cosmo* even though it's a summer edition. Hell, looking at all the sunshine and bathing suits considering we're smack dab in the middle of a snowstorm might cheer me up. When Cami and I were younger, we'd always read our horoscopes and take the love quizzes even if we were still virgins. The thought has me smiling as I flip to the quiz.

It's titled "How Exciting Are You in the Bedroom?" and I grab my pencil and start checking off answers.

A few have me bursting into laughter while others seem like legitimate questions. By the end of it, I've been assigned as a *Foxy Fireball*. Apparently, I create the perfect tension between making a man work for it and then giving him exactly what he wants. I'm proud to be a vixen, but now I'm curious which one Ryan would be.

Clearing my throat, I grab his attention. "I have a few questions for you."

He looks over at me, then down at the magazine. Cami and I have pulled this on him more than once over the years. "Real questions?"

I grin. "*Cosmo* questions."

"I really need to…"

"Oh, come on. Don't be like that. You'll have all week to do whatever you need to do. It's not like we're going anywhere anytime soon," I say and stick out my bottom lip, pretending to pout.

"Fine, but make it quick." He gives in much easier than usual, which makes me happy.

"Okay, well you have to answer A, B, or C," I explain, then start with the first question. "If a guy." I stop and look up at him. "I'll change that to girl."

"Thanks," he says. "Continue."

"If a girl decides she wants to move to second base after two dates, you:

A) Lie back and go for it.

B) You tell her to wait until you know each other better.

C) Leave the date."

He gives me an incredulous look. "Are you serious?"

I nod and snicker. "Yep. Those are your choices."

After a few seconds of contemplating the choices, he finally answers. "I guess B."

He opens his mouth to explain further, and I interrupt him. "I don't need all that. Next question. In the bedroom, you're most known for:

A) Making it fun and exciting

B) Teasing before pleasing

C) Doing it quick."

Ryan chews on the inside of his cheek, and my insides burn as I think about him naked.

"All of the above," he says.

"Nope! One. And just one." I lift an eyebrow at him.

"B. I like to make my women work for it."

Holy fuck.

It might be cold in here, but damn, I'm on fire.

After I get out the last few questions, I hurry and add up his

THE BEST OF US

total, then use the key at the bottom. When I figure out which one he is, I burst into laughter.

"What?" He tilts his head at me as I suck in a breath "Come on, tell me," he nearly begs.

"You sure you wanna know?" I tease.

"Absolutely."

CHAPTER SIX

RYAN

KENDALL LAUGHS her ass off at me, and it's absolutely adorable.

"Any day now," I tell her.

She gives me a look. "You're considered a Distant Diva."

My eyes go wide. "A what?"

"You're a Distant Diva!" She points and giggles, then continues to read. "You play by the rules and like to be in control, but you have issues opening up with those you're dating. Try talking about things that motivate and inspire. Share some secrets. Men, ahem, women like to know you're interested, so show it more. You're committed to relationships as long as there's trust, but it takes a lot to break a Distant Diva from his shell." She looks at me with wide eyes. "I'm never letting you live that down."

"And what are you?" I ask, reaching for the magazine, but she doesn't give it to me.

"I'm a Foxy Fireball. I know how to pleasure and be pleasured. I'm not afraid to ask for what I want in and outside of the bedroom, and I'm fun to date. I've got to say, I have to agree with both assessments." She snorts.

I tilt my head, realizing how true both probably are. Kendall's the type of woman who says what she wants and typically gets it.

I wouldn't be surprised if she's like that in the bedroom too. Just thinking about her dominating me makes me hard as fuck, and I have to adjust myself. Hopefully, she doesn't notice.

"So where's the lie in the survey because it seems legitimate to me, Distant Diva," she sing-songs with a chuckle. "You know, I *could* help you with that."

I swallow. "With what, exactly?"

"Your relationship issues."

I bark out a laugh, but I'm also convinced she probably could. "Last time I checked, I didn't need a love therapist."

With a popped eyebrow, she grabs the pen she used to mark the survey as if she's getting ready to take notes. "You sure about that?"

I chuckle. "Most of my relationships end because I work too much. You know that, Kendall. Women want attention, and I'm married to my job. Until I find someone who can appreciate me when I'm around but allows me to do the work I'm passionate about, I'll be single. Maybe forever. And that's okay with me."

She narrows her eyes at me. "Maybe. Maybe not. When you're in love with someone, you want to spend time with them. Maybe you just haven't *actually* been in love, but rather in lust?"

"You could be right," I admit, contemplating her words and the truth that's in them. Though when I think back to the time my ex, Rachelle, and I spent together, it's hard for me to place if it was love or if I just liked the idea of being with someone. I do get lonely.

Kendall stands up and stretches. "It's so gloomy in here."

"Yeah. I know. We should probably figure out lunch soon," I say, checking my watch.

She nods. "True. I wonder if we should try to eat some of the things in the fridge."

"It's a toss-up because if the power comes on, none of it will be wasted. If it doesn't, we'll lose it all. What's in there that we could salvage?"

"Without a way to cook it, not much." She sighs. "You don't have any camping gear anywhere around? A random iron skillet we can throw in the fire?"

This causes me to laugh. "Not that I know of, but we could always check in the cabinets. Mom stored all her old shit here, so we might find a cast iron skillet or a Dutch oven."

"We could eat the lunch meat I bought. And we've got cheese and mayo too. I'll make us some sandwiches if you're up for that," she tells me as she walks toward the kitchen with a blanket wrapped around her.

"Yep, might as well eat what we can," I say. "But you have to be quick and grab everything fast so we can try to save what we can."

Kendall stands in front of the fridge and closes her eyes.

"What are you doing?" I ask.

"I'm trying to remember where the hell I put everything because you said to be quick." She gives me a half-smile.

I cross my arms over my chest and lean against the counter, watching her. She takes the blanket from her shoulders and hands it to me, then as if she were moving at hyper speed, opens the fridge, pulls out the food, and slams it closed.

She grabs two plates and the loaf of bread that won't last us but a handful of days at this point. Carefully, Kendall squirts on the mayo, then stacks meat and cheese a mile high. My eyes go wide.

"I'm not letting this mesquite roasted turkey go to waste," she says as she puts everything back in the fridge. After grabbing some potato chips from the pantry, she sets the plates on the bar, and I place her fluffy blanket back on her shoulders. "Thanks," she tells me.

"Welcome." I sit next to her. "Wow," I say, taking a huge bite. "This is really good."

She snickers. "What kind of lunch meat do you eat?"

"The packaged stuff. I don't have time to wait at the deli."

Kendall places her hand on her chest over her heart. "You should invest in food delivery because the ingredients are worse than what Cami eats in her snack cakes."

"Point taken," I admit. We finish, and I clean up.

Going to the living room, Kendall grabs the notebooks and pencils she brought with her and sits by the windows. The cabin has a lot of natural light. Otherwise, the fireplace and candles would be our only source of light. Picking up my iPad, I turn down the brightness and then continue reading an article about medical research done earlier this year on the mutation of the virus.

After an hour, I glance over at the fire and get up to maintain it. Kendall's busy sketching something, so after I add some logs, I walk over to see what she's doing.

"You can draw?" I ask, bending over and noticing how she captured the snow-capped mountains in perfect detail.

She looks up at me with her big brown eyes and grins. "It's just a little hobby I picked up when I was a kid."

"I'm impressed," I say wholeheartedly. The shading on the slopes and cedars is incredible. She hasn't left a detail untouched. At first glance, it looks like a black and white photograph.

"You're just saying that." She tugs on her bottom lip, and something sparks between us.

"No, I'm not. You should know I don't give frivolous compliments. You've got a real talent with this. I had no idea," I say.

She laughs. "Well, maybe one day I'll draw you like one of my French girls."

I lift an eyebrow and shake my head. When I turn around, I can't help but smile.

After a few more hours, the sun begins to set in the distance. So we're not sitting in the dark, I place lit candles around the living room.

Kendall gets up and throws her hair into a high ponytail. "I really wish I could take a shower. Wash my hair. Soak my weary bones. Put on a face mask and use a bath bomb." She lets out a frustrated groan.

"I was wondering when high-maintenance Kendall would arrive," I tease.

"I shower every single day, Ryan. You don't understand how much torture this is for me right now."

"And it hasn't even been a full twenty-four hours yet." I chuckle. "We've done nothing but lounge around and eat. You're not dirty, just being dramatic."

"Dramatic?" she questions. "Just wait a few more days, and you'll get to meet that side of me," she warns with an evil grin.

I clap my hands together and look up at the ceiling. "Please let the lights come on before that happens."

Kendall rolls her eyes, grabs her phone, and turns it on. She's lost in her text messages, and every few minutes, she looks at me and laughs. This can only mean one thing—she's talking to my sister. I try to ignore her though my curiosity nearly eats me alive. I'm sure Cami is excited we're here together.

As the sun fully falls behind the mountain, we're prepared. The cabin glows from the candlelight, but it also grows colder. I make it my mission to keep the wood burning so it stays comfortable in here.

"We should probably sleep on the couch tonight," I suggest. "We can move it closer to the fire. Even with extra blankets, I think we'll be too cold sleeping upstairs."

Kendall breaks away from her phone. "It's a good idea."

"Good, let's move it then." I stand, and we push it closer. After we're done, we go our separate ways to change into more comfortable clothes and grab the blankets from our beds. When I come back down, I can barely see over the huge pile she has stacked. Thankfully the couch is a sectional. Otherwise, I'd probably be sleeping on the floor.

"You can have this end, and I'll sleep here," she says, grabbing pillows and rationing them to each side. After our temporary beds are made, we sit on the couch and stare at the fire.

She's busy on her phone and looks up at me. "Seems the power is estimated to be off for at least seventy-two hours."

I groan and suck in a deep breath, then pinch my nose, trying to stay calm. We have plenty of food and firewood, so hopefully the estimate is wrong. "We'll be okay."

She locks her phone. "No, we won't. My phone has ten percent now."

"There are plenty of magazines to read," I suggest. "I'm sure *Good Housekeeping* has some great surveys for you to take."

Leaning her head back on the cushion, she looks up at the vaulted ceilings. "I have an idea."

I wait for her to continue.

"Since it's so cold in here, and I bought enough booze to open a bar, as you said, we should drink to warm up." She turns her head, and her eyes meet mine.

A smile touches my lips. While I want to be the responsible one, there's nothing else to do, and if the power will be out for that long, we might as well let loose a little. I'd love to sleep like a brick tonight.

"Deal," I offer.

Kendall claps her hands together and stands. "I'll get the tequila."

I chuckle as she quickly runs into the kitchen and returns with a bottle of Patrón. "We should play a game."

"What do you have in mind?" I ask.

"Never have I ever," she quickly says.

I lift a brow at her, and she speaks up. "You're not pussing out, are you?"

"Hell no," I say. "Just making sure you can handle this."

She places her hand on her chest and lets out a sarcastic laugh. "I'm sure I can. You go first," she tells me as she takes the wooden cork from the top.

I think about it. "Never have I ever purchased a designer handbag."

She narrows her eyes, then drinks. "Oh, so we're playing dirty? Alrighty, I see how it is. Never have I ever helped someone in an emergency room."

I grab the bottle from her and take a big gulp. "If we keep this up, we'll both be trashed in twenty minutes."

Leaning over, she whispers, "That's the point."

"Okay, well then I guess it's up to me to change the pace of this. Never have I ever dated someone for over a year," I say, wanting to get into the nitty-gritty of Kendall with hopes to learn more about her.

"Dated or slept with?" she questions with a smirk.

"Isn't it the same thing?" I hand her the booze.

"Poor little Distant Diva. You can have sex with someone without being official. It's basically just fucking for fun. Maybe you should try it sometime," she offers and doesn't drink. "Next up. Never have I ever finished reading a book in a day."

I reach out and put my lips to the top and take a drink.

She chuckles. "I forgot you were always a little nerdy."

"You mean, smart," I add. "Never have I ever been with someone who was in a relationship."

She drinks. "It's a long story. I didn't know he was married until his wife caught us together. I felt horrible about it because I'm not a home-wrecker. Trust me when I say I was livid. I've also never told anyone that before because it's embarrassing."

My eyes soften. "Wow."

"Yeahhhh." She chugs, and I swear I see her eyes blink at two different times, then she turns to me. "Never have I ever thought about proposing to anyone."

Neither of us drinks.

"No one?" she whispers, shocked. "At *all*?"

Shaking my head, I shrug. "No. Just haven't found the right person yet, I guess. The last thing I want to do is get married for it to end in divorce. I don't want to rush into something that could potentially end badly, so it's easier for me to stop things before they get too serious if I'm not feeling it. They say you know when you've found the one. I haven't."

"I understand that," she admits. "I haven't found that person either. Not even close. So many men have wanted to date me just because of my family. I know you've probably gone through the same thing. It gets old, and I usually can see through it now, but when I was younger, not so much. I thought they were into me, but they were really into buddying up with my dad," she admits.

"I'm sorry you've had to go through that. There are a bunch of assholes out there. You deserve better," I tell her.

She takes another drink and yawns. "Thanks, Ryan."

I can't help but think how goddamn beautiful she is and how she shouldn't have to put up with men using her. Kendall sinks into the cushions and stares at the fire. The candlelight illuminates her face perfectly, and she seems to be lost in thought.

I get up and put another log on it until the flames lick up the chimney. When I sit, I seemed to have settled closer to her because I can feel the warmth of her body next to mine. It's cozy and feels like home.

Kendall scoots closer and places her head on my shoulder. I wrap my arm around her, and there's no denying the electricity that streams between us. The alcohol has made us both too brave. While I refuse to cross that line with her, I feel as if she's shown me a different side of her—one that isn't so focused on superficial things. One I should've seen all along.

We listen to the crackle and pop of the wood, and there are so many things I want to say but don't. After a moment, her breathing softens, and when I tilt my head, I notice she fell asleep. Slowly, I move, and she wakes.

"You should lie down and get some rest," I whisper.

Her eyes stare at my lips, then she meets my gaze. "Yeah."

I pull the covers down, and she snuggles in on her side of the couch.

"Good night," I say, giving her a warm smile.

She blinks, her long lashes touching the top of her cheeks. "Good night, Ryan."

It doesn't take long before she's out. Seems Kendall can't hold her liquor, and the thought makes me chuckle. I take two big gulps of tequila, then climb under the blankets. Though I'd like to fall asleep, I can't because all I can think of is Kendall and the things she shared with me tonight.

CHAPTER SEVEN

KENDALL

DAY 4

WARMTH COVERS my body as I slowly blink open my eyes. It's a major contrast to how I woke up yesterday when I was freezing my ass off. The tequila's certainly having an effect on my head, and I wonder if I'll suffer from a hangover all day.

"Mmm…" a husky voice next to me mutters in my ear. Ryan's bare chest is pushed up against me with a leg arched over mine. One of his arms is wrapped over my waist, and the closeness feels nice, *too nice*. He nuzzles his nose in my neck and moans again.

Fuck my life.

There's no way he realizes what he's doing.

How the hell did we even get into this position? When I fell asleep last night, I was on my side of the couch, and he was sitting on his. But somehow, he ended up next to me, holding me in a way that's making my mind run wild with possibilities.

As if he senses my thoughts, he moves against me, and it pushes his hardness into my side.

Holy shit.

I blink and slowly look down at the tent in his sweatpants. His erection is…*impressive*. Definitely wouldn't say no to that.

As he squeezes me closer, I realize I have to pee. Though I'm enjoying how warm he is and our bodies being together, I'm going to explode. Not to mention, I really don't want Ryan to wake up and freak out the second he realizes what he's doing.

Slowly, I do my best to slide out from under his arm and leg. Though not very gracefully because my ass ends up falling on the floor. Quickly peeking at him, I blow out a relieved breath when he didn't wake. I tiptoe to the stairs and go to my room. Once I'm in the bathroom, I look at myself in the mirror and see a hot mess staring back. Jesus.

Once I'm done, I grab a bucket of water from the tub so I can flush the toilet. This is so weird, and I hope we don't run out before the power returns. The first thing I'm doing when that happens is taking a shower.

I'd never survive living in the woods.

After I change into clean clothes and brush my hair and teeth, I casually go downstairs. My head is throbbing, but maybe some meds and food will help.

I notice Ryan isn't on the couch anymore and wonder where he went. The kitchen is empty, so I grab a Pop-Tarts, then return to my side of the couch.

As I slowly eat, Ryan returns wearing gray sweatpants and a T-shirt this time. Too bad. He has nice abs.

"Morning," he says groggily. I can tell he's still tired. "Please tell me I'm not the only one with a hangover."

I chuckle and shake my head. "Nope. Please tell me you brought meds."

"I sure did." He walks over and drops two white pills in my palm. "I'll grab some water."

"Thanks," I say softly, wondering if he remembers what position we were in this morning. His hooded eyes tell me he's still half-asleep and probably doesn't.

Ryan returns with two bottles of water, gives me one, then sits on his side of the couch. Though I'm covered with blankets, I'm shivering. When he notices, he stands and puts a couple more logs on the fire.

"Think we'll get power today?" I ask optimistically.

"Not sure. I'll turn on my phone and check for updates."

As he does that, I swallow down the meds, then continue eating.

"Eli and Cami texted me and said there's more heavy snow coming."

"Great," I mutter. "Another night on the couch."

While I don't mind, I'd rather sleep in a warm bed and be able to flush the damn toilet. And have a hot meal.

"It's only been twenty-four hours," Ryan says, chuckling. "At least the couch is comfortable."

I blush as I think about how his erection was saluting me this morning. Especially the way he pushed himself into me and moaned.

Fuck, I gotta stop thinking about that, or he's going to wonder my face is red.

"That's true. Plus, the fire gives a nice cozy feeling."

"The plows won't be coming down the private road for a while, but hopefully, the crews can fix whatever power lines are down." His tone changes as if it just hit him that we can't leave today.

"You okay?" I ask and turn toward him.

He brushes a hand through his hair, messing it up even more, which is hot as hell. Even sexier is his facial hair. I wouldn't mind him scratching my thighs with his jaw.

"Just frustrated and worried I'll get penalized for being gone."

"You work a ton of hours. They should be happy you're taking some time off. It's good for your mental health," I tell him matter-of-factly.

"Staying busy is better," he retorts.

I can think of something to keep us both busy, but I don't say that aloud. At least not now.

"Are you hungry?" I ask. "I can try to make something."

Though my head is still throbbing a little, I hate seeing him like this. Perhaps getting some food in his stomach will help him from worrying so much.

"You don't have to—"

"Let me!" I pop up and immediately regret it when a dizzy spell hits me. Ryan stands, then grabs my arms.

"Whoa, you okay?"

Blinking at him and noticing how close we are, I nod. My face flushes with embarrassment, but the way he holds me doesn't go unnoticed, and I wonder if he feels the connection too.

"I'm fine, just stood too fast." I stay rooted in place and wait for him to make a move or run away.

"I'll go with you to the kitchen and make sure you don't pass out or something," he teases, then flashes a wink. "Plus, I'm pretty sure our options are limited anyway."

"Yeah…" I blow out a breath when he releases me. We go to the pantry and look at the shelves.

"Peanut butter and apples." He reaches in and grabs the jar.

I look up at him in shock. "You eat PB and apples too?"

"Yeah, it's the best snack, especially when I only have a couple of minutes between patients."

Smiling, I agree. "Cami always teased me for snacking like a kindergartner, but there's just something about it…"

"It's sweet and salty."

"Yes!" I laugh. "The perfect combination."

Picking up the apples off the counter, I cut two of them into slices, then put them on a plate. While I do that, Ryan scoops peanut butter into a bowl, and we both go back to the couch.

We set everything on the coffee table and share.

After a few minutes, it grows awkward, and I wonder what he's thinking.

"So, guess we're both lightweights, huh?" I say, easing into the conversation.

"Pretty much. Though to be fair, when I do have a drink, it's usually beer. I don't have time to go to a bar and get shit-faced."

"Oh you should," I cackle. "It's pretty fun when you're with a bunch of your girlfriends."

He pops a brow at me, and I burst out laughing.

"Well, I've only done that a few times since the bars opened up again. Otherwise, I usually just drink wine or have a margarita for lunch."

"For lunch?" he asks.

"You can't go to a Mexican restaurant without having a margarita, especially with chips and salsa. It'd be a sin not to."

He snorts, covering an apple slice in peanut butter. "If you say so."

"Hey! You're taking it all." I push his hand away.

"I'm twice your size. I need to eat more."

I scoff, then roll my eyes. "Oh please. You wish."

He smirks, then backs away to let me get some more.

"So, Distant Diva…" I grin. "It wasn't so bad hanging out with me last night, was it?"

Or pressing your dick into me…but I don't think he's ready for that conversation yet.

"You're alright when you aren't being all…"

"All what?" I press.

"*Gossip Girl*."

"What?" I screech. "I'm not a teenager! If you're going to compare me to a TV show, at least have the decency to pick a good one."

Ryan crosses his arms with a laugh. "Okay, fine. What TV show are you?"

It only takes me a few seconds to respond. "*Sex and the City*. And according to the BuzzFeed quiz I took on 'Which *Sex and the City* character are you,' I got Carrie. So there ya go," I say smugly before taking a drink of my water.

"I have no idea what that means."

I laugh as I swallow, but it comes out as more of an embarrassing snort-choking.

"That was adorable." Ryan grins.

I'm still trying to recover when I notice the faint flush of his cheeks.

"Carrie's the star of the show," I tell him once I can breathe again.

"Oh God, then I'm not even surprised."

"I'll take that as a compliment," I remark. "She's a fashion icon, which clearly I'm not at the moment, but on a good day, then yes."

"Well of course," he mocks.

"Carrie loves to have fun but can be serious and work hard when she has to. She loves love but is better at being a friend than in a relationship."

"Now that—" He points at me with his bottle. "I can relate to that."

The intense way he's looking at me gives me the confidence to say what's been on the tip of my tongue since I woke up.

"Well, considering the way you were all snuggled up to me this morning, my guess is you really want to be in a relationship, but as you said, you're married to your job."

I wait impatiently as he processes my words, and neither of us speaks as our eyes lock. My breathing grows rapid as my heart flutters.

"If I was snuggled up to you, it was only because I was looking for body heat."

"Oh really?" I gasp, offended.

"Yes, *really*." He taps his knuckles on the coffee table before standing. "Don't read into it, Kendall. If I crossed a line while I was sleeping, I apologize, but it wasn't on purpose."

He walks away before I can respond, which is actually for the best because I'm speechless. He can lie to himself all he wants, but I know he's attracted to me. Years of us bantering and getting into heated arguments over stupid shit tells me the electricity I feel isn't one-sided. Sure I've pretended I wasn't into him, especially in front of Cami, but that was only because I couldn't face rejection. I knew Ryan wasn't ready for a relationship, especially with a needy woman like me. It's time we both stop pretending there's nothing between us and go for it.

"I'm gonna change and clean up," he calls out from the other room. "Be back in a bit."

"Okay."

I'm completely bored out of my mind and wish I'd brought more things to do. Flipping open my sketchbook, I decide to draw until Ryan returns.

After an hour, I start to get worried and head upstairs to put on another layer of clothes before searching for him. I don't want things to stay awkward between us, and I hope that tension dissolves.

"Hey, Ryan?" I ask outside his bedroom.

"Come in," he says, which I wasn't expecting. I thought he'd come to the door.

Slowly, I turn the knob and peek inside. He throws on a sweatshirt, but I still manage to get a glimpse of his bare chest.

"Sorry I've been gone a while. Trying to clean up with limited water and looking for clothes with a flashlight took some time."

I'm not sure how much of that is true, considering how eager he was to get away from me earlier.

"Oh, that's fine. I'm bored and wanted to see if you could grab the Christmas decorations. I figure since there isn't much else to do, we could make the best of the daylight and decorate while we can."

"Sure, we'll need some flashlights since most of it is in the basement."

I suck in my lower lip as I watch him walk across the room. "Or you could just bring it all upstairs for me, and I could help from there?"

He shakes his head with a chuckle. "That's the only reason you wanted me to come."

"Well…" I stall, then shrug. "Not the *only* reason."

CHAPTER EIGHT

RYAN

THE MOMENT SHE SPEAKS, I stiffen and contemplate asking her what she meant. Considering how awkward things got downstairs when she mentioned our sleeping situation, I'm sure I know what she was referring to. It's no secret there's an attraction between us, but getting involved with Kendall Montgomery would be equally good and bad.

Good because there's no denying she's gorgeous. I'd gladly devour her for breakfast, lunch, and dinner.

Bad because she's my sister's best friend, and if either of us caught feelings, it'd only end badly. I'm not in the position to have a relationship or give her the attention she deserves. Not to mention, I can't think of anything we have in common besides being from wealthy families.

Kendall couldn't be happy with someone who'd only give her a few hours of themselves a week. She's an all or nothing kind of woman. It's why most health care professionals end up marrying people in the same industry. We understand the dedication, long shifts, and exhaustion after working a double.

However, it's not like I haven't thought about it a time or two. Especially now when she's dropping obvious hints, but I can't allow myself to go there. Not when it could end with her getting hurt.

After she brought up fucking for fun last night combined with how we woke up this morning, I needed space. The best I could do was walk away so I didn't stumble over my words. The truth is I do remember moving to lay closer to her in the middle of the night. As I fell asleep, I must've snuggled closer to feel her warmth, then held on.

I haven't been that comfortable sleeping with someone in years.

It was hard not to move closer to her when she stirred awake. I wondered if she'd reciprocate and lean into me, but it was like she couldn't get away fast enough. Mixed feelings swirled as we went on about our morning, but then the moment she brought it up, I denied it.

Knowing I need to grab the decorations, I grasp my flashlight and move toward the basement. She waits by the door as I go down the steps. Kendall reminds me she brought some décor but wants all the extras that are stored down here.

"You might have to put your big girl panties on and help me with all of this," I tell her after dragging the heavy ass storage containers to the bottom of the staircase. "Everything is heavy as fuck, and I don't want to fall down the steps today."

"You really think me helping is going to do anything?"

"Valid point." I chuckle at the way she roasts herself. Kendall might be good at charity events and serving food, but she's not one to get her hands dirty and lift shit.

After a solid five minutes of trying to pull the plastic container up the steps, I finally make it to the top, and Kendall helps me drag it across the floor until we're in the living room. I take a few more trips and bring every decoration we have to the living room. I'm sweating my ass off, and my muscles burn from lifting so much.

"See? Easy peasy!" She smirks once I bring the last of it.

"Don't push it, *Diva*."

"Ha! You're the diva…" she reminds me.

"I got the decorations up here. Now you get to put up the tree."

"What? No way! I'm five and a half feet. There's no way I could."

"Are you serious?" I fold my arms over my chest.

"I'll hold the flashlight for you." She flashes a cheeky grin.

"Don't work too hard," I mutter and start removing the branches from the oversized bag I brought up here a few days ago. Almost seems like an eternity has passed since then.

"Stop complaining, I'll do the ornaments," she tells me, "after you bring in the ladder."

"The ladder?"

"Yeah, this tree is gigantic, and I can't reach up ten feet to hang them!"

"Good lord. Is all this really necessary?" I scowl, watching her sort through the ornaments.

"I told you, you're here to do the heavy lifting. Now be a man and…*lift*. Remember, this is for Eli and Cami, so suck it up, *Diva!*"

I want to remind her the honeymooners will probably hardly ever leave their bedroom, but I refuse to put that image in either of our heads at the moment.

"In that case, if we're being stereotypical, get your fine ass in the kitchen and make me some lunch," I bark out teasingly.

"Fine ass?" She perks a brow at me. "You've been lookin'?"

Fuck, that was an inappropriate slip. "Shut up. Be helpful or go away."

Luckily, she drops it with a chuckle. "Fine, you do the branches, and I'll fan them out so we can insert them in the trunk thingy."

"Alright, boss." I flash her a smirk, and she rolls her eyes.

"Too bad we won't be able to see it lit up."

I nod.

"But we can still string the lights. And put on the ornaments," she continues.

"You mean, *you* can. My job's almost done, remember?"

"Har har."

I grin. "Just following orders."

Once it's set up, Kendall continues feathering out the fake pine needles. Looking at it brings back lots of memories. It's been years since my family has celebrated Christmas at the cabin, and a part of me misses it. Mom is a nut about the holidays and always tried to make it special when Cami and I were younger. After we learned the truth about Santa, the glitz and glam became more important than spending time together.

"I wish we could watch a Christmas movie or listen to music."

"Thanksgiving hasn't even happened yet," I say, digging through the boxes for Cami's favorite ornaments.

"So? Christmas season is November first through New Year's."

"Oh you're one of *those*." I snicker.

"Can you grab the box of lights I brought? I wasn't sure if the ones here worked, but I think twinkling white lights would look awesome. You agree?"

I squeeze the back of my neck as I watch her. "Uh, sure."

Kendall rolls her eyes. "That's it, we're singing carols to get you in the Christmas spirit."

"No. I don't sing," I say firmly as I walk toward the extra lights Kendall packed.

"You can let your guard down, ya know? I won't tell anyone." She smiles, then winks. "Even if you suck at it, I won't judge."

The more time I spend with her, the more I warm up to her. Kendall is slowly tearing down my wall, and considering the situation we're in, I'm not sure it's a good idea for us to get closer.

She continues to dig around in the box. "I'll start, and you chime in." Kendall starts singing "All I Want For Christmas Is You," and it's hard not to laugh at her infectious energy. Together, we string the lights, and though I don't sing with her, I hum the tune as she bellows out the words.

I'm so entranced by her that instead of moving around the

tree with the lights, I stay planted, and she ends up bumping into me. She looks up at me, and I smile back at her. The realization of how stress-free I feel for the first time in months nearly takes my breath away. The way she brightens up a room with her positive attitude and energy is becoming impossible to resist.

We finish with the lights, and she dives back into the ornaments. Some are from my childhood and others she brought. Digging through all the homemade and gifted ornaments that I haven't seen in years takes me on a trip down memory lane.

"Do you remember that Christmas I came here with your family? I think Cami and I were like thirteen?" Kendall asks as we continue decorating.

How could I forget? I was seventeen and knew it was inappropriate to think my sister's best friend was hot. To be fair, she had always looked older than she was and dressed like a typical Upper Eastside teenager in expensive designer clothes and shoes. She could've easily passed for an eighteen-year-old.

"Yeah," I reply. "You and Cami were inseparable."

She chuckles as she pulls out a fake beaded candy cane, then sets it to the side. "True."

"You want garland? Or this tree topper?" I ask, changing the subject. I'm not sure where she was going with that, but our teenage years only remind me how out of her league I felt.

"Let's save the garland for the mantel and yes to the star." She holds out her hands, and I pass them to her. "I have some glittery ribbon we can add, though. Make it really pretty."

Thirty minutes later, the tree is finally finished to Kendall's liking. She adds a gold tree skirt and makes sure every part of it is perfect.

I cross my arms over my chest and stand back, staring at it. "Cami's gonna love it," I say sincerely. "I wouldn't be surprised if she leaves it up all year long."

"That'd be awesome. It really does add to the cabin."

We clean up our mess and put the boxes in a corner so we can finish decorating the rest on another day. It's starting to get dark in here, so I light some candles around the room.

"Are you getting hungry?" I ask.

"Starving! I'm craving seafood pasta so bad right now." She pouts.

I walk to the kitchen, chuckling as I open the pantry. "Well, I can't do that, but maybe a can of tuna?"

"That's just depressing." She laughs. "We can't even make a tuna melt."

"Well, you can put it on crackers," I add.

"I guess. And maybe some wine."

"That's the grossest combination I've ever heard," I say, laughing.

"Okay, save the wine for after. We're gonna need it tonight."

I give her a skeptical look. "We will?"

A soft pink covers her cheeks as she avoids eye contact. "Yeah, to stay warm."

Once we eat random things and she pours her wine, we go to the living room. I add more logs to the fire and sit next to her.

"Wanna play another game?"

"I don't trust you," I tease. "Depends what it is."

She takes a drink, then turns toward me with a cracker in her hand. "If you only had twenty-four hours to live, what would you do?"

I pop a brow. "That's morbid."

"C'mon, just answer it." She pushes my arm. "Twenty-four hours, what are you doing?"

"I guess…spending time with my family and letting them know I love them. Making sure my will is updated and that everything's taken care of for after my passing."

Her mouth opens. "That's it? Wow, you're boring."

"That's logical," I retort.

"Okay, something *fun*. If all that shit was taken care of already and you said your goodbyes to your family, what would you do?"

I take a breath and reflect on it for a moment. It's odd thinking

63

about something like this even though I witness people dying every single day.

"Then I'd go to New Zealand and visit Fiordland National Park. I'd spend the whole day hiking and capturing the mountain views."

"From the photos I've seen, it's beautiful. I've never been there, though," she says. "But now you're giving me ideas for a trip."

I chuckle, grabbing a cracker topped with tuna. Sadly, it's not the weirdest dinner I've had. When I'm working, I eat whatever I can whenever I can.

"Alright, I told you. What about you?"

"Hmm…I'm not sure I should say." She grabs her wineglass and sucks down the liquid as if she's trying to find the courage. After it's empty, she sets it down.

"Why the hell not?"

Kendall inches closer to me. "Because I think it'd be better if I showed you."

My heart races when she licks her lips, then stands in front of me. *What the hell is she doing?*

"If I only have twenty-four hours to live, then I'm gonna come clean," she states, straddling my lap and wrapping her arms around my neck. Instinctively, I grab her hips and hold her still.

"Come clean about what?" I ask with a raspy voice.

"That I'm attracted to you, and I don't think it's one-sided." She rocks her body against my groin.

Fuck. Me.

"Kendall…" I warn as my eyes lower. "I think you're a little drunk."

"Not really. Plus, I only have one day to live, Ryan," she mocks. "There's something between us and has been for a while, so if this is my only chance, then I'm gonna take it."

My breath hitches as we stare at each other.

"Admit you like me too," she whispers, grinding her hips into my cock that's now hard thanks to her. "Even if you say you don't, I can *feel* that you do."

I slide my hand up her arm and grab her chin so our eyes lock. "I'd be lying if I said I didn't, but I can't give you what you deserve, Kendall. I'm not good at being in a relationship and would only let you down."

"I'm not asking for a relationship."

"Then what do you want?"

"You. Just sex. It doesn't have to be anything more than that. We're attracted to each other and stuck in this cabin together. We might as well take full advantage…"

"So you'd be alright with just sex and nothing more?"

I hear the way her breathing increases as she rubs my dick between her thighs. A groan escapes me as she moves faster.

"Yes, that's all I'm asking for. We've both failed at relationships, so let's just stick to the fun parts."

"You're seriously testing me right now…" I whisper as I slide my fingers under her shirt and touch her soft skin.

With her eyes locked on mine, Kendall lowers her hand and removes her shirt. I watch as it drops to the floor, and my gaze hardens as I take in her perfect breasts.

"Fuck it," I growl as I cup her face and press my mouth to hers. She immediately responds, holding me as I slide my tongue between her lips and taste the red wine she was drinking. Our hips move in sync as she rubs her pussy over my cock. It's practically begging to be released and fuck her raw.

"Kendall, are you sure?" I ask as I move my lips down her neck. "You're driving me insane."

"Yes, God, yes. I want this."

"Good because stopping would kill me."

She chuckles as she gives me more access to her silky skin.

"I want to see your tits bounce as you ride me," I tell her when I unclasp her bra and slide the straps down her arms until it's off. "Goddamn. They're perfection."

As I move my mouth down her chest, I massage her other

breast with my free hand. Kendall arches her back as I suck her nipple, and the little moans that escape her drive me wild.

"Sit up a moment," I order so I can unbutton my jeans. As soon as I slide them down my thighs, Kendall drops to her knees and grabs my cock out of my boxers. Before I can say another word, she wraps her lips around the tip, and I nearly go blind by the sensation. Her hot mouth feels incredible, and there's no denying the current streaming between us.

"Holy shit," I hiss as my head falls back on the couch. Fisting my hand in her hair, I move with her as she bobs her head up and down. Gripping my shaft with her palm, she strokes me and teases the tip.

Kendall's little moans are burning in my brain as I fuck her mouth, and though I don't want to come yet, I can't deny how good it feels having her cherish me.

"I can't take it any longer," I say, pushing her away until I can wrap my arms around her and pull her down on the couch beneath me. "I gotta taste you."

She helps me remove her leggings and panties, and as soon as she's bare, I dive between her legs. She squeezes her thighs against my head as I lick up her slit and suck on her clit.

"Oh my God, Ryan. Holy—shit, yes. Right there…"

Kendall's hips go wild as I tease her pussy, and moments later, she screams out her first orgasm.

Yes, *first*…of many more if I have anything to say about it.

CHAPTER NINE

KENDALL

HAVING Ryan's mouth between my thighs is pure fucking heaven.

I knew straddling him was a bold move, and I had no idea how he'd respond. Part of me thought he'd push me away, but all of me had hoped he wouldn't.

That first kiss we shared was *hot*. It burned me from the inside out, and I've never experienced that kind of electricity before. As I rocked on top of him, I could feel how hard he was and couldn't resist tasting him. But the moment he flipped me on my back and dived headfirst into my pussy, I nearly lost it.

Given that Ryan's a doctor who probably knows a woman's anatomy better than I do, I should've expected he'd be good. However, I've never had a man make my eyes roll to the back of my head and my toes curl at the same time.

I can hardly breathe.

"Goddamn, you taste so good…" he growls after he licks up my slit, and I love how his facial hair scratches my skin. "The way your body shook…I hope you can keep up."

Fuck, his confidence…turns me on even more.

I snort as we make eye contact. "I hope you have good stamina…" I bite my lower lip, hoping he never stops touching me.

"I'm a doctor, Kendall…stamina is the first requirement of the job." He crawls up my body, then sucks my nipple into his mouth.

"Then we're about to have some fun," I taunt, threading my fingers through his hair.

His head pops up with wide eyes. "Shit. I don't have any condoms."

"I don't either."

"Fuck, well…" He frowns.

"I'm on birth control and got tested a few months ago," I explain. "What about you?"

"I got tested a year ago after my last relationship ended. I haven't been with anyone since."

"Perfect." I thrust my hips up, and he groans.

"You're so fucking tempting. Always teasing me in your tight dresses and low-cut shirts."

"So you liked what you saw?" I ask as he moves his lips to my neck.

"I think you know damn well I did…" he whispers in my ear. His deep gravelly voice sends shivers down my spine, and I lower my hand to reach for him.

"Good, then let's get started," I say eagerly, reaching lower.

"Not so fast."

Before I can respond, he grabs both of my wrists with one hand and secures them above my head. Then he pins my body to the couch with his hips and flashes a devilish smirk.

"What're you doing?"

"I don't like being rushed," he states calmly with a wink.

Heat rushes to my cheeks from the anticipation of what Ryan's going to do. It's almost too much for me to handle.

"I like you like this…defenseless and restrained."

I wiggle underneath him and groan. "Funny."

"Don't worry, Angel." *Angel*? Why does him calling me that give me goose bumps? "You cooperate, and you'll be thanking me later," he continues.

Does the reserved, stick-up-his-ass doctor have a kinky side? Well, fuck. Would've never guessed that, but I'm not complaining.

"Keep your hands there," Ryan orders as he slowly removes his grip.

I watch as he leans back, fully removing his jeans and boxers. His cock bounces, tempting me to touch and suck it again. He takes off his sweatshirt, and though we have no power or heat, just watching sets my entire body on fire.

Standing, he grasps his erection and watches me as he strokes himself. I lick my lips, swaying my hips as he pumps faster.

"This is torture. Let me touch you," I beg.

"Put one hand between your legs," he orders. "I want to see how wet you are for me."

I slide it down my body and rub my clit to the same rhythm as his motions.

"Good girl. Build it up slowly."

I've never had a man watch me touch my pussy before, but I'd be lying if I said it wasn't unimaginably sexy. Watching him while pleasuring myself is like a habit-forming drug.

"Now pinch your nipple with the other hand," he demands.

I cup my breast and squeeze before pinching the hard bud. The double sensation makes it hard to keep my eyes on him though I don't want to look away. Moaning as the climax builds, I feel my pussy tighten as I grow closer to the edge.

"Spread your legs wider. I want to see the come spill out of you."

"Oh my God…" I pant and obey him. Ryan ordering me in a deep, demanding voice nearly has me combusting on command.

He moves his eyes from my breasts, to my pussy, then back to my gaze. It's as if he's trying to take all of me in at the same time.

"Jesus Christ…" he hisses as he increases his speed.

His other hand balls into a fist as if he's trying to calm himself down. It's so damn sexy watching him struggle with his self-control, and if the thick vein in his cock is any indication, he's close to his own release.

"I'm so close," I tell him, arching my back as the intense sensations roll through me.

"Let me see, Angel."

I squeeze my eyes tight as I step over the ledge. Fireworks shoot through me as I ride the wave of pleasure and moan out his name.

"Fuck, yes. I love hearing you say my name like that."

When I open my eyes, he's no longer standing next to me. Instead, he's kneeling between my legs on the couch and towering over me as though he's about to devour me.

Hell to the motherfucking yes.

Ryan's hand lowers to my pussy, then slides up my slit and coats his finger with my arousal. I watch as he brings it to his mouth and slowly sucks on it.

My body shudders at the prospect of what's to come. This is a side of Ryan I've never seen, and I have a feeling not many have. The thought makes me smile because I want this part of him all to myself.

"I can't wait to fuck you until you can't walk straight. Then everyone will know I was inside you." He nips my skin before he sucks below my collarbone.

"You want people to know?" I ask as his cock brushes my pussy, and I instinctively arch my hips to feel more of him.

"I don't give two shits who knows, Kendall," he whispers in my ear. "This is just sex, remember? Hard, rough, passionate sex. You okay with that?"

Another shudder.

"Yes," I breathe out. "Stop torturing me now."

He smiles against my neck as he sucks the soft skin. "Why do you taste so good all over?"

"Ryan…" I warn. Getting impatient, I wrap my legs around his waist and pull him into me. "Fuck me. Hard and rough, like you said. I want it." I'm nearly begging at this point, hell—I *am* begging. Being teased by him is worse than the years I spent pining over him in private. Watching him from afar and spending years in his presence but never having the courage to admit my feelings has no comparison.

He pulls back until he lines my entrance with his dick and slaps the tip against my clit before sliding down and thrusting in.

And just like that, I know I'll never *only* want just sex with him. It doesn't matter, though. We made a deal, and Ryan isn't ready for anything more than that. So I'll enjoy every second and live in the moment instead.

"Fuuuuuuck, Kendall," he growls before sliding out, then roughly back in.

Our hips rock against each other as the buildup gets stronger. His muscles flex as his body moves, and I can't help admiring how fit and sexy he is. He manages to slide in deeper, and I nearly lose my breath as my eyes roll to the back of my head.

Ryan wraps his palm around my throat, and I instinctively tense up.

"I'm only going to press on the side of your esophagus. It won't hurt," he explains. "Are you okay with that?"

The fact that Ryan can fuck me into blindness and then ask for permission before going too far makes him even sexier.

"Yes," I tell him. "I trust you."

He smirks, then lowers his mouth to mine. "My only desire is to pleasure you, Angel."

With his hand around my throat, Ryan worships my body as he forms a rhythm and hits the right spot every damn time.

Without warning, my body shakes, and an orgasm takes over. My pussy squeezes, and his body tenses.

Ryan buries his face in my neck as he thrusts deeper and comes inside me. I widen my legs and arch my back so I can take all of his release. Knowing he hasn't been with someone in a year and he chose me gives me great satisfaction.

With a deep groan, Ryan pumps once more inside me before pulling out. Instead of getting up like I expect, he curls up next to me. He wraps an arm around me and moves me to his side.

We're still breathing heavy as we settle into the sofa. I wrap an arm around his waist and a leg over his.

Silence passes between us until he looks over and tilts up my chin. "That was pretty amazing." He winks with a smirk.

"Agreed."

DAY 5

I wake up with a mild headache and a stiff body—one that's pressed to Ryan's. Slowly looking up at him, I exhale in relief when I see he's still asleep. I'm not sure how he's going to react being this close now that we've actually had sex.

Though I drank some wine last night, I'm not waking with an ounce of regret. If anything, it gave me just enough liquid courage to say what I've been holding in. Now I finally have confirmation that Ryan has feelings for me too. Maybe not 'jump into a relationship' type feelings, but at least I know mine aren't one-sided.

Maybe we can have fun for now, knowing it won't turn into anything. Of course it'd be nice if he was ready for that, but I won't push that on him. I'm happy with whatever he's willing to give me, even if it's just sex.

I manage to slide off the couch without disturbing him and pick up my clothes from the floor. Without Ryan's body heat, it's freezing in here. The fire has long died, and there aren't any hot coals. If he doesn't get up soon, I'll have to wake him so he can make one because I have no idea where to start.

Before I do that, I head to my room and use the bathroom before putting on clean clothes. I can't wait to soak in the tub and take a shower. We're lucky the cabin has so much natural light during the day, so we only have to use the candles at night.

I brush my teeth and try to fix my hair. It's long and thick, so I typically have to use a lot of product to maintain it. I'm used to washing it daily, so not being able to is driving me crazy. But I'm doing my best to just go with the flow, even if that means eating tuna on crackers and Pop-Tarts.

Once I'm done, I head to the kitchen and find Ryan standing shirtless behind the counter. He's chugging a bottle of water, and when our eyes meet, I try to read him.

"Morning," he says.

"Good morning," I reply, walking closer to grab some water too.

"How'd you sleep?"

"Pretty good, actually. Though I have a little headache now, but nothing major. How about you?"

"Yeah, good. Freezing my ass off, but I got the fire going again."

At the mention of his ass, I blush. It's because he woke up naked, and I was already gone.

"Oh awesome. Yeah, I was pretty cold too…" I say, testing for a reaction.

"Well, it should warm up in a few minutes. I'm gonna change, then check for updates. Then we can figure out what to do for breakfast if you want?" He rounds the island and walks toward the stairs.

"Oh, um, sure. I'll start looking."

I'm too stuck in my head to even think about what to eat but peruse the pantry anyway. I'm not really sure how I expected him to act the morning after, but this…he's being so *normal*. Like we're just two roommates hanging out.

And even though I've never had a roommate before, I'm pretty sure most of them don't just have sex and act like nothing happened the next day.

I grab the box of Pop-Tarts even though I'm sick of them already. After this, there won't be any left. Moments later, Ryan returns in jeans and a sweatshirt, but in my head, I'm still picturing him naked and on top of me.

"You okay?"

Blinking hard, I shake my head and force a smile. "Yeah, just wishing we could get a hot meal." I hold up the strawberry Pop-Tarts. "I'm gonna have a sugar crash from all this processed food."

He chuckles and walks closer. My heart races as he steps toward me, then picks up an apple off the island. "Here. Maybe try this instead?"

I stare into his eyes, wondering if he'll mention anything about last night. The intense way he looks at me gives me goose bumps, and I nearly shiver.

"No, thanks," I say.

He lifts it and takes a large, crunchy bite. "As soon as the power's back, we'll make something hot and delicious."

Hot and delicious? Is he trying to kill me?

If I wasn't annoyed by having no electricity before, I definitely am now since I can't use my phone to text Cami and Piper. Not that Cami would want the details, but it'd be nice to talk with someone who can give me advice on what the hell to do.

Knowing Cami, she'd say to be truthful with him and wait for him to open up. However, Piper would just tell me to jump his bones again to get rid of the awkwardness.

Which *might* actually be a good idea.

"Any news?" I ask.

"My phone's dead but…hold on, I'll be right back." He walks toward the garage where his SUV is.

Instead of waiting for him, I go to the couch and get comfortable. I pick at the weird icing and obsess over everything that happened between us last night.

When Ryan sits down next to me, I don't bother looking at him. My mind races with a million different thoughts.

Does he regret it? Does he think I regret it? Did he not enjoy it?

When I hear his phone turn on, I snap my eyes toward him. The screen lights up, and there's a cord attached to it.

"What the fuck? What is that?" I point at him.

"My emergency portable charger. I don't travel without one."

"Oh my God! And you're just now mentioning this?" I frown with annoyance.

"Yes, because it's for *emergencies*," he emphasizes. "I knew if I let you use it, you'd waste the battery checking Instagram and texting my sister. So I saved it for when we needed it, which is now."

I glare but don't respond because he's right. But *still*.

I need to talk to a girl about this, or I'm going to have an anxiety attack over it.

"Okay, checking my messages now. Just Cami and Eli asking how we are and wanting us to call as soon as we can."

"What about the weather and road conditions?"

"Looking now…"

"Nothing new on the roads yet. Still dealing with an overwhelming amount of snow and haven't made it this far yet," he explains. "Oh, we have a power update. They're working on it and are saying surrounding areas should all be up and running by the end of day today."

"Oh thank God!" I exhale with relief. "I hate that I have to say a little prayer every time I flush."

Ryan bursts out laughing. "What the fuck are you doing in there?"

Playfully, I smack his arm. "Shut up! You know what I mean. I pour the water in, but I'm still worried it's going to malfunction or something."

"You'll be a pro by the end of this. I'm just gonna check my work emails, then I'll text Cami and Eli and let them know how we are doing."

We sit in silence for a bit while he types on his phone. If we don't talk about the elephant in the room, I'm going to combust. For someone who doesn't do casual sex, he's sure acting like nothing happened.

Is there any chance he forgot?

No way. He wasn't even drinking. So what the hell then?

"Okay, Cami says to make sure I find food for you so you're not living on booze." Ryan snorts. "I'll tell her too late for that."

I smirk, then decide to just go for it.

"Oh, can you give her a message for me?" I ask.

"Sure. What do you want me to say?"

Without hesitation, I reply, "Tell her we fucked on the couch last night."

CHAPTER TEN

RYAN

My heart jumps into my throat as I stare at Kendall.

The calm way she mutters those words makes me wonder if she's been itching to say something all morning. I'm a little thrown off, but I do my best to act casual.

"You know she'll call the second I tell her, and we need to preserve battery power. You'll just have to wait to talk about me after the electricity gets restored." I throw her a smirk.

Kendall glares at me, and I'm bracing myself for her rebuttal, but she stays silent. I almost feel bad that she's going crazy thinking about last night, but I like that she is. Though we agreed it was *only* sex, it felt deeper than that. But I can't confess that to her because once we leave the cabin, I won't be able to give her the relationship she deserves.

After Rachelle and I ended things, I buried myself in work even more and didn't process the breakup for months. I put up my guard and didn't let anyone in—including my family. It was easier to keep people away than to deal with the emotional fallout.

By the time the holidays rolled around, the pain of not being with her hit me like a wrecking ball. The year prior, I had spent the holidays with Rachelle and her son, Joey. He was only five at the time, and it was so special for me to see Christmas through his eyes. It was our first and last Christmas together.

A month later, the pandemic hit, and I worked more in my life than ever before. There was no time to think about broken hearts or dating. My only focus was to save as many lives as I could. Rachelle still checked on me, which I appreciated, but I didn't have much time to give her. I loved hanging out with Joey and hated that when things were over, it meant our relationship ended too.

"You're not as transparent as you think you are," Kendall blurts out, taking me out of my fog.

"Huh?" I arch a brow, looking at her.

She shakes her head, and mutters, "Never mind."

Before I can respond, the lights flicker on.

"Oh my God," Kendall squeals, jumping off the couch. "Yes, I can finally charge my phone and take a shower!" She rushes toward the staircase.

I quickly call out her name. "Kendall, wait. You need to let the water run for a couple of minutes first."

"Fine by me." She nearly sprints, and I chuckle at how eager she is to text her friends. *About last night, no doubt.*

I'll call my boss and get updates on my patients too, which gives me some relief. Once I return, I'll be working extra hours. I'm okay with it because I'll need a distraction from spending this time with Kendall.

My phone beeps, and I see a text from Rachelle. She messages me every once in a while, but when I read it, I know it's not coincidental.

Rachelle: Hey…Cami told me you were trapped at the Roxbury cabin. You doing okay? Can I do anything to help?

I slowly exhale and hesitate to respond.

Kendall returns with her cell and charger and plugs it into the outlet next to the couch.

"Looks like we'll finally get to have a hot meal today," I say.

"Thank God." She breathes out. "Are you gonna take a shower? I have the water running in my bathroom."

"Yeah, I will."

Kendall stands, leaving her phone plugged in. "Or we could shower together and fuck through this awkwardness between us?"

She licks her lips and challenges me with a popped brow. The last thing either of us needs is to catch feelings.

"Uh, no. I'm gonna call the hospital and check on my patients."

Her face drops, and I see the disappointment written all over it.

"Alright, suit yourself." She spins around and heads back upstairs.

When she's out of view, I return to my messages.

Ryan: I'm doing fine. Thanks for checking on me. I'm here with Cami's maid of honor. We're making it work for now.

Rachelle: Kendall? Yikes.

Instead of responding, I stand with a fuck it attitude.

I want Kendall as much as she wants me, and the only thing coming between us is my insecurities.

Heading to her room, I let myself in and hear the water running in the bathroom. Slowly, I push the door open and see her sexy silhouette as she runs her fingers through her wet hair. She's a fucking goddess.

Instead of waiting for her to notice me, I strip off my clothes and walk closer.

As soon as I step in, she spins around, and I close the space between us. I cup the back of her neck as our mouths collide and slide my tongue between her lips. She moans and wraps her arms around me as the water cascades down my back.

"I can't stay away," I whisper in her ear. "Fuck, I want you so bad, Angel."

My cock throbs between our bodies, and I know she can feel how hard I am. When she brings a hand down, she grips my shaft and strokes me.

"I'm all yours. Fuck me," she begs.

"God, yes." I spin her around until her back is pressed to my chest and slide my hand between her legs.

"Ryan," she whispers my name.

"Ride my fingers," I demand when I thrust two inside her. "I wanna feel you come."

Kendall places her palms on the shower wall as I rub her clit with my other hand. When her body begins to shake, I kiss her neck and suck her earlobe.

"Yes, right there…" Moments later, she's moaning my name.

"That was hot." I kiss, then suck on her lip. "Now spread your legs so I can fuck that tight cunt."

As soon as she does, I stroke my dick a few times, then slowly thrust inside her. I can't go as fast as I want because we could fall on our asses in this shower. But it doesn't stop me from going as deep as I can while rubbing her clit.

"So good, Angel," I tell her while holding her tight to my chest. Her breasts bounce as I increase my pace, and moments later, her pussy squeezes my cock while she moans out her release.

"Oh my God," she pants. "That feels amazing."

"I can't wait to bend you over and fuck you hard and deep," I tell her as my release builds. "And maybe take that ass cherry."

"Holy fuck, I—" Kendall's back arches as her hips go wild with another intense orgasm. Seconds later, my body tightens, and I come inside her.

"Jesus Christ," I hiss.

It takes a moment for us to catch our breaths, and when we do, I press her against the wall and steal a kiss.

"I think it worked."

"What?" she asks.

"Fucking through the awkwardness." I flash her a wink.

She smirks. "It only works if we don't stop."

"Count me in."

A few hours have passed since our hot shower sex, and we're both starving for some real food. Kendall's on her phone while I empty the fridge and freezer. As soon as she got a whiff of the smell, she bailed and escaped to the living room.

"Are you coming back in here?" I call out.

"Does it still smell like rotten eggs in there?"

"Quit being a baby." I chuckle. "I sprayed some Febreze."

Seconds later, she slowly walks over and wrinkles her nose. "That smell will haunt me for the rest of my life."

I roll my eyes at her dramatics, and when she walks past me, I smack her ass.

"Hey!" she squeals and tries to get me back.

I laugh and run around the island, staying out of her reach. She tries catching me, but instead, I grab her from behind and lock her arms in place.

"Promise you'll be good, and I'll let you go," I taunt in her ear.

"Why? I already know you like me when I'm bad."

I twirl her around and lift her onto the counter. Standing between her legs, I grab the back of her head and thread my fingers up her scalp.

"Only when it involves my dick…" I pull her hair until her head falls back. "And your pussy," I whisper in her ear.

She sucks in her bottom lip, and I know she's getting worked up again. I bring a hand between her thighs and rub over her leggings. Her eyes flutter closed, and when her breath hitches, I know she's close.

My cock gets hard as her body trembles, and she moans out her release. If we weren't starving right now, I'd bend her over the counter and fuck her again. But we're never going to get anything done if we can't stay off each other.

As soon as Kendall comes down from her high, I flash her a smirk.

"Time to make dinner now."

She glares as if she was hoping there'd be more. Giving her a wink, I walk to the pantry and look through our options.

"Do you even know how to cook?" she comes over and asks.

"I can follow a recipe."

She chuckles and shoves me aside. "Let me cook for you tonight. A nice hot meal."

"You know how?"

"Don't sound so surprised! I'm a great cook. Might be a bit difficult with the limited ingredients, but I'll figure out something."

"Okay, be my guest. I'll finish cleaning the fridge while you do your magic."

"Deal."

Kendall gets to work, pulling out cans and pouring them into a large pot. As it heats on the stove, I wipe down the inside of the freezer.

"I hate how much food we threw away," Kendall says. "Such a waste."

"Yeah, it definitely sucks. But we can't risk getting sick, especially since we're stuck here."

She nods and continues cooking.

An hour later, I sit at the table and patiently wait. We chat as she moves around and serves two bowls.

"Bon appetit!" She sets both down with a proud smile.

"Thank you. What is it?"

"Well, I had to improvise and use what we had, but it's a vegetable-based soup with beans and corn. I added tons of seasonings, so hopefully, there's enough flavor with the diced tomatoes," she tells me and sits across from me.

I give it a try and am pleasantly surprised by how good it is. Kendall's eyes light up as she watches my reaction.

"You like it?"

"I love it. Wow, it's *really* good." I eat another spoonful. "I could live off this for a month."

She smiles and chuckles. "Well you might have to, considering our options. Good thing I made a large pot."

I grab some bread and let it soak up the juices, then take a bite. It earns me a weird expression from her.

"You've never dipped bread in your soup before?"

"No, I tend to avoid carbs unless it's something worthy, like pasta."

I snort. "Trust me on this. Try it."

She takes a piece, folds it in half, then dunks it. As soon as she chews and swallows, I know she's in heaven.

"Told ya." I snicker.

After we finish eating, I rinse the dishes and wipe down the counters. Since Kendall cooked, I told her I'd clean. Once I've finished, I meet her in the living room where she's flipping through channels.

"Now that we have power, we can watch Christmas movies." She beams. "It's literally the perfect setting—snowed in, fireplace, hot guy. I think I'm living in a Hallmark movie."

"I swear to God." I shake my head, moving the blanket so I can sit down next to her. "Why are all chicks obsessed with Hallmark?"

"Hallmark Christmas," she emphasizes. "And you'd know if you actually sat down and watched one."

"Like I have time when I work a hundred hours a week."

"Well, you do now." She grins.

Even though I couldn't care less about understanding the hype, the opportunity to spend time with Kendall is enough for me. I wrap my arm around her and pull her in close.

"*A Christmas Cottage*," she says. "It's one of my favorites!"

"Hope there's nudity."

She elbows me in the ribs, and I wince. "Not cool." I groan, but she just smirks at me.

"Hallmark is wholesome. Don't ruin it with your dirty thoughts."

"Too late. I'm already thinking of ways to get you naked again in *this* Christmas cottage."

"Oh my God." She snort-laughs, and settles in next to me.

Overall, the movie isn't horrible. Having Kendall so close while smelling so damn good almost tempted me to throw her on her back and lick between her thighs. But I could see the way her eyes lit up as she watched the movie and didn't want to distract her.

Once the credits roll, I stand and stretch. "I think I'm going to bed."

"Okay. I'm pretty tired myself."

"You going up?" I ask as she adjusts her pillow and blanket.

"I prefer it down here. I've gotten used to hearing the wood burn and watching the fire as I fall asleep. It doesn't feel as lonely."

Though I don't think she meant to, I hear the sadness in her voice.

She's lonely?

Fuck that.

"Sleep with me in my bed," I say. Not giving her any room to argue, I rush to say, "I'll keep you warm *and* make sure you aren't lonely."

Kendall arches a brow. "Double bonus."

I smile and reach for her hand. "That's right. C'mon."

Though I made it sound like it was for her benefit, I love the idea of having her in my bed. Next to me, smelling like me, having me inside her. A possessiveness I've never experienced before sweeps over me. But when it comes to Kendall Montgomery, I can't help it.

If only we could stay in our little bubble forever.

CHAPTER ELEVEN

KENDALL

DAY 6

When I roll over to find a warm, strong body next to mine, I realize where I am—in Ryan's bed. Lifting the sheet, I see that I'm naked. A smile touches my lips as I replay what happened last night after we came upstairs. Flashes of him on top of me, riding him, and multiple orgasms nearly drive me wild.

Damn.

I let out a content sigh and hold back a squeal, considering Ryan's still asleep next to me.

Carefully, I slip out from under the sheets and grab my leggings off the floor, then search for my phone. Unlocking it, I open a group text with Cami and Piper and think about what I want to say. Yesterday was incredible. Being with Ryan so intimately seems like a dream. If I close my eyes, I can almost imagine us in a real relationship. He already knows how to please me and has my body memorized.

Just thinking about him and his mouth on me drives me insane, but I try to calm the hell down even though I feel like a horny teenager. It's tough when the man is so damn sexy with his looks and dirty talk. It's official...I'm hopeless.

Kendall: I think I might be dead!

Cami: What? Are you okay?

I snicker.

Kendall: I can't get enough of Ryan. Where has he been all my life?

Cami: I am so happy! Now get married and have kids immediately!

Piper: Give me all the details PLEASE!

Cami: Please spare me. I don't want to hear that about my BROTHER!

Piper: Don't listen to her. I want every damn sexy detail.

I send an eggplant emoji with the three water drips and have to hold back laughter.

Cami: KENDALL, PLEASE MESSAGE HER PRIVATELY!

Cami's reaction has me snickering.

Kendall: Let me just say, if I could have him every night for the rest of my life, I'd be a very, very happy woman. The sex is FIRE. I wouldn't be shocked if I've lost the ability to walk.

I can almost hear Cami groaning as I send ten fire emojis. Ryan rustles, so I hurry and type my next text to them.

Kendall: I'll fill you in later, Piper. Gotta go.

Before he wakes, I slip back under the sheets and wrap my arm around his firm body. I love how warm he is and snuggle closer.

"Morning," he says in a sleep-raspy voice, then rolls over and meets my gaze.

Leaning over, I paint my lips across his, needing more of him. By the time we pull apart, we're both smiling. I can't believe this is really happening. Sure, we've had sex several times, but just kissing him like this causes emotions to swarm through me.

"You're beautiful," he tells me, giving me another soft kiss. I've imagined what it would be like to wake up next to him, and here we are.

"Thank you," I whisper.

He nods, tucking loose strands of hair behind my ear so he can look into my eyes. "I mean it." His words are sincere.

My cheeks heat, and I can't stop smiling. Before we can say anything else, an alert goes off on our phones, and I know it's related to the weather. If I never hear that sound again, I'd die a happy woman. Ryan sighs and grabs his.

"What's it say?" I ask.

He sits up as he finishes reading. I watch his reaction, and it almost seems hopeless. "Looks like we're getting another snowstorm."

I suck in a deep breath. "Do you think we'll lose power again?"

With a shake of his head, he grins. "Nah. Doesn't look like it'll be as windy as before, but it means we might be stuck a little longer. They haven't plowed the private roads from the first blizzard."

I move closer to him when he opens his arms, and he holds me tight. "So, guess that means we still can't go into town."

"Right. We'll have to check our food supply and see what's left. Might have to get a little more creative," he tells me with a chuckle.

"This is starting to concern me. We didn't prepare to be here this long, or I would've bought even more food for you to complain about. We're going to starve."

Ryan chuckles. "I wouldn't let that happen. We'll make it work. Plus, I've got really great news."

"Great news?" I ask.

"Yep! We can make coffee now."

I sit up and look into his eyes. "Coffee? Oh my God. I totally forgot about that. That's the best thing you could've ever said to me because I've been having withdrawals."

"We have enough to last us a year. How about I get up and brew a pot?" he offers.

Tucking my lips inside my mouth, I nearly squeal. "I think I just had an orgasm thinking about it."

His eyebrow lifts, and he clears his throat after he catches a glimpse of my bare breasts under the sheet. Undoubtedly, he's replaying yesterday too, and I'm almost tempted to have him for breakfast. Though, I'm trying not to be so pushy, considering he is a *Distant Diva*.

However, I'm still interested in learning more about him. While I've gotten to know a side of him he's never shared with me, I feel as if we have more in common than I thought. I'm kinda sad we were too stubborn to act upon it until now.

Maybe Cami was right. Maybe the cabin really does hold some magical love powers.

"What are you thinking about?" he asks.

I shake my head. "Nothing. You'd think it was stupid."

"I promise," he offers. "And if it is, I won't laugh."

I meet his eyes again. "Would you be willing to bet on that?"

"My poker face is the best in all of New York. Lots of practice being a doctor, remember?"

"Oh yeah. That's true." I laugh with hesitation. "Well, your sister said there was something magical about the cabin."

"Don't start with that," he mutters, and I'm sure Cami has pulled that crap on him too.

"It wouldn't be so crazy, would it?" I ask, trying to figure out where his head is.

Ryan thinks about it for a moment, then brushes his fingers against my hand. "Weirder things have happened. I'm sure you filled her in on everything."

I giggle. "I did."

"So she already knows? I'm surprised she hasn't texted me yet," he admits.

"I'm sure she will. And don't worry, I didn't discuss any details. Promise."

"Thanks, spare her. She might throw up or something. When Eli told me about him and Cami...trust me when I say I'm glad he *didn't* share certain things."

"Says the doctor who sees nasty things on a daily basis," I mock.

He leans closer and gives me another kiss. Ryan catches another peek under the sheet. "Damn. I should go make that coffee now, or we might not leave this bed until it's dark."

"I wouldn't complain," I say.

Ryan gets up and slips on some joggers, and I watch his every move, admiring the muscles that cascade down his back. "Meet me downstairs," he says over his shoulder before leaving the room.

When I know he's downstairs, I squeal into a pillow. When we left, I never imagined anything like this would happen. Now that I've had him, I'm greedy for even more.

I climb out of bed, happy the cabin is the perfect temperature. I'm grateful we have heat again. While I was cold and miserable from not showering, I'd choose being snowed in with him a hundred more times if I could. I learned things about Ryan that I never knew and shared things about myself that I've kept locked away. He makes me want to be a better person, considering he's sacrificed so much of his life for others.

After I slip on my clothes from yesterday, I go up to my room and freshen up. My second suitcase is still full, and I'm glad I brought extra jeans and sweaters. After I change, I put on my slippers and make my way downstairs, where I find Ryan pouring two cups of coffee.

"You look nice," he says and hands me a mug.

"Thank you." I take it and stare at it. "I imagine there's no cream, right?"

"Actually, there are some creamer singles in the pantry. Once they're gone, though, that's it."

I'm so excited, I nearly jump out of my skin. When I walk into the pantry, I scan around and immediately find them close to the top shelf. Standing on my tiptoes, I reach up and pull the small container down. There are about twenty little plastic cups of creamer, but if the snow alert is any indication of how long we might be here, I need to be conservative, so I only grab a few. This might last me a few days at best.

I go back to the kitchen and notice Ryan leaning against the counter. He's holding his coffee in one hand and phone in the other. When I catch a glimpse of him, I instinctively chew on my bottom lip because for as long as we're here, he's mine.

"Did you want some?" I offer and hold out my hand.

He shakes his head. "No thanks. I like it just how it is."

"Not sure how. The only time I've ever drunk my coffee black was when I tried dieting fads. Wasn't easy having a best friend who had the paparazzi taking pictures every time we went out," I admit, peeling back the top and pouring in the cream. "Way too many pictures with bad angles were printed for my taste."

He gives me a look, but I can't read him. "You've always been gorgeous, Kendall. And fuck the paps."

"It's hard not to feel self-conscious, though. I avoided the limelight as much as possible. I know how it affected Cami's life. Hell, mine too when I was with her," I say.

"Yeah, and everyone wonders why I broke away from all of that. I'm the forgotten child, and while my parents would love to rope me into their fundraiser pictures and everything else, I'm happy not to be seen. I just want to live my life and do as much good as I can in the world while I'm here. Nothing's guaranteed, and if the pandemic has taught me anything, it's not to take things for granted. I don't. Not anymore, at least."

I swallow hard, loving how he's opening up to me about it but also hating how much it's affected him. "You're changing the world, Ryan. I truly believe that."

He gives me a smoldering look over the rim of his mug before taking a sip. "I'm trying. Sorry to change the subject, but any chance you're hungry?"

"Starving. I'd love some bacon, a big fat omelet, sausage, pancakes, waffles—with extra butter and syrup."

He lets out a hearty laugh. "I think we've got Beanee Weenees, tons of chili, beans, corn, and other random canned goods."

I get up and go back to the pantry to see what's available. "Beanee Weenees? That actually looks gross." I chuckle.

"I've never been a fan, but my dad loves it. Not surprised there's a bunch of weird shit here."

"Well, we've got gourmet macaroni," I say with a raised tone, grabbing the box.

"Gourmet?"

"It's only gourmet because it'll be made with love."

Ryan smiles and fills a pot with water, then places it on the burner. We wait for it to boil before I add the noodles.

"This is going to be so good," I sing-song, mixing in the Velveeta cheese. "A hot meal is much better than a cold one."

"You know, if anything, this time we've spent here has humbled me a bit. Makes me think about all the people you help at the shelter."

I suck in a breath, thinking about everyone I've met while volunteering. They all have unique stories, and it's hard not to feel guilty that you were born into wealth and they weren't. "I feel the same."

I'll be devastated if we're still here over Thanksgiving and I can't help serve lunch because it's something I've done for the past decade. While I'm enjoying spending the time with Ryan, it means a lot to me to give back every year during the holidays.

When our food is done, I divide it into two bowls. We move to the bar top, and when Ryan takes a bite, he lets out a hearty moan.

"Oh my God. I haven't eaten this since I was a kid."

"It's delicious, isn't it?" I take another bite and savor the taste.

He nods. "So good. Much better than Beanee Weenees."

I chuckle, and when my phone buzzes, I swipe my screen to find a message from my sister.

Piper: Just checking to make sure you're still breathing after all that good sex.

I snort, and Ryan looks at me.

"Wanna share with the class?" he asks.

"Not in a million years."

CHAPTER TWELVE

RYAN

KENDALL CONTINUES TYPING on her phone while taking breaks to eat.

After a few minutes, Kendall lets out a moan, and I nearly choke. She covers her mouth and laughs.

"Sorry," she says. "It's just so damn good."

I lick my lips, thinking about how she tastes. "Like you."

Kendall blushes, then gets up and refills her coffee. She grabs mine and does the same.

"Thanks, babe," I say.

She grins wide, and I swear her cheeks get redder. "Babe? Hmm. I could get used to that."

"Oh yeah?" I shoot her a wink and empty my bowl.

"Mm-hmm. Though I certainly like it when you call me *Angel* in the bedroom." Kendall's smile doesn't falter as she finishes her food. "This might put me in a carb coma for the rest of the day."

"Same," I admit, grabbing our dishes and rinsing them in the sink. "What're your plans today?"

"After being without water for so long, I wanna soak for an hour in that amazing tub," she admits.

"You should. Self-care is important."

With a nod, she laughs. "Glad Cami had it stocked from the

last time she was here a few months ago. Though I did pack extra bath bombs."

When I think back to how irritated I was about her two suitcases, it makes me laugh. She's the only one prepared to be snowed in. "I'm sure you are. I regret not bringing more with me now. Speaking of, I'm going to wash clothes, so if you have any dirty stuff, put it in the laundry room, and I'll take care of it for you," I tell her.

"That'd be great," she says, humming after she takes another sip of coffee.

After I dry my hands, she comes over and wraps her arms around my waist. I love how she isn't scared to show affection. Most women are timid around me, so I'm usually the one to make most of the moves in a relationship. This is a nice change of pace.

Kendall's body molds to mine, and when she meets my gaze, I dip down and brush my lips against hers. Our tongues tangle together, and I thread my fingers through her hair, deepening the kiss. While I'm trying not to lose too much control with her, it's easy to get lost in this isolated world.

By the time we pull apart, we're breathless, and my cock is hard. Kendall bites down on her bottom lip, then smiles.

"Bath time," she teases, tugging at the hem of my shirt. "Wanna join me?"

I groan at the thought. "Tempting, but can I take a rain check?" I want to give her time to relax because if I join her, that won't be happening. Hell, we wouldn't even make it to the tub at this rate.

She taps her lips with her index finger. "I will this time, but you owe me."

Her response has me grinning from ear to ear. When she turns and walks away, she purposely shakes her ass more than usual. Before she's out of sight, she winks at me over her shoulder, and I mentally slap myself for turning her down. Just watching her makes my heart race.

With Kendall on my mind, I sit on the couch and pull out my

phone. I was so preoccupied while we ate, I didn't realize Eli had texted me.

Eli: Just checking on you, man. Saw more snow was coming. Are you surviving over there?

Ryan: I'm actually doing really good. It's been a while since I've had a vacation, even if this one was forced.

Eli: That's good. How are you and Kendall getting along?

I was waiting for that question, considering my sister knows what's going on. She's probably been talking about it nonstop.

Ryan: Great, honestly.

Eli: I'm gonna need more details than that, considering your sister has been giddy as fuck lately.

I figured he'd say something like that, but openly talking about relationship stuff isn't easy for me.

Ryan: I'm taking it one day at a time, but I've realized how much I didn't know about Kendall until now. Makes me feel bad about how I treated her over the years. It was unfair.

Eli: I get that. It's like how Cami and I treated each other, and you know how that ended.

The two of them used to be at each other's throats, but I always knew Eli had a thing for my sister. It took being locked in the cabin together for them to realize their true feelings for one another.

Ryan: Yep, you put a ring on it and will probably knock her up soon.

I laugh because it didn't bother me at all when I heard the news. I'm happy for my best friend and sister.

Eli: I wasn't gonna chance losing her :)

Ryan: Well, not sure that's in the cards for me, but I'm enjoying my time with her while we're here. Just taking it one day at a time.

Eli: Well I'm happy for you either way, man. Cami has talked nonstop about Kendall having a thing for you, so you never know what could happen.

Ryan: What's frightening is I can almost imagine myself dating Kendall. She gets me on a different level. Surprising, but it's true.

Eli: Well, I guess getting stuck there was the best thing for you two. Gave you a real chance to talk and get to know each other better, but I hope you're not there too much longer. Cami's going nuts with the wedding so close, and I know you're probably losing your mind not being at work.

Ryan: True, but I'm making the best of it. We'll be fine here, though. The food choices are getting slim, but we have plenty. I'm not happy about using my vacation days, and I do miss being at work, but it's not the end of the world.

Though it felt like it over the past two years.

Eli: You never use them anyway. HR always forced you to take a vacation, then you'd complain about it the whole time.

I chuckle because it's true. I have a handful of weeks available to use, but it's always hard for me to break away.

Ryan: You're right. Trust me, even I'm shocked that I'm enjoying myself.

Eli: Maybe the snow will miss you guys, and the plows will come.

Ryan: Doubt it, but thanks for the positivity.

Eli: If you need anything, let me know. Could probably get your parents to hire a private company to get you if you really needed out.

Ryan: Please do NOT get them involved. It will be a media nightmare, and I'd rather be trapped here than deal with that.

Eli's probably laughing because he knows exactly how to push my buttons, but I know he'd never do that to me. Anything involving my parents becomes a news story.

Eli: I'd never. When you get back, we should have a drink. Miss you, man.

Ryan: I'd be down for that. Miss you too. Be safe, and we'll chat soon.

Eli: Perfect. You too.

Before the fire goes out completely, I add more logs, then decide to check the garage for more wood. The cold nearly slaps me in the face as I look around the massive space. I find some stacked in a corner. Thankfully, either Eli or Cami made sure there was backup the last time they were here.

Once the wood pile is replenished, I grab my laptop and settle into the couch.

Eventually, Kendall comes downstairs after her bath, smelling like heaven, and we're lost in our own worlds until dinnertime. We eat a pasta concoction of noodles and jarred sauce, and it does the job. At this point, I've accepted I'm only eating to live and not for enjoyment. When I get back to the city, I'll have to make it up to Kendall and take her for a nice dinner like she deserves.

After we finish, we move back to the living room and get comfortable. She rests her feet on my lap as she flips through the TV channels. Carefully, I knead into the pads of her foot, giving her a massage. Her head falls back on her shoulders, and she fully relaxes. "God, your hands are…"

"Magical?" I finish when she doesn't speak.

"Yes, I'm like putty," she whispers with a moan.

"Won't be the first time," I tease.

She sits up and playfully smacks me. I pull her close and swipe my lips against hers, stealing a kiss. This is becoming far too natural, considering how we were just days ago, but I don't even care. "I could even offer you a proper full-body orgasm massage. With oils…"

"Oh God." She moans as she rolls her head back. "That honestly sounds amazing. However, we should probably finish decorating now that we have electricity and can test the lights. That way, we can check off one of the big things on our list we were sent here to do," she suggests, looking at the tree and the lit garland we strung around the staircase.

"Another rain check then." I flash her a wink, then move across the living room with Kendall behind me.

I grab the cord for the lights, but before I do anything, I quickly realize it's not going to reach the outlet.

"I think we need an extension cord," she tells me.

"There's a few in the basement. I'll go find them," I say, heading to the basement stairs.

Once I find what I need, I go back to the living room. "Damn, it's chilly down there."

"Stand by the fire and warm up," she says as she takes the cord. Carefully, she plugs in the tree and as it lights up, so does her face.

Kendall gasps as she looks up at the tree. "It's *perfect*."

I move behind her and kiss her shoulder. "You did a great job picking out the right decorations."

She leans into me and smiles. "Cami's gonna love it."

"Definitely. Christmas was always her favorite." I see a few of the old ornaments from my childhood and smile as the memories flood in.

"We have a few more things to do to make it complete." Kendall grabs something, then turns to me. She stands on her tiptoes and holds up the mistletoe. "Have to hang these in a few places."

I steal a kiss when she raises it, but before we break apart, she pulls me closer. Her soft lips memorize mine, and I slide my hands down her waist, then cup her ass.

Kendall moans against me and undoes my jeans while sucking on my neck. I can't even explain the way she makes me feel, almost like I'm alive again. Something I wasn't sure I'd ever experience after all the loss I've endured.

"I need you," she begs.

I slide my hand under her shirt and palm her breast, feeling her hard nipple. Quickly, we're undressing each other until we're down to our underwear. I take a step back and admire how goddamn beautiful her sexy curves are.

With a lifted eyebrow, she smiles.

"I can't wait to fucking taste you," I growl as I lay her down on the couch and bury my head in her neck.

She props up on her elbows as I lean back and lower my eyes down her body. Hooking my fingers in her lace panties, I slide them down and pull them off her ankles. I drop to my knees and position her so I can devour every inch of her sweet pussy. As soon as my lips touch the soft skin on the inside of her thighs, she gasps and runs her fingers through my hair.

She spreads her legs wider as I lick and flick her clit, then she's screaming out my name. She's a greedy little thing and rides my fingers when I slide them inside.

"Damn," I whisper between finger fucking her and teasing her clit. "You're so wet."

Kendall breathes hard as she watches. When her eyes roll, I reach up and pinch her nipple. The sexual chemistry between us is so hot and like nothing I've experienced before. I can't get enough no matter how many times we end up in bed together.

"Mmm," she whimpers as she rocks her hips against my hand.

Slowing my pace, she trembles under my touch. "Ryan," she hisses. "*Please*. Don't stop."

"I love hearing you beg, Angel," I hum against her pussy, then ravage her clit as she hangs on a string. Her composure snaps, and as her body convulses, she squeezes her thighs around my head. I allow her to catch her breath, but we're not done yet.

She looks up at me with hooded eyes and grins. "You've ruined me."

"That was only the warm-up." I grab her legs and flip her over until she's on all fours. She squeals as I tease her slick opening with my cock. I'm so goddamn hard and can't wait to be inside her.

Not being able to hold back any longer, I grab her hips and slam inside her. She moans as she sinks her body against mine, creating the perfect amount of friction.

"You have a tight cunt, baby," I say, not knowing how long I'll be able to last. "Feels so goddamn good."

"Harder," she demands breathlessly. I slam my cock deeper into her, and our skin slaps together as our heavy pants fill the air.

"Goddammit, Kendall," I groan, then slap her ass. I love the way my hand sounds against her skin.

"Yes, yes, yes." Her walls tighten, and I know she's seconds away. "I'm about to…" Kendall screams out her release as her body shakes.

"Yes, good girl," I growl. "Keep your ass up, Angel."

She arches and widens her legs, allowing me to fuck her as deep as possible. I thrust all the way out and slam back inside until I nearly lose myself.

"Fuck, yes," I grunt, digging my thumbs into her hips, steadying her as I sink farther.

"Come inside me, baby." When Kendall reaches between her legs and gently massages my balls, that's all it takes before I'm falling off the ledge and riding the wave.

"Jesus Christ." We sink to the floor and catch our breaths. I cup her cheeks and softly kiss her.

After we've cleaned up, I pull a blanket over us and hold her naked body against mine on the couch. I can't control the stupid smile on my face. It's scary to have these intense feelings about Kendall in such a short amount of time, but it already feels more real than any of my previous relationships. However, I know this isn't real life. We won't be stranded here forever, but I'm going to enjoy every second I have with her while I can.

As we watch the flames of the fire lick up the chimney, our eyes become heavy. The smell of her hair and skin is so sweet that I can't help but let out a content sigh. With Kendall wrapped in my arms and molded to my body, we fall asleep in no time, completely elated.

CHAPTER THIRTEEN

KENDALL

DAY 7

I WAKE up on cloud nine. Ryan's pressed against me, and when I rustle, he tightens his arms around me.

The fire has died down, leaving nothing but glowing embers in the bottom. Needing to use the bathroom, I shimmy out of Ryan's grasp. Once I'm free, I pick up my clothes off the floor and slip on my shirt.

As I climb the stairs to my room, I think about how Ryan and I keep losing control with each other. Even though our agreement is just sex, something more sizzles between us, and he'd be blind to deny it. He's everything I've ever wanted in a partner, but I have a feeling this is all we'll have. However, I'm hanging onto the possibility of more after we leave the cabin. Ryan's a workaholic and has already admitted he's not good at balancing his job with a relationship. But whatever's happening between us is special, and if he'll let me, I'll show him he can have both—his career and a girlfriend.

After I go to the bathroom and brush my teeth, I slip on a clean T-shirt and some jeans, then head downstairs.

Right now, I'm on a mission to drink the biggest cup of coffee I can find.

As soon as my foot hits the bottom step, I see Ryan is still sound asleep. I make my way to the kitchen to brew a pot, then try to figure out what we'll eat today.

I go into the pantry and start rearranging the cans and boxes. My eyes go wide when I see a box of pancake mix. How in the hell did we miss this? I feel as if I just won the lottery, but then I laugh at myself. When I get back to the city, I swear I'm ordering takeout for a month straight.

Wanting to surprise Ryan, I mix in the proper amount of water with the powder, then grab a skillet. I pour enough oil to coat the bottom of the pan, then get to work. As I wait for them to cook, I grab plates and fill a mug to the top with coffee. Carefully, I move between stacking pancakes and pouring batter until the large bowl is empty.

With a big grin, I grab the syrup I found, and when I turn around, I slam into a hard body.

Ryan grabs my waist to steady me, wearing a sleepy grin. "Sorry," he says. "Didn't mean to startle you."

"I thought you were sleeping! I wanted to surprise you with breakfast in bed or rather, on the couch, well, you know what I mean." I stumble over my words.

He chuckles. "They smell delicious. How can anyone sleep with that wafting through the air?"

I smile and notice how his pants hang low on his hips. I take him in, then meet his eyes.

"That's true. Welp, dig in."

We go to the bar top, and Ryan hands me a fork.

"This looks amazing." He takes a mouthful, and I'm not sure he even chews before he swallows. His eyes go wide, and he nods, continuing to eat.

A sly smile spreads over my lips. "All I did was add water," I admit, then take a bite. They're cooked perfectly, and the maple pecan syrup makes them even better.

"Damn, I'd marry me." I snort-laugh because it's evident I'm no chef, but I do try. Before Ryan can say anything, he pulls his phone from his pocket, looks at the screen, then silences it.

When I catch a glimpse of the name on the screen, my stomach drops.

Rachelle. His ex. Why the hell is she calling?

The mood in the room changes, and I have a million questions, though it's none of my business.

"Answer it if you need to." I hurry and shove food in my mouth so he doesn't hear the confusion in my voice. Ryan looks down at the screen, then back at me.

"Nah, I'm good," he replies. After a couple of minutes of awkward silence, he continues, "You're being quiet. What's on your mind?"

I suck in a deep breath. "Do you guys talk regularly?"

Ryan shrugs. "Sometimes. She'll call me to catch up or to chat about Joey."

"If you two still care about each other, why did you break up?" I ask since I never heard the story. I'm not sure if Cami knows the exact reason, but Rachelle still occasionally calls her.

He stiffens, and I know I've crossed the line. "I'm sorry. You don't have to answer that," I quickly add.

"No, it's fine. She couldn't handle how much I worked, and after a while, she had trust issues because of all the women I work with, though I never gave her a reason to doubt me. I'd never cheat on her and even told her so, but that wasn't enough to reassure her. When we first started dating, my hectic work schedule wasn't a problem, but the longer we were together, the more it became a wedge in our relationship."

"Sounds like you guys were able to remain friends at least. Do you blame her for the breakup?"

"No, but I've harbored guilt about it. We could've had a good thing, but my job is non-negotiable. Either it's something my partner accepts or it's over." He's almost emotionless as he says those words. Ryan shrugs, then grabs the syrup and pours more on the few bites he has left.

It's clear Ryan will always choose his work over a woman, and while his dedication is admirable, I wonder if any woman can handle that kind of schedule. I'd never make him choose, but it's easier to say that beforehand. I'm sure it causes issues in a relationship when you never actually get to see the person.

Ryan continues when I don't say anything. "Don't get me wrong. I cared about her and Joey a lot, and I miss hanging out with him," he admits, finishing his food. "Rachelle and I were good for each other, but it was more of a right person, wrong time kind of situation."

My heart races, and I swallow down a big gulp of coffee. I'm not sure I like the sound of that, but I keep that to myself.

"She didn't understand why my job came first. I made a commitment not only to my patients but also my co-workers. They depend on me to show up and do my part. Even though I'd get two days off a week, it wasn't enough. We'd spend them fighting, and things weren't fun anymore. I knew I had to end it before things went any further. It was hard to leave, though, because of her son. He'll always hold a special place in my heart," he tells me as his expression softens. "His dad is a piece of shit and doesn't want anything to do with him, so I tried to be a good role model for him and spent as much time with him as I could. We spent many afternoons feeding the geese in Central Park or visiting the Lego Store at Rockefeller. The carefree times we spent together are what I miss the most," he honestly says.

My heart hurts for him because I can tell he truly cared for Joey as well as Rachelle. At this point, I don't even know what to say.

"But I made the right decision," he confirms. "I'm sure you know how it is when things end for the best."

I nod and pick up our empty plates. "If you were really in love, you would've never walked away." At least I hope that's true.

Ryan comes over to me and smiles while reaching to turn on the water. "You're probably right."

After I rinse the syrup from the plates, I place them in the dishwasher, then start it since it's almost full.

"I think I'm gonna take a shower," he tells me. "Need anything?"

"Nah, I'm good for now," I say.

As soon as he walks upstairs, I make myself comfortable on the couch, then pick up my phone and text Cami because I need to know how much she knows about Rachelle and Ryan. While Cami didn't really know her that well, she still might have some juicy details. They were together for almost a year, and everyone was shocked when they broke up, including me. We were all convinced they'd get married, and she'd get pregnant shortly after.

Rachelle is beautiful, blond, busty, and runway model thin and tall—the complete opposite of me. I've only seen her in pictures, and I'm sure they didn't do her justice. From what I've noticed over the years, Ryan only dates insanely gorgeous women with successful careers. Even though he's called me beautiful and I'm not usually insecure about my looks, not being on the same job level as his exes or even him is intimidating. I don't have any expectations for once we leave the cabin, but I'd be lying if I said I didn't hope we could be something.

I stare at my phone for at least five minutes as I think about what I'm going to text to Cami, but instead of letting it drag on any longer, I type out a message.

Kendall: On a scale from 1-10, how in love were Ryan and Rachelle?

Cami: Oh no. What happened?

Kendall: Nothing really. I just wanna know. She called

him today, but he rejected it, so I wonder if they're talking again or if he still has feelings for her.

Cami: I'm not sure. She called me recently to catch up, and I told her he was stuck at the cabin due to the snowstorm. That's probably why. But to answer your question, I'd say it about a 6.5. It was his longest relationship, but he never proposed. So in my mind, it wasn't that serious. Otherwise, she'd have a ring, and they'd be planning their wedding.

The thought of Ryan committing himself to someone else makes my stomach roil.

After thirty minutes of texting back and forth with Cami, Ryan comes downstairs. She continues trying to convince me nothing is going on between them.

Cami: Don't worry about it. Wouldn't be surprised if she's trying to get him back, but I don't think he would.
They've been broken up for almost two years.
Considering you're the one he's sleeping with, you have a better chance at being with him than anyone.

"Who're you texting?" he asks. He pops an eyebrow and smirks, then continues. "Tell my sister I said hi."

"Is it that obvious?" I snicker.

He sits next to me. "Yep. Anytime you talk to her, you get a certain look on your face, like you two are conspiring to rob a bank, then go spend it on a vacation."

It causes me to burst out into laughter. "That's hilarious."

With him sitting this close to me, I can smell the soap on his clean skin.

"So what did you ask her about me?"

I roll my eyes. "Who says we're talking about you?"

"Please, I wasn't born yesterday. Go on, tell me," he says with a wave of his hand.

"Nope. Our text convos are top secret." I pretend to lock my lips and throw away the key.

Just as I tell Cami bye, I get a call from my mother. I let out a sigh and answer.

"Hi, Mom!" I say. Ryan grins wide at my forced tone.

"When are you coming home? You know your father has planned an elaborate Thanksgiving dinner next week, and you're expected to be there," she reminds me.

I watch Ryan as he looks at me. "As long as I can get home, I'll be there after I volunteer in the morning. I'm currently snowed in until the plows come out this way. Could be tomorrow or a week," I explain.

"I guess we'll have to send our pilot out there to pick you up then," she states, but I know she's serious.

"Mother, there's no way a helicopter could land here. There's too much snow. I'm fine for now. If I can make it, I'll be there. If I'm not, well, Dad will get over it."

She gasps. "He won't."

"He'll be forced to. I can't control the weather. It wasn't a part of my plans either."

With a sigh, she gives up. "Alright, darling, please keep me updated so I can keep your father informed. Everything else okay?"

Though I could use a burger right now, there's no way I'd admit that to her. "Perfectly fine."

The line goes silent for a second before she continues. "Well, if you need anything, please call me. Love you, sweetie."

"Love you too, Mom."

She makes the kissy sound, and I do too, then end the call.

Ryan chuckles, shaking his head. "Sounds like my mother."

"She means well, but they can be so overbearing sometimes. Thankfully, Piper keeps them plenty busy."

He grins. "I'm sure they just want what's best for you."

I laugh. "They do, but they also like to be controlling."

"It's because they worry. You're a beautiful woman who's way too friendly. Hell, I worry about you."

I let out an aww. "Really?"

"Yeah, I can only imagine the trouble you and Cami have gotten into that I don't know about." Ryan tilts his head in speculation.

"A lot," I admit. "But still, sometimes I wish I lived a normal life where *Page Six* didn't feature my family name. It's not always the easiest when people recognize you at the grocery store."

He places his hand on mine and squeezes. "I get that more than you know."

I nod. "I'm grateful for the lifestyle they've provided me, but sometimes, I wonder what it would be like to have a simple life."

"It's one reason I became a doctor. Normalcy. Keeps me grounded."

I lean over and kiss him on the cheek. It feels so fucking good to have someone understand what it's like growing up in the spotlight with that constant pressure.

For the rest of the day, we flip between the weather channel and college football. The forecast still doesn't look the best, but I'm okay with staying here a little longer with him. I'm secretly hoping he'll admit he wants our "only sex" agreement to become more.

After we eat macaroni leftovers for dinner, we go back into the living room and return to the couch. I swear this is the most I've lounged around all year long, but it feels nice to relax and spend this time with him.

Ryan hands me the remote. "You choose."

"Really?" I ask, then look around at the warm glow of the Christmas lights and hear the crackling of the burning wood. Immediately, I change it to the Hallmark channel.

Ryan cracks up. "Again? I should've known."

The first movie that comes on is about a rich girl who goes to a small Christmas town to buy the only tree farm. Of course, she falls in love with the young, handsome owner and decides she wants to stay instead of returning to her corporate life.

Ryan snorts. "Yeah right."

"What?" I turn to him. "It could happen."

"No way," he says and gives me a smirk before standing. "Be right back."

"Where're you going?"

"It's a surprise," he tells me before walking to the kitchen.

I grab the fluffy blanket and throw it over my body, then sink further into the couch. After ten minutes, Ryan returns, carrying two mugs. He gives me one, and my eyes widen in excitement.

"Hot cocoa *and* a candy cane?" I gasp, stirring the warm liquid.

"I found some in the cabinet earlier, and watching everyone on this damn movie drink cocoa made me want some," he explains.

"Thank you. So perfect too." I smile, then blow on it to cool it. When I take my first sip, I hum at how delicious and warm it is. "This is happiness in a cup."

"Better be. Looked expensive." Ryan clinks his mug against mine, and we watch another ridiculously cute movie.

When the guy almost kisses the leading lady under the mistletoe, I let out an aww.

"Jesus." He shakes his head in disappointment. "He could've kissed her at least ten times by now."

I place my finger over his mouth and shush him. "That's not the point."

"Really?" He pops a brow.

"Yeah! It's about the chase. Come on, Distant Diva, you should know this!"

"I'm sorry, what did you call me?" He sets his mug on the coffee table, then grabs mine and does the same. Now I know I'm in trouble.

"You heard me!"

Seconds later, he's tickling the hell out of me.

"No, no, no," I yelp. Bending over, I try to fight him off me as he laughs.

"Stop!" I screech. "If you keep it up, I'm gonna pee myself," I warn, but he keeps going. As soon as he pulls away, I go into attack mode and try to get him back.

He jerks around, trying to get me away, but fails. Another adorable thing I've learned about him—he's as ticklish as I am. Once we've both laughed ourselves stupid, I remove the distance between us and slide my lips against his.

"You taste good," I tell him. "Like chocolate and sexy man."

He chuckles against my lips and cups my cheeks. "You taste like Christmas."

I smile. "My favorite holiday."

He presses a soft kiss on my forehead. "And mine, but I have a feeling this year might be the best one yet."

CHAPTER FOURTEEN

RYAN

WHEN I LOOK at the time, I realize it's barely past seven, though we've already had dinner and watched two Hallmark movies. Kendall's getting antsy, and if I'm being honest, so am I. I've never had so much time to sit around and do nothing but overthink.

Kendall grabs us each a bottle of water, then sits back on the couch next to me. "I'm bored."

"I know. I can only check the weather and watch so many G-rated movies before I feel like mush," I admit.

"Are there any board games here?"

I think about it for a second and know there are some in one of the spare closets upstairs. "I believe we have Monopoly and Scattergories. There may be some others. I can go look," I tell her.

"Monopoly!"

I give her a sly grin. "You sure you wanna play?"

"Of course." She laughs.

"Just remember you chose it. Cami stopped playing board games with me when she was ten for a reason," I tease, standing to go find it.

Kendall bites on her lip. "We'll see about that."

I hurry up the stairs to see if it's where we left it all those years ago. When I open the closet door, it's full of old games. I grab the box and head downstairs.

Returning to the living room, I find Kendall on the floor with pillows around the coffee table.

"Hope you're ready to get your ass kicked," she playfully threatens.

I let out a chuckle, setting down the game. "We'll see about that."

Kendall pats the floor, and I add a few more logs to the fire before I sit next to her.

"Do you want to be the banker?" I ask, taking the top off the box and sorting out the money.

"Sure." Kendall grabs the instructions and reads over them. "I need a refresher. It's been a long time."

"So we're not playing by house rules?"

She lifts a brow at me. "Like what?"

"Monopoly isn't fun if you play by the official rules, but go ahead and read them. I learned the summer after fifth grade that they were incredibly stupid."

Kendall continues to read and gasps. "Oh my gosh, did you know *all* property must sell when you land on it?"

"Yep. If you don't want to buy something, it goes to auction, so your opponent, which is me, can buy it for ten dollars."

Her eyes go wide. "And if you land on Free Parking, you don't get all the money in the middle. Uhh, this really does suck."

"So house rules or real ones?"

She shakes the instructions. "You're telling me every single person who's played this game has been doing it wrong?"

A chuckle escapes me. "Yep."

"House rules then because this"—she points at the booklet—"sounds boring as hell."

"Fine by me." I wink.

Kendall counts out fifteen hundred dollars for each of us, then we discuss how we'll play.

"Okay, we're all set up!" she exclaims, and I love how happy she looks. It's been ages since I've played, and I'd be lying if I said I wasn't excited.

"This game could last for hours. One time, Cami and I played a game for all through breakfast, lunch, and dinner. I felt like I worked a job all day after paying bills, buying properties, and collecting rent."

She snorts. "Damn. I usually give up after a few hours. Which piece do you want?"

I meet her lips, then her eyes. "Top hat."

"Good, because I love being the car." She hands me the dice. "You can go first."

We take turns rolling, and it doesn't take long before we're collecting our two-hundred dollars after passing go. I quickly realize Kendall's a savage when it comes to board games, and I may have finally met my competitive match.

She lands on Park Place and immediately buys it, regardless of how expensive it is. "Now I just need Boardwalk, and you're done," she says as I buy my second railroad.

"Okay, Miss Thing. I wouldn't get *too* cocky."

She playfully rolls her eyes, then drops the dice. We go back and forth for nearly two hours, buying properties and drawing chance cards. Not too long after, Kendall gets sent to jail for the second time, and I'm trading in my houses for hotels. One whole side of the board is mine, so there's no way she'll pass my properties without paying. As soon as she does, I hold out my hand for her to pay up.

"You're gonna make me go broke!" she says, slamming the colorful bills in my hand. On my next turn, I land on Boardwalk.

"Don't you dare buy it!" she warns.

I slowly count out four hundred dollars for the bank and give it to her. She groans when she hands over my card.

"Thank you very, very much." I kiss it and set it down next to my others.

"That was supposed to be mine." She scowls before shaking the dice.

"I'll sell it to you," I offer, then look down at her sad little money pile. She has around three hundred dollars left, and if she lands on just one of my railroads, she's done for.

"Sell it? You see how much I have!"

"I'll take it all plus the Electric company and St. James Place, Tennessee, and New York Avenue."

She narrows her eyes at me. "That's not a fair trade."

"Alrighty then. Never mind." I take my turn and draw a Get Out of Jail Free Card. "Hell yes!" I flip it around and show her.

"I'm pretty sure I don't like playing with you," she sneers, then lands on Vermont Avenue.

I burst out into laughter because it's got a hotel. "That'll be five hundred and fifty bucks, please."

She scrunches her nose. "I only have three hundred and twenty-five left."

I tap my finger against my lips. "I guess you'll have to sell some property or..." I linger for a second. "I can think of another way you could earn some money."

She tilts her head. "What do you have in mind?"

Lifting an eyebrow, I smirk. "Three hundred dollars for each piece of clothing."

Kendall's mouth falls open, then she gives me a devious grin. "How about five hundred?"

"Of course you'd negotiate," I say with a chuckle.

"Well?" She teases me by lifting the hem of her shirt, barely showing some skin.

I hurry and hold out my hand. "Deal."

Kendall stands up and removes her shirt, then tosses it toward me while biting her bottom lip. Then she sits and takes money from the bank, then pays me rent.

Thousands of dollars are stacked up in the middle, and when I throw the dice, I land on Free Parking and collect my winnings.

"Oh my fucking God," she says with a groan. "Meanwhile, I'm over here being a prostitute for Monopoly money, and you're getting rich by doing nothing."

I snort at how dramatic she sounds, but it's hilarious. "Exactly. The original point of the game was to prove a single entity can dominate the market. It's proof of how the rich get richer and the poor get poorer."

"Wait, seriously?" she asks as she lands on Kentucky Avenue, another property of mine with a hotel.

"Absolutely. Looks like you owe me ten-fifty." I flip the card around so she can see.

"Fuck!" She counts her money and has two hundred and twenty-five dollars because she passed go. Kendall stands up and removes her jeans. "Dammit. It was a bad day not to wear socks."

Reaching behind her back, she unsnaps her bra. Her breasts are on full display, and I almost forget we're still playing.

"Monopoly is a dark-ass game," she huffs. "But now that I think about it, the concept makes sense. Makes me proud of my parents, honestly. They've set up foundations to help people in need and give back in some way instead of being horrible rich people sitting on mountains of cash."

I beam. "They've done a lot of good, but so many others in the same social class are greedy as fuck."

Just thinking about it makes me sick to my stomach. There have been times when people have come into the hospital and refuse surgeries because of their out-of-pocket cost. When that happens, it makes me strive to work harder and be more involved to make our healthcare system better.

"There are," she admits. "Dad can't stand those assholes, though. I'm glad they don't associate with people who act like that."

I roll the dice and land on one of Kendall's properties, but it doesn't even have a house. I pay her ten dollars, and she shakes her head.

She lands on Reading Railroad with the next roll, and I have all four. "Two hundred big ones, baby."

After throwing the money toward me, she rolls again since she has doubles. Two fives face up, which forces her on Pennsylvania Railroad.

"If I didn't know better, I'd say you rigged these dice." She chuckles, handing me the last of her money.

"It's still your turn," I say.

"I know. I know. I'm just trying to get the courage to go." Eventually, she does and somehow makes it to a property she owns.

I get thrown in jail, use my pass to get out, and Kendall lands on the Luxury Tax.

Shaking her head, she stands up and gives me a little strip show before she slides her panties down and throws them at my face. Finishing this game is the last damn thing on my mind, especially when she stalks toward me completely naked. Before she can straddle me, I grab her hips, then loop her leg over my shoulder. She knows exactly where this is going when I taste her.

Kendall steadies herself but also rides my face as I flick and suck on her clit. Moans escape her as she moves to the rhythm. She's a greedy little thing, and when I pull away, she's flustered and breathing hard.

"Lie down, sweetheart."

Carefully, she moves to the floor. I hover above her and press my mouth against hers. Our tongues tangle together, and I'm so damn hard, I nearly burst out of my jeans. Wanting to please her, I trail kisses down her body to her sweet pussy. I take my time to tease her real good, allowing her orgasm to teeter on the edge. Every time she's close, her body tenses, and I pull away before she can spill over.

"Fuck, Ryan," she pants with frustration. "I'm so close."

Her breathing is erratic, and her back is arched. I dip my tongue inside, tasting her arousal, and as soon as I pick up the pace on her clit, her body convulses. Her sweet moans are music to my ears. Not able to wait another moment, I unzip my pants and lower my boxers.

Kendall widens her legs for me. As I slowly slide into her, she presses the heels of her feet into my ass cheeks and smiles. "You know how I like it."

"I love anything you do." I flash her a wink.

I hover above her, then slam my dick in and out of her. She's so goddamn wet and tight, and no matter how slow or fast I go, I can't seem to get enough of her. My lips are magnetized to hers as I continue my calculated pace, enjoying every second of her. We kiss sweet and slow, but fuck raw and hard.

"I think I'm addicted at this point," I growl in her ear. "I can't get enough."

"Me too," she murmurs. "That wasn't part of the plan, though."

"None of this was part of the plan." I smirk. "Guess we'll have to improvise."

The anticipated buildup has me losing my mind. Kendall somehow manages to flip me over onto my back. I kick the Monopoly board and hear the pieces scatter everywhere. We chuckle at the mess we've made but don't care. She takes control, riding me with her palms on my chest while wearing a satisfied smile on her face.

As her perky tits bounce, I grab her nipples. Kendall's head falls back on her shoulders, and her body tightens. Seeing her lose herself is all it takes for my impending release to build. She continues her pace as she rides me, and moments later, I squeeze her hips and spill inside her.

We unravel together, moaning and panting, then both come down from our high. She topples on my chest, and I hold her until we catch our breaths. Eventually, we break apart, and once we're clean, I look over at the board.

Hotels, houses, and money are scattered everywhere. Kendall giggles when the realization hits.

"Now what do we do?" she asks. "We'll never know who won."

I meet her eyes and smile. "I think we both did, Angel."

After we pick up all the pieces and put everything back in the box, Kendall and I find something to eat. We settle with tuna and crackers, then go back to the couch and watch another Hallmark movie. At this point, I don't even fight it because I know how happy it makes her, and that's all I care about anyway.

This time, we lie down together, and I hold her in my arms. My eyes grow tired, and I realize how much being with Kendall has calmed my anxiety over the past week. I'm usually wound up so tight from work that I sleep like shit. When I'm around her, I'm more relaxed and sleep through the night. Too often, I've woken up from nightmares or flashes of working during the pandemic. The PTSD likes to fuck with me like that.

The past week has been incredible, and though I know our time together will eventually end, I'm not sure if I really want it to.

CHAPTER FIFTEEN

KENDALL

DAY 8

ALL MORNING I've been pacing. The windchill is still below zero, and more snow has fallen overnight. As long as we have power, I'll be able to handle it, but I'm going stir-crazy.

The last time I stayed locked up inside like this was while I was quarantined. Now, it's starting to get to me, and I know it's affecting Ryan too. He wants to get back to work as much as I want to get home. Though I'm not complaining because I love spending time with him and having him all to myself. It's the only saving grace to all of this.

If we would've been arguing the entire time, I would've shoveled myself out of here. Ryan's been busy on his laptop all morning, so I don't want to disturb him.

He looks up from his screen when I stand. When our eyes meet, a gush of excitement courses through me. It's ridiculous how much he affects me just by being here.

"Where ya going?"

"Was thinking a hot shower might be good."

Ryan chews on his lip with his perfect teeth. "Have fun."

"I will," I say, popping a brow, then walking upstairs.

Once I'm in the bathroom, I grab my razor and shaving cream along with body butter, then turn on the water. Once it's warm, I step inside and let the stream fall over my body. When I close my eyes, all I can think about is Ryan and the way it feels when he touches or kisses me. It hasn't even been a full week since we agreed to "only sex," but all those underlying feelings I've held back over the years are boiling over. I'm already getting attached to him, and I'm scared to death I'm falling for him. The way he looks at me is enough to bring me to my knees. I don't know how I'm going to go back to my life before being with him. It's possible Ryan St. James has broken me and ruined me for all men.

After I shave my legs, I scrub my arms and legs with the body butter. Ryan thought my skin was soft before, but now I can't wait for him to touch me after this. I take my time, allowing my mind to wander, and I decide that I need to call Cami as soon as I'm out of the shower.

She's the only person who understands us both on a personal level and can talk me off the emotional ledge.

Once my hair is cleaned, I allow the strong beads of water to massage my back, then I suck in a deep breath and get out.

My skin is steaming as I dry off and wrap myself in a fluffy robe. After I twist my hair up into a towel, I grab my phone to FaceTime my best friend.

"Hey, future sister-in-law! What's up?" She answers on the second ring.

"Just wanted to chat and see how things are going over there while I get ready."

"Get ready for what?"

I blush at the thought of what tonight will be. "I guess to seduce your brother?" Laughing, I shrug. "Not that it's much of a challenge at this point."

She smiles wide, then makes an obnoxious gagging noise because I know she doesn't want to hear the details. "How's it going between you two? Engaged yet?"

I suck in a deep breath as she watches me. There's no way I

can hide how I feel when she's right in front of me like this. "I...well. It's going amazing. But that's kinda the problem."

She furrows her brows. "How is that a problem? Honestly, you both needed to get laid, and I'm glad you two decided to finally fuck it out."

I snort, remembering our recent conversation about how he used to drive me crazy. "It's not so much a problem because the sex is…I'll spare you the intimate details, but it's amazing. I've never felt the kind of connection during sex like I do with him. But now the issue is my heart." I suck in a breath as I think of my next words. "I'm confused because I can't catch feelings and—"

"But you are," she says. "And you don't know where this will lead, and you're getting all in your head about it."

I grin. "Yes, exactly."

I move to the vanity and pull my hair out of the towel, then brush it.

"Honestly, you can't cross out being in a genuine relationship with him. And maybe he used his job as an excuse in his previous relationships because he wasn't ready for something so serious. He's changed, and even if he doesn't see that, I do," she explains. "Plus, I selfishly want the two of you to fall madly in love, get married, and have babies so our kids can be cousins."

I burst out laughing, but it warms my heart. That sounds amazing even though it's a really far-fetched reality.

"Honestly, I think he has a lot to work through, and he hasn't found the right woman yet. But you're exactly what he needs in life, Kendall. He's always had a thing for you even though he'd never admit it. I love my brother, but when it comes to his family, he's a horrible liar."

Her words have my heart racing as I grab my makeup bag. I start with moisturizer, then foundation. "You could be right. I just don't want to get hurt," I admit as I continue my routine with powder, bronzer, and blush.

"If he hurts you, I'll castrate him, and I'm pretty sure he knows that. That's probably why he always stayed away from you in the first place. Also, you and I both know it's impossible to fuck without feelings when they were there first. Neither of you is fooling me. You're both putting on an act. Convince me otherwise." She stands and brings me with her to the bar top.

"See, this is exactly why I called you. You make me feel better when my thoughts are trying to suffocate me," I breathe out, relieved.

"When Eli and I first got together, I had no idea where it would lead, but I knew I had feelings for him. And sometimes, you just have to let your heart lead instead of your head. You and my brother are meant to be together, but only when you're both ready. Plus, you know the power of the pussy." She flashes a cheeky grin, and I snort.

"Damn right. Trust me when I say he will never forget being with me."

She immediately shakes her head. "No details. For the love of God."

"Okay, okay, I'll spare you," I mock. "How's the last-minute wedding stuff going?"

"Everything is officially done, just dealing with anxiety that everyone is going to do what they're supposed to. I'm also trying to avoid chocolate, but Eli found my secret stash of Twix. He took them and hid it."

I laugh. "Surprised you didn't murder him for that."

"Well technically, I told him weeks ago to make sure I didn't fall off the chocolate wagon. Now the honeymoon? That's a different story. When you go to restock, I want all the chocolate, got it?"

Smiling, I say, "You got it. That skintight dress is going to be painted on you, and you hardly had room to breathe."

"Guess I shouldn't mention I found an entire bag of Kit Kats and ate them today." She lets out a contagious laugh, and I join in. Cami's naturally thin, and no amount of sweets will make her gain a pound anyway. "I don't know why I'm stress eating so much, but the anxiety of everything coming together is overwhelming."

"Well it's not like you're having the biggest wedding of the season or anything," I tease. "Don't worry. It's going to be perfect, and fingers crossed Ryan and I actually get to leave before the big day."

"Don't even say that!" Cami groans. "I will send Eli to plow you out himself if it gets to that point. Speaking of," she says, clearing a notification. "I need to call him back."

"No problem," I tell her. "I'll call you when I have an update on the weather."

"You better," she says, then we say goodbye. I stand, sucking in a deep breath, and think about everything Cami said. I'm going to let Ryan take the lead and not rush anything but make it clear that I'd be game to make it work with him.

As I walk into my bedroom, I open my suitcase and pull out a dress I packed. We had only planned to be here for two days, but I brought a variety of clothes, knowing I'd be with Ryan. Considering the cabin is warm, I decide to slip it on, minus my bra and panties. I wonder if Ryan will notice I'm going commando.

After I blow-dry my hair and put on some red lipstick, I go downstairs. When my foot hits the bottom step, I look for Ryan on the couch but don't see him.

I go into the kitchen, where he's standing at the stove. Looking over his shoulder, he scans his eyes down my body, then gives me a sexy ass grin.

"Whatcha cookin'?" I ask, removing the space between us and coming up behind him.

He wraps an arm around me. "Canned chili and rice. Might have to start calling me Chef."

I can't stop smiling as he squeezes my shoulder with his strong fingers and pulls me closer. "You smell so damn good."

"Just think how I taste."

Ryan swallows hard and turns off the stovetop.

"I am now," he admits, taking a step back and staring at me. "Fuck, Kendall."

He adjusts himself, and the last thing that's on my mind right now is lunch. Ryan moves forward, and his lips crash against mine. Moments later, my hands are in his hair, and we're walking backward until my ass hits the edge of the kitchen table. With one swift movement, Ryan spins me around and guides me forward until my breasts touch the cool wood. Considering the material is thin, I feel it against my nipples.

He groans behind me as he slowly slips his hands under my dress. He lifts it over my hips, then leans over my back. "So fucking sexy," he whispers in my ear.

I turn my face to kiss him, and our tongues twist together with white-hot passion.

Gently, he removes the dress from my body. "Bend over the table and spread your legs," he instructs, sliding a finger up my bare spine.

I arch my back and ass so he gets the perfect view.

Seconds later, Ryan's on the floor, devouring my pussy from behind. I'm so goddamn worked up, I feel like I'm going to combust when he slips two fingers inside me.

"Yes, yes," I scream out, standing on my tiptoes to give him full access.

Ryan goes slowly as I lose myself in the sensation. Before I can say anything, he's tongue fucking me, then takes me by surprise when he licks from my pussy to my asshole, then back down again.

My entire body shivers with pleasure, and I'm ready to fly the white flag of surrender.

As I take in the sensations, Ryan pulls back, and I immediately feel the loss.

"I need to feel that soaking wet cunt," he growls, kissing up my back. Ryan's strong hands wrap my long hair around his fist, then tug. "Tell me how you want it."

I try to gain my footing as the adrenaline comes rushing in. "Hard. Rough. Fuck me like you've never fucked anyone before."

His breathing becomes ragged, and right now, I just want to be dominated. I stay bent over, giving him all the access he needs to do whatever he wants to me. I look at him over my shoulder and see something swirling in his eyes as he enters me.

Ryan ravages my pussy, and a strong palm strikes my ass cheek. My entire body clenches, enjoying the intense pleasure sprinkled with a little pain. He touches me with purpose, squeezing my hips hard and making sure I won't forget he's the one who made me feel this way.

"Again," I say.

Ryan grunts, pounding against me, and delivers another hard slap. "Mine, all *mine*."

"God, yes," I pant at how good this feels and how I never want it to end. Our ragged breathing echoes throughout the room, and I know neither of us will last long at this rate.

"Kendall," he whispers, moving my hair and pressing a soft kiss to my shoulder. "I want to try something. Do you trust me, Angel?"

"With my life."

Ryan pulls out and kneels. His mouth is on my asshole again, and moments later, his tip is circling my hole.

"Yes, please," I beg, and Ryan slowly enters my ass. As soon as he goes deeper, an explosion of pleasure soars through me, and I lose my breath.

"How's that feel?" he asks, moving slow. "You okay?"

"Ryan," I mutter when my insides tense. "Fuck. I'm gonna—"

I try to give him a warning, but my body crumples too quickly. The orgasm practically blinds me as it shakes through my soul, and I nearly lose my footing when Ryan comes too.

"Angel," he rasps. "Fuck, the way you squirted was hot. I love making you come."

I stand, and he steadies me as I look and see how wet my thighs are, then sit my ass on the table. "Wow," I say, still trying to catch my breath. "Guess I can mark two things off my sex bucket list."

"I promised I'd take that ass cherry," he says with a smug grin, standing between my legs. "Did you like it?"

His hand moves down to my swollen pussy, and he massages my clit. My mouth falls open as I claw my nails into his back. "Yes. It was weird at first, but as soon as I relaxed, I came, and it felt amazing. No one's ever gone there before," I admit as he picks up the pace.

"I wanna make you come all night long."

"You have for the past five days," I tease. "Not that I'm complaining."

"I think we have some records to break, sweetheart," he taunts, gently kissing me, right as I crumple beneath his touch again. My body convulses, and I lie flat on the table, taking it all in.

"Trust me, we've already broken records," I say breathlessly.

"Then it's time to make new ones."

CHAPTER SIXTEEN

RYAN

AFTER WE CLEAN UP, Kendall and I sit at the breakfast bar and eat our chili and rice. There's no way I'll ever be able to look at that table the same. While Kendall admitted she's experiencing many firsts with me, the truth is, I am too.

I've never had a partner who's been so open to try new things in the bedroom. When I was with Rachelle, the sex was more routine but not the focus of our relationship. It makes me realize how special my connection with Kendall actually is, and I'm not sure I want this to end.

I know we'd discussed just fucking for fun without the feelings, but I can't deny what's brewing between us. It's almost too much for me to handle because I know what she deserves, but I just don't know if I could give her that.

"Whatcha thinking about?" she asks right before she takes a big bite of chili.

I put on a smile. "Nothing. Nothing at all."

She points her spoon at me. "You're a bad liar, Ryan St. James."

I chuckle as she drops my full name. "It's why I'm a doctor and not a lawyer," I admit with a wink. I've learned to tell the truth, but in a respectful manner. Patients expect doctors to deliver bad news with compassion, and it's partially why I'm so devoted to my job. I'm not just their doctor. We form relationships, and I truly want the best for them.

"So, I spoke with Cami earlier." Thankfully, she changes the subject.

"Really? What level of stressed-out is she about the wedding today?"

Kendall takes a sip of her water. "Eh, I'd say between six and seven. She's already devoured a bag of candy from her secret stash."

I let out a hearty laugh. "Sounds about right. I'm sure everything will go fine. My parents hired tons of security, so she has nothing to worry about on that front. And she's more than ready to settle down with Eli. I'm sure it's just anxious nerves for it to be here already."

Kendall meets my eyes and smiles. The realization hits me that Kendall and I are following the same path as my best friend and sister. My entire body is on fire.

After we finish eating, Kendall and I clean up the kitchen, then we go to the living room. Instead of sitting on the couch, we pull two chairs close to the large windows and look out at the new blanket of snow covering the ground. At this point, I've been trying to keep my boss updated as much as possible, but I'm not convinced we'll be leaving in the next few days. As soon as the main roads were clear, we got bombarded with more snow and another delay in the private road leading to the cabin getting cleared.

Kendall changes into some leggings and a tank top, then loops her legs over the edge of the chair, sitting sideways in it. I'm checking emails and trying to go over charts as she draws.

Every once in a while, I find myself staring as dark hair falls in front of her face. She's mesmerizing, and I can't help but watch her work. Randomly, she'll chew on the inside of her cheek when she's shading something. I can't wait to see what she's working on because I was blown away by the snowscape she painted. The more time we spend together, the more I learn about her.

She stops what she's doing, then stretches her arms and rolls her neck around. "Why did you decide to become a doctor?"

I stop typing and meet her eyes. "I knew when I grew up, I wanted to directly help people. I didn't want to run a business like my dad. Sure, he helps people by paying their salary, but I wanted it to be more personal. Have you ever seen *Groundhog Day*?"

Kendall thinks about it for a second. "That old movie with Bill Murray? Where he lives the same day over and over?"

I nod. "Yeah, that one. Do you remember that scene in the alley when he finds the homeless man dead?"

"I think so."

"Well, Bill Murray goes back to the old man over and over to try to figure out a way to save his life. He tries everything, and eventually, he realizes there's nothing he can do. In the end, he still fails to save the old man. As a kid, I understood that on such a deep level, and I knew I wanted to save people's lives. Like Bill Murray, I might fail at times, but it's better than doing nothing, and that's where the difference is." I give her a smile. "I've never told anyone that before."

"At least we're both experiencing firsts." She grins, and I know we've both shared things with each other we've never told anyone. "I know how dedicated you are. In a roundabout way, it's why I started volunteering. There was a need, and I knew I could fill it. I respect you so much for dedicating your life to helping others. Not many people do that. In fact, most people I know are quite selfish," she tells me. "However, being here with you has taught me some things about myself."

I smile. "Oh yeah?"

"You mentioned the other day about me starting a business to help charities. I've been thinking about it more and am highly considering it."

My eyes go wide, and I stand. Kendall sets down her drawing pad and wraps her arms around my neck when I hug her.

"Really?" I ask, so damn delighted she came to this conclusion.

"Yeah!" She's all smiles as she slides her lips across mine.

"Okay, we have to crack open some champagne. This is a huge deal."

She laughs. "I will never deny champagne, but I still don't know where to start with any of this. It's gonna take a long time to get going."

Walking to the kitchen, I pull down some flute glasses, then crack open the bubbly and pour it.

I hand it to her, and we clink the rims together. "I'd be happy to help you come up with a business and marketing plan if you want."

Her mouth falls open. "Seriously? You already have so much going on."

"You're right, so much going on as we're locked in a cabin for God knows how long," I tease.

A blush hits her cheek as we walk back into the living room. We move in front of the fire with our drinks.

"I'd be honored to have your assistance. Honestly, I don't know why I didn't think of it myself," she admits.

"Sometimes you need an outside person's perspective to show you what you've always been destined to do. I think you would've eventually done it, but trust me when I say I'm happy to have pushed you in the right direction."

She comes in closer, and I paint my lips across hers. "I needed this break." Though I'd never take this much time off willingly, it's helped me decompress and given myself a mental break.

"I did too. Being here has helped me work through some things," Kendall says, then pulls back and chugs her glass. "That was really good."

"I know. I opened the bottle that was reserved for the honeymoon."

Kendall's eyes go wide. "No. You. Did. Not."

Chuckling, I shrug. Cami can't stay mad at me forever anyway. "I did. This was worthy of a celebration. Do you have any idea how many people's lives you're going to change? This is monu-fucking-mental, and don't you dare discredit it."

"You give me *too much* credit," she says, but she's smiling.

"No." I brush my thumb across her jawline. "You just don't give *yourself* enough."

When her eyes meet mine, there's something more behind it, a twinkle I've never seen before. Unspoken words stream between us, and there's no denying she's knocked me off my axis. A blush hits Kendall's cheeks, and she clears her throat.

"Guess I should get back to my drawing," she tells me, taking my now empty glass. She brings them to the kitchen, and I take a moment to catch my breath. Settling back in my chair, I open my laptop, trying to focus on emails over my pounding heart. Is it possible I'm falling for her so quickly? Did she feel the sparks between us too?

When Kendall plops back down in her spot, I force myself to keep my eyes on the screen, but it's hard. When I'm around her, I feel happier than I've felt in months and more like myself. I honestly can't remember the last time that's happened to me. Years, maybe? A decade?

While I hate I can't be at the hospital, I'm happy for the time to work on myself. I've been running from my feelings for so damn long, and Kendall has made me realize I can't stay closed up forever. Within a week, she cut through my hard exterior with her confidence and kindness. I needed her persistence more than she'll ever realize.

After another hour passes, I decide to get up and add more wood to the fire. I admire the Christmas tree as the lights twinkle, and the ribbon Kendall added was the perfect touch.

"Do you usually put a tree up at your place?" she asks.

I chuckle. "Nope."

A gasp escapes her. "Oh my God, Ryan. Are you a scrooge or something?"

I think about the answer my colleagues would probably give. "You know, I might be."

"Hell no. Unacceptable. Tonight, we're watching nothing but old traditional Christmas movies to get you in the holiday spirit!"

I lift a brow at her. "I'm game, but only if we're naked."

I watch her swallow before biting her bottom lip. "When did you become so bold?"

"Oh baby, I've always been like this. You just never knew it." I flash her a wink and watch how flustered she gets.

I wonder if she's thinking about the same thing I am—pressing her naked body against those windows and fucking her from behind.

"Great," she says, slamming her pencil down. "I'm never gonna finish this drawing now that my brain is going crazy."

I walk closer to her and lean over the back of the chair. My eyes go wide, and my mouth falls open when I see a portrait of myself.

"Kendall..."

She places her hand over it and tenses. "They say take a picture, it lasts longer, right?" I hear the uncertainty in her tone, and I want to make sure she knows exactly how I feel about her.

I tilt her jaw and collide my lips with hers. "It's perfect, just like you."

"I can't get you out of my head, Ryan," she whispers as my heart throbs hard in my chest.

"The feeling is mutual," I admit, but we agreed on the terms of our only sex relationship from the start. She set the ground rules to this game. I'm just playing them, hoping we both survive. "Come with me, Angel," I say, holding out my hand.

Kendall doesn't hesitate and takes hold of my grasp. I lead her up the stairs to my bedroom. Slowly, I peel off her clothes, then lay her on the bed to admire every ounce of her beauty. Once I'm naked, I move on top of her. As we kiss, something inside me shifts, and I know she feels it too. Emotions swirl around us, and at this moment, I know we're no longer fucking, but instead, we're making love.

Our heavy breathing fills the room as I whisper how beautiful she is. Feeling this way about Kendall is scaring the fuck out of me. It could end badly. I could break her heart, or she could break mine.

We are so opposite from one another, but when we're together, we fit like two pieces of a puzzle. I wonder if I could give her everything she needs since my work life tends to be a deal breaker for most women.

As our orgasms take over, I'm blinded by the emotions that consume me. I study her face, kissing her lips, and wish I was Bill Murray so I could live this day over and over a thousand times with her. Even if that happened, I doubt it'd be enough because Kendall has already burrowed herself deep inside my heart.

Pushing the thoughts away as we hold each other, I should emotionally prepare myself for when this ends, but I don't want to.

"We're staying in this bed until the sun rises," I say in the crook of her neck.

She laughs and pushes herself onto her side, studying me. "Is that a promise?"

"Considering I can't get enough of you, you bet your sexy ass it is."

CHAPTER SEVENTEEN

KENDALL

DAY 12

THE PAST FOUR days with Ryan have been amazing. Something has shifted between us, but neither of us talks about it. It's easier than admitting we were too weak not to fall for each other. But now I wonder if I'm creating a false scenario in my head that we could actually be more after this is over. Either way, I'm taking it day by day.

It's Thanksgiving Day, and I wake up with sadness in my heart that I won't be able to go to the shelter. The only thing that makes up for it is spending today with Ryan.

Rolling over to an empty space on his side of the bed, I stare up at the ceiling wearing a smile, knowing he's probably downstairs making coffee and breakfast. Before joining him, I grab my phone and check my texts.

Cami: Looks like the private road to the cabin has been cleared! Mom and Dad are having the driveway plowed tomorrow! SO YOU GET TO COME HOME AND HANG OUT WITH ME!

I don't know how I should feel about that news. One part of me is happy to leave, but the other half knows this means my time with Ryan is ending.

Kendall: Wow, that's great! Not sure how I feel about leaving our bubble, though.

Cami: Aw. It's gonna be fine. Trust me!

Kendall: Haha okay. Whatever you say.

My phone buzzes, and I see it's my mom calling.
"Hey, Mom!" I turn on a cheery tone.
"Kendall! Sweetie, how are you holding up?"
I walk to the window and look out. "Doing good! The St. Jameses are having the driveway cleared tomorrow so we can finally drive out of here. Should be home in a couple of days. We need to head into town and restock the cabin for Cami and Eli's honeymoon, but other than that, everything else is taken care of here for them."
"That's great, but I was referring to how *you* were doing. I know how important volunteering at the shelter is for you today. Wanted to check on you and wish you a Happy Thanksgiving. Also, your father is disappointed he won't see you today. He asked me to send his love."
I smile. "Thanks, Mom. Tell him I love him too. Of course I'm upset, but there's nothing I can do. I came to terms with it a few days ago when I realized the snow was still falling." Now, if only I could accept that Ryan and I are going our separate ways sooner than later.
"You'll just have to make up for it over Christmas. I had teatime with Trish last week, and she told me about the Salvation Army Angel Tree program, so I adopted an entire tree."
I snort. "An entire one? Aren't you just supposed to take one?"
"Yes, sweetie, but I thought it would be great to just take all

five hundred. So if you need something to do when you get home, we have presents to buy and wrap. I know how much you love doing that."

"That's awesome, Mom. I'll be happy to help," I tell her. She has a personal shopper who could do all of this, but I think I'd enjoy it, and perhaps, it'd take my mind off Ryan.

"If you need anything, let me know. We love you," she says again, then I end the call.

After I get dressed, I go downstairs, where Ryan's actually listening to Christmas music. He's moving around the kitchen, preparing something. Leaning against the doorway, I watch him and notice how happy he looks. When he turns around, his eyes meet mine.

"Good morning," I say.

He grins. "Is it still morning?"

I look up at the clock on the wall and see it's just past ten. I slept in, but that's to be expected when I was up all night rolling between the sheets with him. I squeeze my legs together just thinking about it.

"Come see," Ryan says, pulling a mug from the cabinet, then pouring me a cup of coffee. I can't believe I've recently learned to drink it black. It's not my favorite, but it's better than nothing.

Once I'm close to the stovetop, I realize he's been cooking.

"What is all this?"

"Our Thanksgiving meal. The first one I've spent with anyone in the past five years." He shrugs. "I'm usually working."

"Aw. That makes me feel kinda special," I admit. "Having you cook for me makes it even better."

"We've got beans and cornbread. I even found a box of no-bake cheesecake too."

Moving closer, I stand on my tiptoes and kiss him. "Thank you. Sounds delicious."

"You're welcome," he whispers against my lips. Ryan pulls away and stirs the beans again, then puts the lid back on.

"Wanna watch the parade?" I ask, my face lighting up.

Ryan turns the stove down to a simmer, and I grab my coffee. We go to the living room and sit on the couch, then he turns on the TV and holds me.

"When Cami and I were kids, our parents would bring us to watch the parade from the comfort of a condo so we didn't have to stand in the cold. There's nothing like seeing those huge ass balloons in person," Ryan says.

"That sounds amazing. Growing up, my parents liked to fly us to Colorado and spend the holidays in the mountains. Watching it on TV is the only way I've ever seen it, but maybe I should add that to my bucket list," I say.

Ryan's fingers brush against my skin, causing goose bumps to trail up and down my arms.

"You cold?" he asks.

I shake my head and smile. "Warmer than you know."

The giant balloon of Charlie Brown and Snoopy passes by, then SpongeBob SquarePants.

"Did you know this has been going on since 1929?" Ryan asks.

"Really? I had no idea." The floats, cheerleaders, and marching bands walk past the screen. Then last, but not least, Santa and his reindeer. I can't stop smiling and feel like a kid again. After it's over, the Disney parade begins.

Ryan checks the time, then stands. "I think the beans might be ready. Well, based on the recipe I found online."

I look up at him and grin. "You're gonna be a professional cook by the time you get home."

"Pfft, we'll see. I think I've expanded my menu from sandwiches to canned foods," he says with a chuckle, then walks to the kitchen.

I lie back on the couch and let out a happy sigh just as Piper texts me.

Piper: HAPPY THANKSGIVING, SIS! Wish you were here, but I know you wouldn't be here anyway.

Kendall: Thanks, you too! How are things at Mom and Dad's?

Piper: Annoying AF. I need a drink, but the chef just brought out the food. I'm going to start volunteering with you to escape them every year too. They won't accept any other excuse.

Kendall: You should do it because you want to! We could use your help, anyway. Plus, having a YouTube star there might bring awareness to the cause.

I laugh because I already know what her response is going to be.

Piper: Yeah. I wouldn't record it. People have been canceled for doing shit like that for notoriety and attention.

She's filled me on all the drama with content creators. It's man eat man, worse than the fashion industry, and many collaborate just to build their own brand. I thought private school was bad, but this is nothing compared to that, which is another reason I stay out of the limelight. I wouldn't be able to handle the criticism like Piper does. She has thick skin, that's for sure. However, I'd take it too personally.

Kendall: I know. Plus, I know how you are when you donate. All anon.

Piper: That's right. Not trying to impress my fans like that. When can you come home? I miss you!

I explain what Cami told me this morning, then I realize Ryan hasn't mentioned anything about it.

"Ready?" Ryan asks from the doorway.

I stand, then send Piper a final text that I have to go.

The table is set with candles and a holiday-themed cloth with cornucopias on it. Not sure where he found this old thing, but I love it. He pulls out a chair for me, and I take a seat.

Moments later, he's returning with cornbread muffins and giant bowls of beans.

I look down at it. "What are these?"

"Lima beans," he says. "Ever had them before?"

"I don't recall," I tell him honestly, picking up my spoon and dipping it in. I blow on the white beans, then take a bite. "Wow."

"I know, right? They don't taste like beans, do they?"

"No, they're nutty but sweet. I can't describe it." I take another bite, then eat my cornbread. I feel so much joy, knowing Ryan worked to make today special for me, and I plan to show him just how much later.

"I added garlic and onion powder. Some red pepper flakes and used the chicken stock from the pantry. This recipe online was easier than I thought," he says proudly.

I smile and abruptly change the subject. "You know your parents have scheduled the driveway to be plowed tomorrow, right?" I ask.

He lowers his eyes. "Yes, my mother called and informed me this morning." His tone is formal, but there's a hint of something behind it. Sadness, maybe?

There's awkwardness in the air, but neither of us mentions the real question at hand.

"That's good news!" I add, trying to lighten the mood. "I can't believe we've been here for twelve days," I say, taking a sip of water.

He gives me a grin. "I know. I was thinking we could go to town and restock the fridge and pantry for the honeymooners tomorrow. Then maybe make a nice dinner for us since we've been roughing it."

"Yeah, I love that idea. Plus, Cami needs her Pop-Tarts and candy or she might not survive for two weeks."

A hearty laugh releases from him. "Yeah, well if we can live off random food for days, she'll be just fine."

"Very true." I chuckle, meeting his eyes. We eat in silence until we're both done. The awkward tension streams between us, and I wish it would go away.

"Did you tell your boss the good news?"

Ryan stands and picks up our dishes. "No, I was going to text him tomorrow morning and let him know," he says as he walks to the sink. I make myself useful and pour the rest of the beans in a plastic container, then put it in the fridge.

After the kitchen is clean, Ryan pulls me close to him. His body feels warm pressed against mine. He places his index finger under my chin and lifts my eyes to meet his. "You okay?"

I nod, but I feel my emotions getting ready to spill over. I suck in a deep breath and push it away. "It's nothing."

He tilts his head. "It's not just nothing."

"I'm being melodramatic." I chuckle, not wanting to talk about this right now. "Today was amazing. Thank you for making it special for me. It means a lot."

Ryan dips down and kisses me softly. "You're welcome. I know how important it was for you to volunteer at the shelter. I never imagined we'd still be here," he admits. "Not that I'm complaining."

"Me either. I'm just happy I got to spend time with you. And..."

He kisses me again, interrupting my words. When he pulls away, he leads me to the living room. When we sit, I notice he has a bottle of whiskey in his hand.

"What's the occasion?" I ask with a smirk.

"Thought we could play a game to get us through another night," he mocks.

I'm intrigued. "A game, huh? You remember how Monopoly ended?"

He smirks and grabs the remote, probably reliving the

moment because I sure as hell am. Flipping through the channels, he stops at *National Lampoon's Christmas Vacation*.

"This is the end of the movie!" I exclaim, sad that we missed it.

He laughs. "I know, but *Elf* is coming on next."

"I love that movie!"

"You might actually hate it afterward," he warns. "You have to take a drink anytime Buddy eats something nasty, someone sings, and the Naughty or Nice list or Christmas Spirit is mentioned."

"So what you're saying is you wanna make sure I'm trashed before the sun sets." I lift an eyebrow at him.

"Wouldn't be the worst thing that could happen." He laughs as the credits roll so fast and small it would be impossible to read them. "Afternoon drinking at its finest."

"Is this a real game?" I ask as soon as the movie starts with the damn list. We both drink.

The sound of Ryan's chuckles fills me with warmness. "I looked it up on the internet."

"Seriously?" I smack him. "Sounds like something you made up."

"I swear! I googled it, and *Elf* just so happened to be coming on. It was like it was meant to be." He drinks again and hands me the whiskey.

I do a full-body shake because it's so damn strong. "I need a chaser."

Ryan glances over at me. "I need *you*."

With an arched brow, I meet his eyes. "How badly?"

He looks down at his groin, and I see his hard cock pressing against his pants. "Like now."

I tap my finger on my mouth, then stand and take off my shirt. Ryan drinks again, and I take a sip, then bend over and take off my jeans and panties. Not waiting for him, I unbutton and unzip his pants, then climb on top of him.

Though I don't want to think about it, this could be one of the last times we're together. He holds me close as I ride and kiss him, not rushing, and wanting to take in every second of being with him like this. I want to remember the way I feel right now and hope it'll be enough to keep me going when we're apart.

There's no way I can predict what's in store for us, but I hope and wish it's more of this. After we've finished making love, I lay on his chest, and we finish watching *Elf*. As I listen to his heart beat, I wonder if a part of him will be reserved for me once we leave the cabin.

I wasn't supposed to feel this way, but I am, and there's no denying it.

CHAPTER EIGHTEEN

RYAN

AFTER THE LONG, emotionally exhausting day we've had together, I wanted to do something super special for Kendall. I knew how much it meant to her to volunteer today, and I hate that we were stranded here on Thanksgiving especially. I typically stop by my parents' since they serve a feast large enough for an army. Even if I have to work, I always make it a point to visit them. It doesn't help that we don't have as many food choices either, but I'm happy to have whipped something together that somewhat represented a lunch. Though we're both a little tipsy from drinking, it's not enough to ruin our evening. If we would've finished watching *Elf* with that bottle of whiskey, neither of us would be coherent right now. While she's busy on her phone, probably chatting with my sister or hers, I excuse myself and sneak upstairs.

She nods with a small smile, then returns to her conversation.

Not wanting to be gone too long, I hurry and grab all the extra candles we have. I move to the large tub, pour in some of Cami's bubble bath that I found under the cabinet, and turn on the water. Once it's full, I place the candles around the tub, light them, and then flip off the light.

When I return wearing a devious smile, she looks up at me with a curious expression on her face. "What are you up to?"

"I have a surprise," I say, then hold out my hand for her to take.

Immediately, she drops her phone and stands. Interlocking her fingers with mine, I lead her up the stairs and into the bathroom. A gasp releases from her mouth, and her jaw drops as she looks around.

"I told you I'd take a rain check on taking a bath with you. I think I'm ready to cash it in."

"Wow, this is so sweet." She bites her bottom lip. "I love this idea."

As I carefully undress her, my fingertips brush against her soft skin, and I feather kisses on her neck. Goose bumps form over her arms, and she shivers against me. Kendall runs her fingers through my hair when I kiss her collarbone, and I notice her breathing increases. Taking a step back, I drink in her curves and think about how fucking lucky I am to have been able to spend this time with her.

She's too goddamn beautiful for her own good. She's kind and caring, and I'm honestly shocked she isn't taken. However, I also know how hard it is to seriously date someone in the kind of families we have. I got to see her in a way not many people have. Jogging pants or leggings and T-shirts with a messy bun and no makeup. It doesn't matter if she's dressed up or down, she's naturally pretty, and I've always thought so. Seeing her like this, though, standing so confidently naked in front of me— *damn*—I'm speechless.

After I'm undressed, I lead her to the tub and assist her as she steps in. I sit behind her, then pull her closer so her back presses against my chest. Kendall lets out a sigh as she rests her head on my shoulder. We watch as the candles flicker and cast a warm glow in the room. It's so relaxing, and I could be content holding her like this forever.

Kendall closes her eyes and hums. "This is just what I needed."

THE BEST OF US

I tilt her chin up and softly press my lips to hers. Something rushes through me, and there's no more denying I'm falling for her. It's all happening so fast, and my head is still spinning as I think about it. When we were teens, she was such a pain in my ass. All we did was argue even though Cami begged us to get along. I was just as impossible as she was because I saw her as a spoiled brat, and she always said I had a stick up my ass. Now, I think it was all a cover-up for our mutual attraction.

I've learned it's easier to act how people expect, and that's what she's been doing all this time. Kendall has a heart of gold, and I was so damn stupid to think she was nothing more than her family's money. I saw the exterior and never tried to learn more.

I reposition myself so I can clean every inch of her body. I grab the body soap and wash her back, then take my time with her hair and massage her scalp. Once I'm done, my hands trail over her breasts, then down farther.

"Mmm," she moans as I rub circles on her clit. I nibble on her earlobe, and she sighs again. "That feels so good."

"I know, Angel. Let go," I encourage. Kendall's sexy pants fill the room, and I need her as much as she needs me right now.

I move my fingers faster, and she grabs the edge of the tub before crumpling under my touch. "Ryan. God yes, Ryan," she whispers my name, her breasts rising and falling each time.

She turns her head and paints her lips with mine, and the moment turns more emotional than I expected. We know our time is ending, and we'll soon have to go back to our lives before the snowstorm. I'm not ready, and I don't think she is either.

When I pull away, I notice the need lingering in her eyes. "I want to make you feel good too."

"It was about you tonight, baby. I know today wasn't what you had planned, but I wanted to make the best of it."

She kisses me again, and I love how soft her lips are. Kendall's like a black widow, leading me to her web, and I'm her prey who follows.

"Being able to spend time with you is something I'll never regret," she admits, and it's exactly what I needed to hear.

"I feel the same," I tell her honestly. I hold her in silence, and my thoughts fill the empty space. When the water becomes lukewarm, we get out.

I grab a towel and wrap it around my waist, then get one for Kendall. When she steps out of the tub, I dry off every inch of her beautiful body, then she towel dries her hair. Instead of getting dressed, we stay naked and crawl into the king-size bed together.

Kendall moves close to me, then slides her hand down to my cock. It's so damn hard she might snap it off. She pumps me a few times, causing my eyes to roll to the back of my head. She already knows my body so well and knows exactly how to please me.

"Fuck, baby," I mutter, and she throws me a smirk before placing her plump lips around the tip. She hums and forces my length to the back of her throat. Not leaving an inch untouched, she licks my shaft and massages my balls.

"I want you to come in my mouth," she whispers, sliding her tongue around my shaft.

"Fuck, Angel," I grunt as she strokes me faster. Placing my hands behind my head, I watch as she devours me. Her eyes meet mine, and the intensity of her gaze is almost too much to handle.

I hold her hair out of her face, and when she cups my balls, nearly choking on my cock, the buildup begins. She's definitely aware of how my body's reacting to her. Instead of picking up the pace, Kendall goes slow and steady, sucking me until I can't hold it back any longer. I explode in her mouth, and she swallows all of me, licking her lips with enjoyment. "Mmm."

I chuckle as she moves up my body, then kisses me.

"You're so goddamn sexy," I tell her. "I need to fuck that tight cunt."

Even though we were supposed to come here to get it ready for Eli and Cami's honeymoon, there's no denying we've been fucking like newlyweds.

She leans up and traces her lips around the shell of my ear, then whispers, "Just think of all the time we've wasted over the years."

"I can't get enough of you," I confess.

Kendall straddles my hips and rides me until she's screaming out my name. I love watching her take control.

"Your dick is all mine," she purrs as her body shakes with her release.

"All yours," I reiterate, then flip her over. I bring her to the edge of the bed and slam inside her until I come again.

By the time we're both satiated, we're exhausted and crawl farther onto the bed. I suck in a deep breath, wanting to inhale the sweet smell of her skin before she lays her head against my chest. She turns on the TV and puts on *Miracle on 34th Street*.

While the movie plays, I can't help but think about Kendall's words. Of course, if we would've created this bond years ago, no telling where we'd be right now. Living together? Married? Would we have kids? It's hard to say because that wasn't our reality.

I'm a firm believer that timing is everything, and if we would've gotten together then, maybe it wouldn't have worked out. During the pandemic, I was dealing with so much shit that I'm convinced it wouldn't have. I was stressed, overworked, and in a constant state of worry about my sister, best friend, and patients. My parents stayed in the city and were still having teatime with friends. Constant overwhelm and exhaustion never left me, and that period still affects me.

Every day I went to work, I risked my life. Medical school never prepared me for losing people to that extreme level. Hundreds every day. It will always haunt me. When I think back to those early months last year, I was working on autopilot, and even weeks later, I never dealt with my own personal demons.

Kendall's breathing softens, and I know she fell asleep. I catch a glimpse of her and soak in this moment.

She rustles, and I lightly tap her arm and help her get under the blanket. Moving as close as she can to me, she presses a kiss to my cheek, and minutes later, she's back in dreamland. Her soft breaths brush against my cheek, and I stare up at the ceiling as my mind wanders.

A million questions come to the forefront, and I rationally ask myself if I can be what Kendall needs. If I can give her the attention she deserves. Once we leave the cabin, the obligations we both have will return. Internal doubt along with all the conflicting feelings I've experienced nearly swallows me whole.

Could I be the man to make her happy?

Over the years, we never got along. She was too worried about brunch and getting her nails done. Or maybe that's what I chose to see?

The blinders have been removed, and I've gotten a glimpse of the real Kendall, the woman I'm falling hard for. It makes sense as to why my sister adores her so much and always has. Kendall's an amazing person.

I'm not sure what will happen when we leave. While we haven't had a conversation about what this means to us now, I'm certain neither of us expected sparks to fly.

Maybe Cami was right after all, and Kendall and I are meant to be together. The thought has me grinning, and I get lost in the fantasy of her being mine. As soon as I get back to the city, I know I'll be working nonstop. It complicates things because I know I won't have time for her even though I would if I could. But I'd try. I don't think I can ignore the way she makes me feel or pretend we didn't share something special these past two weeks.

I reach for the remote and turn off the TV. Kendall rolls on her side, and I mold my body against hers until we're spooning. Kendall might very well be the woman of my dreams, the one I've been searching for all this time. She understands me and calms me in ways I've desperately needed. There's no way I can ignore that, but I'm not sure she feels the same.

CHAPTER NINETEEN

KENDALL

DAY 14

THE PAST TWO weeks with Ryan have been absolutely incredible and surreal. The driveway was plowed yesterday, then we spent the day making sure the cabin was clean and ready for Cami and Eli's honeymoon—made sure the bedsheets were washed and all the decorations were up. We went to the grocery store and restocked all the food and beverages. I even got extra chocolate, booze, and candles just in case they lose power too.

Afterward, I prepared a steak dinner with baked potatoes. Our night was quiet and spent holding each other as we talked and watched TV.

He's given me a lot to think about regarding my future and possibly starting an event planning company. It's something that's been on my mind, and his encouraging words meant something to me, making me believe it could become a reality. The past two weeks have changed me in a good way. My parents are going to be confused when I mention starting a business, but I know they'll support whatever I want to do. A smile touches my lips as I think about all that's to come.

Ryan helped me learn so much about myself. Without all the

outside noise and opinions of my family or friends, it was easier for me to realize what truly makes me happy. It was just us together in the cabin, and I could be myself around him for the first time ever.

After we wake up and have a hearty breakfast, Ryan and I go our separate ways to pack our bags. Yesterday, I did a couple of loads of laundry and threw my clothes on the bed. Since I slept in his room last night, I haven't had the chance to fold them. Taking my time, I neatly arrange them in my suitcases. As I suck in a deep breath, my emotions get the best of me. It's bittersweet that our time together is ending. Two weeks with him isn't enough.

I make a final sweep of the bathroom, grabbing the moisturizer I left on the counter. When I go back into the bedroom, I grab my bags and carry them downstairs. As I wait for Ryan, I stand in front of the large windows overlooking the mountain peaks. Everything is still blanketed in white and looks like a winter wonderland. Seeing the countryside like this hardly ever happens, and I'm grateful for the view. If we could stay here another two weeks wrapped in each other's arms, I wouldn't complain a bit. Well, as long as we had electricity and food. The thought makes me smile.

I think about Cami and Eli and how they fell madly in love with each other while they were quarantined here. Now I understand how they fell so hard and fast in a way I couldn't comprehend before. I'm not sure if it's the quietness or how I'm able to be myself behind these walls, but it's refreshing. I came to the cabin with Ryan for a short decorating trip and somehow managed to fall in love in the process.

The thought scares the absolutely shit out of me.

I've always had a thing for Ryan, but the connection and bond we've created is so damn strong. Losing him and having this end so abruptly is so unfair.

As I stand in silence, replaying all the intimate times and laughs we've shared, I begin to break down. When I blink, tears trail down my cheeks, but I force myself to suck it up and wipe them away. I'm trying to believe this isn't the end, and we can continue this, but I don't know for sure. One thing is for certain, though, things have changed. I've gotten used to spending all day with him. He's quickly burrowed himself in the pits of my heart, and losing that will hurt like hell.

Once we're back in the city, he'll be back to working long hours. After all the conversations we've had about his past relationships and how much his career means to him, there's no way I could come between it. I'm selfish, though, and want him as I've had him here, but that's nothing more than a fairy tale.

When I turn around, Ryan's standing on the bottom stair with his stuff in his hand. He looks me over with a smirk, but I give him a sad smile in return. He walks over and drops his bag, then wraps his arms around me. He holds me tight, and I soak in his warmth and touch, not wanting to let go—not wanting this to be over.

We stand for a while, and I'm certain he inhales the scent of my hair. I look up into his eyes, and I think I see pain in his expression and wonder if he feels the same as me. Running his fingers through my hair, he gently tugs on the ends and forces me to look up at him.

"I'm gonna miss seeing you every day so fucking much," he finally admits.

"Me too. Half of me wishes we didn't have to go, but the other half knows we have to."

My heart flutters, and the weight that's been sitting on my shoulders all morning seems to lift slightly. Maybe he does feel the same way about me after all. Maybe we do have a fighting chance in hell to make this work, but I'm too chicken to bring it up. I don't want to ruin this moment.

He grins, then grabs my hand and leads me upstairs.

"Where are we going?" I follow even though I know we need to get on the road. He has to be at the hospital early in the morning, and I don't want him to be exhausted from the drive.

"I don't want to waste this time," he admits.

Ryan brings me to his bedroom, and when he turns around, our lips crash together. I moan against his mouth, sinking further into him, hoping he can feel exactly how I do right now.

The intense connection nearly slices me open as we exchange slow, emotional kisses. It feels like the final goodbye. Just the thought breaks my heart, but I want this last time together. Ryan doesn't say anything, though, and I kiss him with everything I have even though my lips already feel swollen.

He takes his sweet time unbuttoning my jeans, then slides them down to my ankles. I step out of my shoes and remove my shirt. He studies me as if he's memorizing this moment, then slides my panties down and unclasps my bra.

Once I'm completely naked, we move to the bed, and I lie down in the middle. My breathing increases and my eyes flutter closed as I take in how his fingers feel against my skin.

His lips slide from my neck to my breasts and farther down my body. When he's kissed me all the way between my thighs, he stands and removes his clothes, then towers over me. Ryan's piercing gaze meets mine as he slowly enters me. Raw emotion streams through me as he pants in my ear, and I scratch my nails down his back.

He releases animalistic groans as he thrusts into me deeper and harder, giving me everything I need and want. He takes my heart as his prisoner as we make love for possibly the last time. It's an out-of-body experience when I force him on his back and ride him.

"You're so fucking sexy, Kendall," he tells me, palming my breasts as they bounce. As his thumb circles over my clit, an orgasm builds, and I know I'm close. It unexpectedly washes over me, and it feels as if I've been shot out of the atmosphere as my pussy clenches his cock. I continue rocking my hips, riding out my release, and notice Ryan's body tensing.

I move forward, allowing our mouths to connect. Our tongues wage war as I continue the slow, agonizing pace. Ryan lets out a guttural moan, then grabs my ass with both hands and slams his cock harder into me. Soon, he's unraveling, saying my name, telling me how goddamn gorgeous I am as he fills me.

I want to whisper those three words, but I don't want to freak him the hell out either. He doesn't take relationships lightly, and neither do I, but the heart wants what it wants.

I lay in his arms, and my eyes grow heavy, but we have to get going since we have a three-hour drive ahead of us. After we're clean, we get dressed and fix the bed. He interlocks his fingers with mine, kisses my knuckles, and leads me downstairs.

We make one final walkthrough of the cabin, confirming everything is in place for Cami and Eli when they arrive next week. The mood is somber, but Ryan throws me sexy looks and smirks each time my eyes meet his, and I wonder if he's thinking the same thing.

There's so much I want to say, but I don't even know where I would begin to explain what's going through my mind right now. It grows more awkward between us, and I hate how it feels as though we're coming to a crossroads. I could just be thinking the absolute worst, but he hasn't brought it up either, so I'm conflicted. I wear my heart on my sleeve and usually say what's on my mind, but I can't even bring myself to ask what our future holds. I don't know if my heart could handle rejection from him.

The magic of the cabin has quickly come and gone, and I hope we can continue what we started here, but I don't want to add any pressure on him. I know why he and Rachelle broke it off, and I can't say I blame her for wanting more time with him. Fourteen days wasn't enough, and I'm pretty sure an eternity wouldn't be either.

After he remote starts the Range Rover, Ryan grabs my luggage, and I pick up his duffel. It can't weigh more than five pounds.

"This is really light," I tell him, lifting the bag with a single finger. He looks over his shoulder and smirks as he wheels the suitcases out. I think about how furious he was when he saw how much shit I packed. When we lost power, I was grateful I had brought extra food and clothes.

On the way down the long driveway, I catch a glimpse of the cabin in the side mirror. I watch it until it's out of view, and sadness washes over me because I know I left a piece of my heart behind.

CHAPTER TWENTY

RYAN

I KNEW this day would eventually come, but I couldn't have predicted feeling so devastated by it. Once we're on the outside of Roxbury, the mood grows tense. We make small talk and discuss food we can't wait to eat while reminiscing about not having any electricity, but I can't bring myself to say what's really on my mind.

"Next time I travel anywhere, I'm packing three damn portable phone chargers so my battery doesn't die," she tells me. "Especially after you held out on me. I'm not sure I'll ever forgive you for that." She narrows her eyes at me, then breaks into a smile. She reaches up and releases her ponytail, then brushes her fingers through the strands. Her long brown hair falls down her shoulders, and I can't even count the times I pulled it or whispered in her ear while I was inside her. The memories will haunt me for a lifetime.

"It was for emergency use only," I remind her, blinking away my thoughts. "But it's not a bad idea to carry one or two around with you just in case."

"Yeah, definitely." She sighs. "So what do you plan on doing when you get back?"

"Working." I shrug.

"Duh. That's a no-brainer." She chuckles.

"What do you plan on doing?" I ask, trying to keep the conversation going.

"I'm scheduling a spa day and dragging Cami with me since I know she'll be a stress ball. You wanna join us for mani-pedis?" She smirks.

I snort. "Thanks, but I'll let you two have a girls' day without me. Plus, I'll be working doubles until the wedding."

Immediately, I notice her smile falter, but she quickly puts it back on. I honestly wish I could spend more time with her without the distractions from the outside world and take her out on a real date.

After spending two weeks alone with Kendall, I'm a changed man, but I'm fighting a war with myself over the way I feel for her. It's hard for me to comprehend it, and it scares me how fast I've fallen for her. I know I'm going to disappoint her. I hate I'm going to be working longer shifts, but my boss warned me this would happen. It's only fair to try to make up for what I missed. Not to mention, I'm taking off for Cami's wedding next weekend.

"Probably for the best since I need to catch your sister up on everything that's happened. Can't do that with you around." Kendall waggles her eyebrows at me, and I chuckle.

"Oh yeah, please tell my sister all kinds of juicy details about me. I'm sure that won't be weird."

She chuckles. "I had to hear everything about Eli, so it's only fair."

I grab her hand and bring it to my lips, then press a kiss to her knuckles. Not letting go of her, I rest our intertwined fingers on her thigh as she leans her head against the headrest and smiles.

As I continue driving, our conversations become more sporadic. Needing to fill the silence, I turn on the radio and listen to NPR.

"You can change it if you want," I offer after thirty minutes of listening.

"Nah, it's fine," she says. "But I could really use a coffee right now." Kendall gives me big puppy dog eyes and grins. I think back to how pissed she was when I refused to stop on the way to Roxbury. So much has changed in so little time. Once we're about twenty minutes outside of the city, I spot a coffee shop.

When I park on the street, she looks at me with wide eyes, then laughs. "Seriously? Mr. Absolutely-we're-not-stopping has stopped?"

"For you? Yes, I aim to please," I say and throw a wink her way.

A blush hits her cheeks as she chews on her bottom lip. After a few seconds, I get out and run around to open her door. When we walk inside, I smell delicious cookies and coffee and hear Christmas music playing.

"This place looks like it fell out of a Hallmark movie," she says, spinning around, taking it all in. I love seeing Kendall so damn happy and interlock my fingers with hers. We look over the menu written on a giant chalkboard surrounded by string lights.

A woman with bright blue hair and a lip piercing comes to the counter. After a minute of watching us, she interrupts us. "Hi! Do you know what you'd like?"

"What do you suggest?" Kendall questions. "Anything sweet and holiday-like. I'm not picky!"

The woman seems thrilled to answer this question. "We're famous for our gingerbread peppermint mocha latte with our cookie crumble whip cream."

"Oh my gosh. That sounds amazing." Kendall squeals. "I want the biggest size you have."

"Make it two," I add. She gives us the total, and I pay.

While we wait, Kendall and I look at the gigantic Christmas tree that overlooks the street. All the ornaments are coffee-related, with mugs and coffee beans, even tiny coffee makers. I glance out the window, and it's like the world transformed while we were away. The woman soon sets our drinks on the counter, and we both thank her as we grab them.

Kendall takes a sip, and she moans. "This." She points at her red cup with the words Holly Jolly written in cursive letters. "This is magical!"

I taste mine and nod in agreement. "This is basically dessert."

"Absolutely," she says, giggling. "Christmas in a cup!"

Without hesitation, I tilt up her chin and press my lips to hers.

We thank the barista one more time, then make our way back to the Range Rover. Seeing Kendall this excited over the simplest thing was worth stopping. And I have to admit it tastes pretty damn good.

As soon as we're back on the road, my phone buzzes. I look down and notice it's my boss.

"Hey, Nick," I pick up and answer.

"Ryan, how's the drive?"

"Going fine, not much traffic so I should be in the city within the hour," I explain.

"Perfect. Do you think you can swing by the hospital? I'd like to catch you up on a few patients before your morning shift tomorrow."

"Sure thing," I tell him and glance over at Kendall, who's staring out the window.

"Shouldn't take too long. Maybe an hour or two."

He kept me updated while I was away. One of my weaknesses is getting too attached to my patients and constantly checking up on them even when they're transferred to other doctors. I hear codes being called over the intercom in the background, and then his name is announced.

"No problem, sir. I'll be there," I say, then we say goodbye and hang up.

Kendall doesn't ask who it was, but I tell her anyway. "My boss. I have to go in after I drop you off."

"When's the last time you've taken off this long?"

It takes me a minute to think about it. "Not since before my residency."

"Ryan, you have to take time for yourself every once in a while."

"I know. It's something I'm working on. You showed me how much I've missed in life. I love my job, don't get me wrong, but I have to start being kinder to myself. For the first time in years, I feel refreshed and rested." And it's all true. I'm less anxious than usual and don't feel nearly as stressed as I typically am.

"I'll take some credit for that," she teases.

"Undoubtedly." I chuckle. "It's funny the only thing that can force me to slow down in life is Mother Nature. I think it was a wake-up call to slow down."

"You should. I know you've been through a lot in the past few years and needed to build your career, but if you don't want to blink and realize you worked most of your life away, you need to find a healthier work-life balance. You deserve to be happy and have fun too."

I bring her knuckles to my lips and kiss them. She smiles at me lovingly, and I contemplate telling her how I feel about her. But before I can, her phone vibrates. She releases my hand and reaches for it. "Cami," she tells me, showing me the screen.

I take the exit that leads to her street and know we only have about ten more minutes together. I don't know how to bring up *us* —if there even is an us. As I try to find the right words to start this conversation, I also don't want to scare her away.

I'm dying to know where her head and heart are. Though I'm pretty certain I do, we still need to have an actual conversation about it. I'll see her next weekend for the wedding, but I need to muster the courage to bring it up before then, yet I'm running out of time.

Soon, I'm in front of her townhouse.

Being the perfect gentleman, I get out of my SUV and open her door. I help her out, then grab her luggage from the back.

Kendall leads the way up the steps. As she unlocks the front door, I open my mouth to ask her where we go from here but hesitate. Before I can actually get any words out, Kendall grabs the handles of her two suitcases and sets them inside her doorway.

My heart pounds hard in my chest as she stands in front of me.

"Thanks again for everything. I'll see you in a week at Cami's wedding. I know how busy you'll be until then." She gives me a sweet grin. "If you get a spare minute and wanna chat, you know my number."

I nod and keep my thoughts to myself. "Yeah, absolutely."

"Drive safe," she tells me, then steps inside and gently closes the door.

I'm frozen in place. Not allowing my pride to be bruised, I go back to the car and try to replay everything that just happened between us.

We had sex before we left the cabin. Held hands in the car. I kissed her in the coffee place. Then I walked her to her front door.

Was she waiting for me to make the next move? Hug and kiss her goodbye? Tell her I'd call her later? Before I could say or do a damn thing, she acted like she couldn't get away fast enough. Was this her way of letting me down easy? Were we playing pretend up until the last minute when we went our separate ways?

Fuck me. I wish like hell I knew what she was thinking, but now I have to get my mind focused back on work.

I drive across town to the hospital—my home away from home basically.

Grabbing my badge, I walk inside the double doors and scan into the restricted area. Nick's waiting for me with a clipboard and a handful of files. As soon as he spots me, he starts talking.

"How many third-degree burns did you guys treat on Thanksgiving?" I ask.

He gives me a pointed look. "More than we expected or had staff for."

"Damn. Not a good year for turkeys or ovens." Once I'm fully caught up, I head toward the door. "I'll be here tomorrow morning at five. I'm ready to get back to work."

"Hope so. We're ready to have you back. I realized how much we need you around here." Nick smirks.

"I appreciate that, sir. See you in the morning," I say, then walk out the doors.

On the way back to my condo, all I can think about is Kendall. If I did text her, what would I even say? I don't want us to make any decisions over text messaging, but I know I won't have time to see her before the wedding.

The next time I see her, I won't be a chickenshit and hesitate. Whatever the outcome, I just need to know if she felt what I did. There's enough time between now and the wedding for me to figure out what I'm going to say.

After I get home, I jump in the shower, then order a pizza. When it arrives, I nearly inhale it and wish Kendall was here to enjoy it with me. I've gotten quite used to having her near and hearing her little comments about everything. I try to watch TV, but my mind wanders way too much. When I stop on the Hallmark channel, I shake my head and chuckle at what I'm seeing on TV. Two people are snowed in together at a cabin and can't stop flirting with each other. Our story is literally a corny Christmas romance, but hopefully, we get our second chance like the characters in this movie.

CHAPTER TWENTY-ONE

KENDALL

ONE WEEK LATER

I HAVEN'T SEEN or talked to Ryan since he dropped me off last week, so I'm a nervous wreck. Tonight's Cami and Eli's wedding rehearsal, and afterward, they're hosting a dinner. We never discussed what would happen with us once we left the cabin, but I didn't expect radio silence. I froze with what to say the day he dropped me off. He looked like he'd wanted to say something, but when he never did, I lost my confidence and just blurted out he could text me if he wanted. It was like we went from being a couple, holding hands in the car and talking, to awkward goodbyes. Though he's probably working double shifts to catch up, having no communication with him at all has been driving me crazy. I almost texted him a few days ago, but I didn't want to sound needy.

Hey? What's up? Remember me? The woman you banged for two weeks? So are we just gonna pretend that didn't happen or…?

So instead of sounding like an idiot, I said nothing at all.

I'd hoped he'd reach out to me first and reassure me that our time together meant something to him. I've been counting down the days until I get to see him, and it's finally here. He's Eli's best man, and I'm Cami's maid of honor, so we're walking down the aisle together, and we'll be in dozens of photos with each other. It'd be nice if things aren't strained or awkward.

Since I've been home, I've been busy helping Cami take care of last-minute wedding tasks. We also had some fun too, getting mani-pedis and bridal party massages. I even treated myself to a trim and some highlights. I just can't believe their big moment is finally here.

I arrive at the church in a pale blue dress and heels, wanting to look my absolute best when I see Ryan.

Butterflies surface when I notice him dressed in black slacks and a button-up shirt with a tie. I can't stop watching him as he chats with Eli and Cami. The moment my best friend notices me, she beams and rushes over.

"Kendall! You look so pretty!" She wraps me in a hug, and it feels like I haven't seen her in forever.

We break apart, and I smile at her. "Thanks, so do you. You're glowing!"

"I can't believe I'll be married in less than twenty-four hours. After all this time, it feels so surreal."

"I'm so excited for you two. You guys deserve it."

"Have you and Ryan talked yet?" she whispers. He's been one of the main subjects of our chats all week. She's told me to give him time and not to worry, but that's easier said than done.

"No." I frown.

When I look over and see him staring at me, I freeze. A shiver ripples through my whole body, and I wonder what he's thinking or feeling.

"Well, you two better have a conversation before we get started. The last thing you want is for there to be tension."

I inhale a deep breath and square my shoulders. "You're right. I can do this." I give myself a pep talk before walking over to him and Eli.

"Kendall," Eli greets with a hug.

"Hello, groom-to-be." I smile as we pull apart, then look at Ryan.

"You dress up nice, Doctor," I tease.

Ryan touches his tie and smirks. "Not my first party."

"No but it's your first St. James' wedding. Your mother would've killed you had you not," I say.

"Very true."

"Speaking of…" Eli clears his throat just as Clara St. James and Stephanie, the wedding planner, come into view. She claps her hands to get everyone's attention.

I glance at Ryan as we're told the rehearsal is starting soon and to get into position.

"Best man and maid of honor in front of the bride and father of the bride," Stephanie orders, then directs the other members of the wedding party into position. "Eli up front. The minister is ready."

Cami and I head to the end of the line. When Ryan stands next to me, I give him an awkward smile. "Been busy at work?"

He brushes a hand over his jaw and blows out a breath. "Complete madness. I have about a dozen shifts to cover for those who worked mine when I was gone. At this rate, I should just move into the break room. I had to offer some extreme favors to get this weekend off even though it was scheduled months ago."

"That sucks. Sorry."

"Not your fault, even if it was your idea to drag me with you," he teases, flashing me a wink. Those stupid giddy butterflies return, and I wonder if we'll talk about the elephant in the room.

Before I can respond, Stephanie shushes everyone, then gives detailed instructions. She makes us go through the ceremony twice.

After an hour and a half, it's over, and I'm so relieved. I'm starving and can't wait to eat. I hope I can get a few minutes alone with Ryan, but he's been pulled in every direction by his mother, father, and the groomsmen.

Thirty minutes later, we're arriving at the upscale restaurant for the dinner Cami planned. I manage to take the seat next to Ryan before anyone else does. We chat about something that doesn't include us or the two weeks we spent fucking. Cami and Eli keep the conversation going, and I'm relieved when it doesn't feel awkward.

Halfway through dinner, Ryan's phone vibrates on the table between us. He responded to a text earlier and left it out so when a call pops up on his screen, it's impossible not to notice Rachelle's name.

"I gotta take this. Be right back," he tells Cami and Eli.

Jealousy immediately rips through me, and my insecurities take over every thought.

Is she the reason he hasn't texted or called me? Are they back together? Did being with me make him realize she was who he wanted?

How stupid do I sound right now?

Something must be going on if he's leaving his sister's rehearsal dinner to answer a phone call from his ex-girlfriend.

Perhaps we shared the best of us while stranded, and that's all I'll ever have of Ryan St. James.

Between having our hair and makeup done, getting dressed, helping Cami into her gown, then taking a thousand photos, I'm exhausted.

And even though I'm busy as hell, memories of Ryan fucking me all over the cabin still live rent-free in my damn mind.

After he left to take Rachelle's call, the rest of the evening felt off. I didn't bother trying to speak to him again and kept my attention on Cami and the other bridesmaids.

Whatever we had at the cabin is long gone, and I need to accept it. I thought we shared more than just a physical connection, but apparently not. I won't beg a man to be in my life.

If he wanted to be with me, he would be.

Period.

No matter what I tell myself, deep down, I'm still obsessing over every moment we spent together. I had a sliver of hope that he'd make time for a relationship with me.

Stupid, stupid, stupid.

Eventually, we line up for the ceremony, and my breath catches when I see Ryan in his sleek black tux. Damn, of course he'd look amazing. When he notices me, his eyes scan down my body, and by the time they meet mine, he's wearing a mischievous smirk.

"Wow, Kendall. You look beautiful," he whispers as I stand next to him.

His words cause heat to meet my cheeks.

"Thank you," I say, not returning the compliment even though he looks good enough to eat.

He gives me a strange look as if he's just realized I'm not happy with him, but there's no time to discuss it. Cami and her father walk up, and I focus on her, and how happy I am. Stephanie barks out orders and makes sure everyone's ready.

As soon as it's our turn, I loop my arm through Ryan's and feel warm electricity streaming between us. I focus on the excitement of my best friend getting married to the love of her life.

The ceremony is gorgeous. By the time Eli and Cami exchange vows, there's not a dry eye in the house. As soon as they're pronounced husband and wife, Eli kisses his bride, then they walk down the aisle. Everyone's cheering for the newly married couple, and we fall in line behind them.

I can't stop wondering if Ryan's getting back together with Rachelle. Self-doubt and insecurities flood in, and I think maybe I'm not good enough for him.

After the receiving line, the wedding party is summoned for photos. It's two long hours of smiling for the camera and watching Eli and Cami be madly in love. The photographer does such a good job capturing their perfect love.

I avoid Ryan unless we're forced to take pictures together, then I act like nothing's wrong. When we're apart, I stay with the other bridesmaids and chat.

We take a massive party bus to the reception, and I sulk in tequila shots to numb my thoughts. Next come the champagne and dancing. Aside from my internal obsession with Ryan, the wedding is a blast.

Cami and Ryan have always been fun to be around, but their guests make it even better. Since money is no object, the St. James' went all out on everything. Not to mention there's enough liquor here to serve the entire city.

I manage to stay plenty busy with my maid of honor duties—making sure Cami eats, helping her to the bathroom, and giving my epic best friend speech. The alcohol flows through me, which definitely helps ease my frustrations. Maybe after a few more shots, I'll be able to find my no shits given attitude.

"Kendall, darling…you look lovely," one of Cami's aunts tells me. I'm drawing a blank on her name, but I smile and thank her. She mentions the weather, but I stop listening as soon as I see *her*.

What the hell is she doing here?

Rachelle.

Ryan leads her to the dance floor, and when she smiles up at him with lust in her eyes, my stomach drops.

Unable to watch them together any longer, I excuse myself from the conversation, and Cami finds me.

"What's wrong?" she immediately asks.

"Your brother sucks." I force a grin, nodding my head in their direction.

She looks over, and her eyes widen when she spots Ryan and Rachelle inches from each other on the dance floor.

"I don't understand what the hell she's doing here." She groans, rolling her eyes.

"I had the same question," I mutter, chugging back another glass of champagne.

"This is really weird…" She narrows her eyes, studying them.

"It is what it is." I shrug, trying to act unbothered, but I'm certain she can see through it. "I'm gonna grab another drink. Can I get you anything?"

"No, thanks." She gives me a hug before I walk to the bar.

Now that I'm done with my duties for the night, I decide to get shit-faced to forget that man ever existed. The crowd at the bar fills up, but I eventually place my order. I hear Eli behind me, and when I glance over my shoulder, I see Ryan next to him. Neither seems to realize I'm close because I hear Eli mention me.

"I'm surprised to see Rachelle here. I thought you and Kendall hooking up was gonna lead to something more." Eli says what I've been thinking all night.

Ryan chuckles, and I grow more annoyed.

"I-I don't know. It was fun while it lasted," Ryan says as if he's already uncomfortable talking about me.

"She's not your type or something?" Eli asks.

"We don't have a lot in common. She's a spoiled princess, and I work fifteen-hour days at the hospital," Ryan responds. It takes everything inside me not to turn around and give him a piece of my mind, but I refuse to make a scene at my best friend's wedding. So I bite my lip and let the rage burn inside me instead.

How dare he fucking say that about me? It feels like a giant slap in the face after I confided in him and shared personal details about myself. He knows there's more to me than that, so his words cut deep. *That fucking asshole!*

I'm filled with so much anger that when I get my drink, I immediately suck it down.

I walk to the opposite side of the room, not wanting to overhear any more of their conversation. Quickly, I find a group of friends to dance with and let loose so I don't have to see Ryan and Rachelle flirting.

At some point, Marc, a guy from our friend group, starts dancing with me. He gets handsy and rocks his body back and forth with me, but I don't even care. I lost my shoes hours ago and let him hold me close as we sway to the music.

When the song ends, I excuse myself and decide to get some fresh air. The coolness slaps me in the face and helps sober me up for a few minutes. The hair on my arms stand up when I hear the door open, and I glance over my shoulder to see Ryan.

"Hey," he says casually.

"What're you doing out here? Shouldn't you be entertaining your date?" I snap.

"Who, Rachelle?"

I glare, then roll my eyes at him. "Who else?"

"Kendall...it's not like that. I didn't know she was coming. It's —" He steps closer, but I hold up my hand to stop him.

"Don't waste your breath. I'm just a *spoiled princess*, right?"

His eyes widen, and I see regret written on his face, but I don't care.

"I didn't mean—"

"For me to overhear that? I'm sure you didn't, but I'm so fucking glad I did. At least I know why you didn't text me all week." I push past him, and he stops me. "Ryan, don't."

"Kendall, please. Just..."

I yank my arm from his grip and scowl. "*Fuck off.*"

CHAPTER TWENTY-TWO

RYAN

TWENTY-FOUR HOURS AGO

MY HEAD'S consumed with thoughts of seeing Kendall again. We never talked about what would happen once we left the cabin, so all the unspoken words between us have been circulating through my mind all damn week.

I've thought about texting her a hundred times. Between my shifts and on my breaks, I'd type out a message, then delete it. All the overthinking I did led to not texting her at all. I'm sure it's going to be awkward now.

The "only sex" rules were her idea, but things definitely went beyond that. Even now, I don't know how she feels. My mind goes between not being enough and her not wanting to be with someone who works so much.

Those thoughts stopped me from reaching out. Now we'll be reunited at my sister's rehearsal, and I'm already sweating over it.

The St. Jameses expect nothing less than perfection for Cami's big day, so I dress in a nice suit that'll satisfy my mother. My wardrobe usually consists of scrubs, so wearing slacks and a button-up is a nice change.

When I arrive at the church, I spot my best friend and give him a hug.

"Hey, man." He slaps my back. "Haven't seen you in ages."

"I know. Talk about a crazy couple of weeks."

As soon as I returned to the city, I was buried in work and had no time to hang out.

"I'd say. Cami almost lost her damn mind."

I chuckle. "Yeah well, I think I did too."

My sister comes over, and I give her a hug. When I look across the room, I'm nearly blinded by Kendall. She's in a gorgeous pale blue dress and is wearing fuck-me heels. The thoughts that consume my mind are completely inappropriate.

Cami rushes toward her, but I stay put. The awkwardness already streams through the air, and I'm not sure how Kendall will act. When she walks over, I'm relieved when I see a smile and hear her friendly voice. She speaks to Eli first, and I watch their casual interaction. Kendall seems fine, but as I've learned, she's good at covering her emotions when needed.

"You dress up nice, Doctor," Kendall teases as her eyes roam down my suit.

"Not my first party." I smirk, sliding a hand down my tie.

We manage to have a short conversation before the wedding planner cuts in and directs us to line up. We continue to talk, but it revolves around work and nothing else.

I wish we could have a few minutes alone to talk, but that doesn't happen. We go through the ceremony twice before we're dismissed. Cami planned a dinner for the wedding party at one of her favorite restaurants. Hopefully, I'll get a moment alone with Kendall there.

As I leave the chapel, I get a text alert.

Rachelle: Hey, sorry to bother you, but it's Joey. He has a cough.

When the vaccine was distributed, people who worked on the

front line—like me—and those deemed high risk received the first round. A month later, it was open to the masses. However, plenty of people still declined, and Rachelle didn't have Joey get one since his pediatrician didn't think it was needed since he didn't have any pre-existing conditions. This isn't the first time she's reached out to me in a panic about him being sick and worrying about the worst. She's a single parent, so I try to help her when I can.

I wait until I'm parked at the restaurant, then call her.

She quickly picks up. "Hey."

"Does he have a fever?"

"It's low grade, so I haven't given him anything yet."

"Give him some Tylenol to see if that gets his fever down and cough medicine. Then put some vapor rub on his chest."

"Okay, I'll do that right now."

"When did his symptoms start?"

"A few hours ago. I had to work this morning, and when I got home, I noticed he was coughing, but it's gotten more severe."

"Shit. Well, keep an eye on him, okay? I just got to my sister's rehearsal dinner, so call me if his fever gets worse."

"Thanks, Ryan. I appreciate it."

"You're welcome. I'll talk to you later."

The call ends, and I head inside. I hate that he's not feeling well and that she's worried it could be more serious. There's no other reason she'd call me. Honestly, her tone alone has me concerned about him.

I find the private party room and grab a drink before taking a seat across from Cami and Eli. My heart beats wildly when I watch Kendall walk in and take the empty chair next to me. Some of the weirdness has evaporated as we make small talk, and we manage to keep the conversation moving while we eat. She tells me what she did this past week and how she and my sister got a massage and their nails done. I'd talk about anything just to stay next to her.

Halfway through my meal, my phone buzzes, and when I see it's Rachelle, I know it's about Joey. *Shit.*

"I gotta take this. I'll be right back," I tell Cami and Eli, then excuse myself.

Walking out of the room, I head down a quiet hallway and answer.

"Hey," I greet.

"The Tylenol seems to be working. His fever is down, and he's not coughing as hard."

"Oh thank God," I breathe out. "Hopefully it's just a cold."

"I hope so. Poor guy looks miserable."

"If he's up to it, can I speak to him?" I ask.

"I'm sure he'd love that. Hold on."

I talk to Joey for only a couple of minutes before we say goodbye. Rachelle gets back on the line and asks how things are going.

"Good, Cami's so excited."

"I bet she is. Are you bringing a date?"

I snort. "No. I'm walking down with Kendall and will be doing best man duties for most of the night I'm sure."

"A man as handsome as you should have a date," she teases. "I might just have to come so you aren't alone."

"Don't worry, I won't be alone. You know my parents invited like four hundred people." I chuckle. "Shit, I better get back in there before my mother comes searching for me. You know how she is."

"I do. Give Cami my best, and thanks again for helping."

"You know I always will. Give me an update on Joey tomorrow, okay?"

"Will do."

We say good night, then I head back to the table. Kendall's turned the other way, talking to one of the bridesmaids and acts like she can't stand my existence. I try starting another conversation with her, but she's short with me. As soon as she's done eating, she stands and heads to the bar with another girl, and we don't talk for the rest of the evening.

Watching my best friend marry my sister is one of the highlights of my year. Things are still tense between Kendall and me, but I don't know why. When she grabbed onto me and we walked down the aisle, my thoughts took over. She hasn't touched me since the cabin, and I couldn't stop thinking about what it'd be like to be with her every single day. It's nearly impossible to keep my eyes off her in that dress that shows just enough skin to tease.

After the ceremony, we pose for wedding party pictures, and I take every opportunity to be close to her. I know she feels what's brewing between us, but for whatever reason, she's fighting it. As soon as we get another moment alone, we're hashing this out. I'll get to the bottom of her sudden mood change.

Between the party bus and dinner, Kendall's taking shots and drinking like it's her last day on earth. I've never seen her like this before, and it concerns me.

I lose track of her as family members talk my ear off. I haven't seen most of them in years, so they have dozens of questions about my work and personal life.

"If one more person asks me why I'm single…" I groan when I find Cami and Eli.

"Don't feel bad. I've been asked when we're going to have kids thirty-six times." She forces a smile that makes me laugh.

"Did you tell them we're starting tonight?" Eli flashes her a smirk.

"Please spare me," I groan.

Cami laughs, then her eyes widen as she looks over my shoulder. "You didn't tell me Rachelle was coming."

Wait, what?

I spin around and see her walking toward me with a smile. Instead of waiting, I move forward and close the gap between us.

"Rachelle," I greet. "What're you doing here?"

"Hey." She pulls me in for a hug. "When you said you didn't have a date, there was no way I could let you be here alone. I wanted to save you from your family asking why you're not taken."

"Well, you're kinda late then." I chuckle.

"Shit, sorry." She laughs. "Wanna dance?"

"Yeah, sure." I lead her out to the dance floor, and we catch up on how Joey's doing and her job. We actually haven't talked in person for months, and I'd be lying if I said it wasn't nice to see her again.

"I'm gonna grab a drink. Want one?" I ask when the song ends.

"Sure, anything's fine. I'm going to use the restroom quick."

I find Eli at the bar, then wait in line to order.

"I'm surprised to see Rachelle here. I thought you and Kendall hooking up was gonna lead to something more?" he asks.

This isn't really the place to talk about her right now, so I try to end the conversation before it starts. Plus, this isn't the time or place to discuss my dating life.

I chuckle to ease my anxiety. "I-I don't know. It was fun while it lasted," I say, hoping he'll drop it. I wish I could say we were going to date or were giving each other a chance. The last thing I want is to make it seem like there's more to us than there is. Even if I wish there were.

"She's not your type or something?" Eli asks.

Ugh, come on. I grow more uncomfortable with each question and wonder if Cami put him up to this.

So I say what I think will end the conversation and play it off the best I can. "We don't have a lot in common. She's a spoiled princess, and I work fifteen-hour days at the hospital."

My stomach turns as soon as the words spill out, but it does the job.

After we finally order our drinks, I see Kendall out of the corner of my eye walk outside. This might be my only chance to get her alone for the rest of the night, so I set down my beer and Rachelle's wineglass and follow her.

"Hey," I say casually when I find her near a bench.

"What are you doing out here? Shouldn't you be entertaining your date?" she snaps, and I see the fiery glare in her eyes.

"Who, Rachelle?" I snort. She's far from being my date, considering she's a wedding crasher.

She rolls her eyes at my response. "Who else?"

"Kendall…it's not like that. I didn't know she was coming. It's—" I step toward her, wanting to be closer to her, but she holds up her hand and stops me.

"Don't waste your breath. I'm just a spoiled princess, right?"

The hurt is written all over her face, and I hate that she overheard me. *Fuck.*

"I didn't mean—"

"For me to overhear that? I'm sure you didn't, but I'm so fucking glad I did. At least I know why you didn't text me all week."

Wait, what? She was waiting for me to text all this time?
Shit.

Kendall pushes past me, and I grab her arm so I can explain this giant misunderstanding. I regretted saying those words the moment they left my lips. It's not how I feel, but now thanks to my dumbass, she thinks it is.

"Ryan, don't." She's seething.

"Kendall, please," I beg. "Just…"

She pulls her arm out of my grip and scowls. *"Fuck off."*

I watch as she storms off and instantly feel defeated.

Great.

I've just given the only woman I've ever truly fallen for a reason to hate me. I should've learned at the cabin when she overheard my convo with Eli that my words hurt her, but here we are again. Now I need to figure out how the hell I'm going to fix it before I lose her forever.

If she'll give me the time of day, I'll do whatever it takes to make it up to her. Maybe tomorrow she won't be as heated and will agree to meet me before my shift. All I can do at this point is apologize like hell and beg for her forgiveness.

However, Kendall Montgomery is a strong, independent woman and getting a second chance with her won't be easy.

CHAPTER TWENTY-THREE

KENDALL

IT'S BEEN two weeks since Cami and Eli's wedding.

Two weeks since I last saw Ryan.

Two weeks since he broke my heart.

The morning after the wedding, he texted and asked if we could meet before his shift. I was still so pissed and hurt that I went off on him and told him to never speak to me again. Then I blocked his number.

Since then, I've contemplated unblocking and messaging him, but I've talked myself out of it. Being intimate with Ryan and then hearing him be so mean has messed with my emotions.

Instead of dwelling on it, I kept myself busy. Since I couldn't volunteer at the shelter on Thanksgiving, I started a canned food drive to help stock the food pantry. I'm overjoyed by how successful it's been. With only six days until Christmas, several families will have everything they need to make a nice dinner.

On top of that, I met with my lawyer to discuss business options. I found a realtor I like and even looked at a few office spaces. As excited as I am for this new venture, I'm also sad that I'm not sharing the news with Ryan because he's the one who pushed me in this direction. Perhaps forgetting about him is for the best. He's admitted he doesn't have time for a relationship, so it'd probably just lead to heartbreak.

I've stayed busy to avoid wallowing in my sadness, but eventually, it caught up to me. Four days ago, my emotions got the best of me, and I broke down and cried in the shower. It felt amazing to get it out. As angry as I am with him, I still miss him. I miss what we shared and the connection we had. I also miss the small things like his laughter and the way he looks at me. The physical relationship was mind-blowing, but it was more than that. I fell deeply in love with him emotionally too.

I just wish I had my best friend around to talk to about it in person. Cami's been on her honeymoon at the cabin for the past two weeks and doesn't return until this afternoon. I've texted and kept her updated with my business plans, but anything Ryan related has been off-limits. She knows why I blocked him and respects my decision even though she still wants me to give him a chance.

Piper: We still on for dinner and drinks tonight?

I read my sister's message and smile. She's been dying to hear the details about Ryan and me, and I can't put her off any longer. I also want to see her and catch up with her as well.

Kendall: Yep! Gonna soak in the tub, then get ready.

Piper: Can't wait! We have so much to talk about :)

Kendall: See you then!

As I start my bathwater, I think about Ryan and my new business venture. I still need a company name and wish I could ask him for ideas. He's brilliant and would probably come up with something I'd instantly love.

I hate that our amazing time together ended so abruptly. It's hard to reminisce about the great memories when it ultimately leads to the pain. What's worse is I would've done anything to be with him. Dealt with his crazy work schedule. Met him for lunch breaks just to kiss him. Made sure he had something hot to eat after his long shifts. I would've bent over backward and gave him my all to prove we could work. But that's what hurts the most. It ended before it really could begin.

After I add some scented oils into the water, I slide into the warmth and am immediately brought back to the night Ryan and I took a bath together. He couldn't keep his hands off me, and every time we had sex, another piece of me fell for him.

I shave my legs, wash my body, and soak until the water cools. With an hour until I have to meet Piper, I FaceTime Cami while I do my makeup.

"Hey!" she answers with a big smile. "Where are you going?"

"Meeting Piper at The Rose at six, but wanted to check and see if you guys made it home yet."

"We did, safe and sound! The cabin was perfect. I know I've said this already, but you did such a good job decorating."

"I'm so happy you guys had a good time." I beam.

"That cabin holds so many wonderful memories."

"It really does." I sigh.

"And you really stocked me up on the candy and booze."

I laugh, applying my foundation. "I know you well enough to know what you need."

"I'm already counting the days until we can go back."

"I bet it's gorgeous in the spring and fall. Do you have plans for when you'll visit again?" I ask.

"I'm not really sure. Eli's pretty busy with work through the winter until late spring, and now that I've graduated, my parents want me to get more involved in the company. But either way, I think we're gonna try to make it an annual thing. Maybe during our anniversary week."

"That'd be romantic, especially with the snowy mountains, but you better go prepared!" I tease. "You just might have an arctic blast and get snowed in for *weeks*."

She chuckles. "Yeah, wouldn't be the worst thing, though, as long as we don't lose power."

"Uh, no kidding. Did you know you can't flush the toilet without adding water to it?"

Cami bursts out laughing and nods. "Yeah, the pump eventually stops working."

Eli pops into the frame with a big smile. "Hey, Kendall."

"Hello, Mr. St. James," I tease. Even though Cami took his last name, everyone calls him that because he married into one of the country's wealthiest families. "Married life looks good on you. Did no-shave November run into December?"

"No-shave honeymoon," Cami clarifies. "He's gonna trim it tonight or *else*."

"Or else what?" I mock.

"No going below the equator. That shit scratches when it's that long," Cami says.

I snort, nearly poking myself in the eye with eyeliner. "Is it too early to ask about making me an aunt yet?"

"Don't worry," Eli chimes in. "We practiced twenty-three times."

The devilish smirk on his face has me blushing. "Jesus. I think that's the number of times—" I quickly pause. "Never mind."

Cami blinks at me with a frown. "Speaking of *him*...is he still blocked?"

"Yes," I say. "It's better this way."

"Is it, though?" she genuinely asks. "I know you believe it is because of his work schedule and past relationships, and you're afraid of getting hurt, but I swear, I've never heard him so down. He misses you."

"What? When did you talk to him?" I swallow hard.

"A few days ago. Called to check on him, and he sounded sad as hell. When he mentioned you haven't responded to a single text or answered his calls, I had to pretend I had no idea why. I would've told him, but I wasn't sure if you wanted me to or not."

I blow out a frustrated breath. I feel guilty about it, but then again, I have to do what I can to get over him and move on.

"Well, I'm sure he'll figure it out eventually," I say with a shrug. "I'm sure Rachelle is keeping him plenty busy."

"I don't think they're back together," she says. "At least he hasn't told me."

"Hasn't said a word to me either," Eli speaks up.

I sigh, not really wanting to know one way or another, so I abruptly change the subject. "On Monday, I'm going to view another office space. This one's in Lenox Hill on Madison."

"Oh my God, really? That's your dream location." She beams.

"I know! I'm really excited. If I love it as much as I think I will, then I'll be able to start buying furniture and office supplies."

"I'm so proud of you, Kendall. You were born to be an event planner. Have you thought of a company name yet?"

"No, I'm kinda stuck on that part. If I wanna start marketing, I need to figure it out. Of course my mother thinks I should use Montgomery in the name somehow, but I don't want it to be about my family. It's about the charities and small businesses that I wanna cater to."

"You'll come up with something great. I mean, St. James is a *great* last name too."

"You can use mine!" Eli shouts from the background. "Ross Events Planning. R.E.P." His face comes into the frame with a big cheesy smile.

Cami snorts, and I laugh.

"Why would she name it after you? You didn't even help come up with the idea!"

"Well no, not directly but…" He taps his temple. "I'm the one who talked Ryan into going on that trip, which ultimately led you to this career realization. So, technically, I *did* help."

"Nice try." Cami snickers. "If anyone gets credit, it's me. She's my best friend, and Ryan's my brother. So, you could do St. James or Cameron. I'd accept either." She flashes a cheeky grin, and I roll my eyes.

"As *helpful* as you two are being, I'm gonna pass on the suggestions and take a few more days to brainstorm. Maybe something brilliant will come to mind."

"Okay, fair enough. Hope you have fun tonight. Tell Piper I said hi."

"Will do. Glad you two are home safe. Love you guys!"

We wave goodbye, then hang up. I love seeing how happy they are together. I wonder if it's in the cards for me. Just when I think it could be, something happens and reminds me it's just a fantasy.

I arrive at The Rose around six, but of course my sister isn't here. She's notorious for being late, so I find an empty table and order a drink while I wait. As I scroll through my Instagram, I come across a photo of Ryan. It shocks me because I can't remember the last time he's posted on social media. It's a photo of him in front of the Rockefeller Christmas tree. He's wearing scrubs like usual, but it's obvious someone else took the picture. That leaves me with one guess.

"Hi," a deep voice grabs my attention, and I look up.

"Hello," I respond nicely, though I have no idea who he is.

"I'm Edward." He holds out his hand.

"Kendall," I reply, taking it.

"I was wondering if I could buy you a drink. Yours looks almost empty." He nods his head toward my watermelon martini.

I suck in my lips, unsure of how to respond.

"Oh, um...that's so kind of you, but actually, I'm meeting my

sister here and don't want to get drunk waiting for her," I say
kindly. While I'm technically single, a part of me would feel guilty
accepting a drink from a strange man.

"Okay, well let me know if you change your mind." He flashes
me a wink, then walks away.

I blow out a breath, wondering if I'll ever move on. I'm
twenty-four and should want to meet new people, but Ryan's
embedded in my heart.

"Hey!" Piper squeals as she comes to the table, plopping her
ass down across from me. "Sorry, I'm late. I was filming a video
and lost track of time."

I laugh. "I figured. You're a celebrity."

"Oh shut up. Who isn't YouTube famous these days?" She
waves me off.

"Literally millions of people." I snort.

"Okay well anyway, I need a dirty martini stat. Then you and I
are talking all about boys."

"Boys? Are we thirteen now?" I take a sip of my drink and am
ready for another.

"Men, whatever." She rolls her eyes and waves over a
waitress. Piper orders a drink and an appetizer, and I get another
martini.

Once the server walks away, I continue, "Well, maybe you're
dating boys, but I'd rather not be seen with anyone under twenty-
five."

"You're not even twenty-five!"

"Exactly! Older men are where it's at…or so I've learned." I
shrug because I've never had a preference before *him*.

"Good, we're diving straight into Ryan gossip."

"No, thanks. Already had that unpleasant convo with Cami,
and I'm done for the year."

"That's not fair, I wasn't there. I need to be caught up!" she
demands.

After our drinks arrive, I tell her everything and give her all
the dirty details she wants even though it hurts to repeat it.

"So you think he's with this Rachelle bitch now?"

"Piper!" I scold.

"Well, am I wrong? She's swooping in on your man. If she was someone with a following, I'd make a video about it and expose her."

"Jesus. YouTubers are ruthless." I laugh.

"You have no idea. Speaking of which, Dad hired a bodyguard."

I scrunch my nose because this is news to me. "A bodyguard? For what?"

"For me, apparently. There's been this stalker…he's been commenting on my videos and sending me messages for the past six months. He completely crossed the line when he sent me naked pictures of himself. Then he emailed photos of my apartment building, so he knows where I live. Dad found out and lost his shit. Demanded I shut down my entire account! I have twenty million followers. I'm not giving that up for some psycho."

"Piper, are you serious? How could you not tell me that?"

"Because I didn't think it was that big of a deal. I get crazy fans all the time. Dad's just being overprotective."

"So where is your bodyguard now?" I ask.

"He's standing outside the restaurant," she says, nodding toward the door. "Really fucking fine too."

"For real? He just follows you around all day?"

"Only when I leave the house." She taps her long nails on the table and smirks. "Which means he's basically on call twenty-four seven."

"Wow…that's intense. How long is he supposed to guard you?"

"Dad says until they find the guy and can be sure he's no longer a threat. Could be a month, could be a year. I honestly don't know."

"Wow, Pipe. That's…unsettling." Instinctively, I look around. "So why's he outside?"

"He walked the perimeter and knows what my stalker looks like. So if he happens to show up, he'll stop him before he even gets in. Honestly, I think the douche is harmless and just wants my attention, but Dad seems to think it's motivated by money. So to give him reassurance, I let the hot bodyguard be my shadow."

"What's his name?"

"The stalker or the bodyguard?"

I laugh even though this isn't a funny situation. I'm worried about her. "The guard."

"Tristan Belvedere." She smiles as she grabs her glass and sips her drink. "Even his name sounds hot, right?"

"What's he look like?"

"Tall and muscular—obviously. He has a short brown buzz cut and a full face of dark facial hair. I think he's former military. I haven't really gotten him to talk much about himself, but I will. I plan to go to lots of holiday parties, so he'll have to come with me." She waggles her brows and smirks.

"You cannot get involved with your bodyguard," I demand, knowing exactly what she was implying. "That's trouble waiting to happen with a capital T."

"Okay, *Mom*…" She rolls her eyes. "There's no harm in flirting with him. Plus, he barely says two words to me. I text him when I'm leaving, and he shows up with the car."

"I feel better knowing he's with you now that I'm aware you're being stalked." I sigh. "I can't believe this. Maybe you should consider taking a break from YouTube."

"And disappoint my followers just because of one bad apple?" She gasps. "No way! I will be more careful, though, about showing where I am and posting my location."

"You should've been doing that in the first place," I mutter.

"Yes, I know. I already got lectured from both Mom and Dad."

I finish my second martini. "Good. You're young, beautiful, and social—the perfect target for sick, perverted men. You have to be careful."

"I will be, promise. Mom, Dad, and Tristan can track me on my phone now. I'm certain Dad was ready to put a GPS device around my ankle too."

"Well, can you blame him? You're his baby," I tease.

She snorts into her drink, nearly spilling it on the table, and we both laugh. Piper and I were close growing up and best friends during our teenage years. She loves the spotlight and has an addictive personality that draws people in. I always preferred a small circle of friends and stayed away from the paparazzi. After hearing about her stalker, I have no regrets.

"So now that you've lectured me, let's get back to how you're going to repair this broken heart. I could ask Tristan if he has a brother," she says with the corner of her lips tilted. "Or sister, if you're writing off men?"

"I'm not looking to date or ho myself out with anyone right now. I'm focusing on me and my new business venture."

"Alright, I can support that. But just in case you change your mind, I'll get Tristan's brother's number."

CHAPTER TWENTY-FOUR

RYAN

I HAVEN'T SEEN or talked to Kendall since my sister's wedding two weeks ago. I've been working every single day, but I have called and texted her every free chance I have. She hasn't answered or responded to me, and I'm starting to think she changed her number or blocked me. But I'm not giving up that easily. I just need five minutes of her time to apologize and explain what happened at the wedding. If she's going to hate me, it needs to be over the truth, not a misunderstanding.

This time of year has been insane in the ER. We see a lot of third-degree burns and cuts from people preparing holiday dinners and not paying attention. Not to mention those who stress themselves out so much with planning the perfect Christmas that they end up with bleeding ulcers and sometimes need blood transfusions. Add that to patients who need emergency surgeries, and well, let's just say it's been one insane day after another.

"How ya holding up, Dr. St. James?" Nick asks. "I've never seen you this focused before."

"I'm always focused," I retort. "Trying to be anyway."

"You are, but I'm worried you'll burn out. You need a day off?"

"Nah." I open a chart and start reading.

"I got New Year's Eve covered. Why don't you take off and spend it with your family or girlfriend?"

"I didn't work Thanksgiving, though. Are you sure?"

"You can work Christmas Eve and Day." He chuckles. "But please, take New Year's Eve and Day off."

"Sure, thanks, sir." I don't bother to mention I don't have a girlfriend.

"You wanna grab a drink after your shift?"

I look up and meet his eyes. He's never asked me to hang out after work. "A drink?"

"Yeah. You look like you could use one. Unless you'd rather go home and drink alone," he mocks. "You kinda look like someone ran over your puppy."

I smile even though it's forced. "I don't have a puppy."

"Don't be a smartass. Your shift ends in an hour. Meet me in my office and we'll go to The Heights."

"Alright."

It's not that I don't consider Nick a friend even though he's my boss, but the last thing I wanna do is drink and talk about Kendall. Inevitably, she'll come up, but who knows, maybe he'll give me another perspective that'll help me get her back. Or at least have her responding to my texts.

As usual, I don't get done on time, but I meet Nick ninety minutes later, and we head down the street to the bar. It's busy because it's eleven o'clock on a Friday night, but we manage to find a table in the back.

"Beer and shots?" he asks.

"Sure, I don't have a fifteen-hour shift tomorrow," I deadpan.

"Eh, just one round, you'll be alright." He waves me off, then orders.

"So, I have a suspicion that you wanted to talk about something."

"Yeah, but before we do, let's get some alcohol in your system."

I chuckle at his honesty and clink my shot of vodka with his before we down them.

"That's better." He takes a swig of his beer next. "I wanna see how you're doing."

"I'm great."

"Mentally…" he reiterates. "We've all suffered from the pandemic, and even though things have slowed down since the vaccine was released, I can tell how the past couple of years have affected you. I was actually glad you got those two weeks off. Even though we needed you, I could see you needed the downtime more."

"I agree," I say with a nod. "It definitely helped me recharge."

"You're passionate and hardworking, and there's no denying that. I highly value you as a doctor, but I also need to make sure my team is emotionally stable."

"You don't think I am?"

"You are, but you can't be a robot twenty-four seven. You get in, do your job, talk to your patients, and overwork yourself until you can't see straight. That's not healthy for anyone."

"I like to stay busy, but if you're saying I need to work less, then just say it."

"You need to do what's best for you, including getting help if you're still suffering from PTSD symptoms. Are you sleeping?"

"I'm a doctor in New York City, what do you think?"

"When you lie in bed, do you fall asleep right away?" he clarifies.

"I pass out fairly quickly, but I wake up three or four times usually."

"From nightmares?"

Brushing a hand through my hair, I feel uncomfortable answering, but I can't deny it. Nodding, I say, "Yeah and anxiety attacks, but when I was off, I had no trouble sleeping." I don't mention the cure was Kendall lying next to me almost every night or falling asleep with her in my arms.

"Are you sure you don't want to see a therapist? You know I can pair you with one."

I shrug, not immediately shutting down the idea but also not sure if that's what I need right now. Kendall consumes my mind, so if I don't stay busy, she's all I think about. I've thought about going to her house, but I never have enough time to go between my back-to-back shifts.

"I'm not against it, but I dunno if that'd help," I tell him honestly. "I'm kinda going through some other shit."

He gives me a weary look, then smirks. "What's her name?"

I'm impressed by how quick he was able to guess. "Kendall."

"Breakup?"

"It's complicated. We weren't officially together, but at the same time, we were. But then our time came to an end, and before I could ask if she wanted more, I fucked it up. Now she won't talk to me."

"And you working nonstop isn't helping, which makes my case stronger," he taunts. "Effective immediately, two days off per week and only twelve-hour shifts. No exceptions."

"Nick…"

"I'll make sure we have enough staff to cover it. Don't make the same mistakes I did at your age or you'll become a lonely workaholic like me."

I furrow my brows and take a drink of my beer. "What happened?"

"I had a Kendall. Her name is Maggie, and I was head over heels in love with her. We went to medical school together and spent every waking hour studying. When our internships took us to opposite sides of the country, she left before I could confess my true feelings. A year later, I was interviewing for residencies, and the hospital she was at had an opening. I thought it was perfect. We would be back in the same city, and I'd tell her how I felt."

"And?" I ask, knowing his story doesn't end well.

"She got engaged." His eyes lower, and he frowns. "Maggie

was so happy, and I couldn't bring myself to tell her the truth. I decided not to move and stayed here."

"Ouch." I see the pain in his expression. "So she never knew?"

"Deep down, I think she did. But I took too damn long to tell her, so she moved on."

"Did you stay in contact?"

"We did because she's still one of my best friends. She moved to an LA suburb after they got married, and she's now pregnant with baby number three," he tells me. "So if this Kendall is *the one,* you better not let her go because someone will sweep her off her feet, and you'll be too late. Then you'll be like me and kick yourself for the next ten years."

My heart aches at the thought because he's right. Kendall's an amazing woman, and there's no way she'll stay single forever. I need to figure out what the hell I'm gonna do before it's too late for us.

"I'm sorry…" I offer. "I hate that for you."

"And I'd hate it for you." He grins. "Are you in love with her?"

Without hesitation, I nod. "Ridiculously in love with her. I can't stop thinking about the way she makes me feel when we're together and how much I've missed her. She overheard me say something I didn't mean, and before I could explain, she told me off and walked away. All my calls and texts go unanswered."

"You better fight for her then. Fight like you've never fought before."

"I wish I knew how or what would get her attention."

"Well, I just gave you off New Year's Eve and Day. That gives you a week to figure out what you can do to win her back."

"My parents host a huge party on New Year's Eve, and since she's best friends with my sister, there's a good chance she'll be there."

"Bingo!" He points at me with his beer bottle. "Don't let her leave without hearing you out. You get on your knees and beg her to forgive you."

I exhale with a grin. "Sounds like a solid plan."

"And if, at the end of the day, she doesn't want to be with you, at least you can walk away knowing you did everything you could. You'll have the closure you need to move on, and that's one thing I never got. Trust me, it's better than nothing."

An hour later, Nick and I part ways since we work tomorrow. As I walk to my car, I decide to call Kendall again but am sent straight to voicemail. Even though she may never hear it, I leave her a message.

"Hey Kendall, it's Ryan. I'm not sure you'll ever get this, but I just wanted to tell you I'm thinking of you and miss you. I'm not giving up on us. I love you."

I end the call before my emotions take over and hope like hell she'll give me one more chance.

CHAPTER TWENTY-FIVE

KENDALL

I SPENT Christmas Eve with my parents and Piper. On Christmas Day, I volunteered at the shelter until dark. I helped cook, then served food until we ran out. For the past week, I've managed to stay so busy that I immediately fall asleep in bed when I get home. Even so, I'd be lying if I said Ryan still hasn't found his way into my thoughts. He's impossible to forget about, but I'm trying to let go.

After I put on some dark red lipstick and finish my smoky eye shadow, I text Cami. Her family's throwing their traditional New Year's Eve party, and I agreed to go even though I'm not in the mood for one. She was relentless and refused to take no for an answer. I don't know if Ryan will be there, so I'm full of nervous energy. If he's not working, he's usually there, but I wouldn't be surprised if he's at the hospital tonight.

I've been thinking about what I'm gonna wear. If he's there, I want his jaw to drop to the floor, and I'm certain this skintight dress and curled hair will do the job.

After I lightly spritz on perfume, I text Cami and let her know I'm on my way. My driver texts me when he arrives, then I check myself in the mirror before grabbing a coat and stepping out. Within fifteen minutes, I'm at Cami's parents' penthouse. A woman stands at the door, checking in those who have RSVP'd. The paparazzi have tried to ruin many St. James' parties, so they take extra precautions to keep their guests safe.

As soon as I walk in, one of the attendants takes my coat, then I'm personally greeted by Cami's mom and dad. Clara gives me a hug and kisses both of my cheeks before Bradford tells me hello.

"Hope you've been well," he says.

"I have. No complaints," I reply as I grab a glass of champagne. When I look through the crowd of older people, I see Cami walking toward me wearing a huge smile. She grabs my hand and pulls me away.

"Thank you," I say as she leads me to the massive kitchen filled with the caterers.

"They would've bored you to death. Trust me." She grabs one of the crystal shot glasses and pours tequila.

I glance at the bottle. "Imported. Fancy."

Cami lifts hers and gives me a wink. "To a new year!"

We shoot it down. She gives me a look, then smirks. "He's here."

"Who?" I play dumb, but my heart rate immediately races.

She tilts her head, seeing right through me. "My brother. I knew you weren't going to ask, so I thought I'd just tell you instead."

"I don't want to see him," I say. Grabbing the tequila, I pour another shot, then down it.

A laugh escapes her. "I would've believed you if you weren't dressed like that, but..." She lowers her eyes as she makes her point.

I roll my eyes, then grin. "You know me too well, but I'm not lying. I don't want to see him, but if I happen to run into him, then…" I sweep my hand down my body. "I'll be ready."

"I'm sure there's an explanation for everything, but you have to quit being so damn stubborn," she says, filling our shot glasses again.

"Wow, way to call me out." I groan. "I'm not stubborn...I'm strong-minded."

"Yeah, you're something." She cackles.

"I just want to avoid him because I don't know what I'd say. I'm not over him yet. It's going to take some time," I admit, swallowing down the liquid. I've been here for ten minutes and have already had three shots. *Great.*

"We should do some karaoke. There's a DJ on the roof by the pool," Cami says, then grabs my hand and leads me through the house. On the way there, we run into Eli.

"Good to see you, Kendall," he says, giving me a hug.

"You too, Mr. St James," I tease, then the three of us exit the double patio doors.

The outdoor heaters make it bearable, and the alcohol definitely helps too. Two people are up on the makeshift stage singing "I Got You Babe."

Cami takes a slip of paper and snickers. I shake my head. "You better not be signing me up."

"It's tradition," she reminds me as if I've forgotten. It's a game we play where we sign each other up and you have to sing whatever's chosen for you no matter what.

Cami hands the slip to Eli. "You know what to do with this, baby," she says, then kisses him.

"You two are so adorably disgusting," I tell her, though I've said that a million times since they became official.

She grins. "I still feel like I'm living in a dream."

I can relate to that more than she knows. As soon as Ryan comes to mind, my mood changes, and she immediately notices. Cami gives me a pouty expression. "None of that."

A handful of people sing, and soon, I hear my name being announced. Thankfully, we got a refill of drinks because I couldn't do this sober.

The emcee speaks into the microphone. "Sorry, I was told I can't tell you what you'll be singing until you're on stage. "

When I take the steps up, I shake my head. "This is your fault, Cami. I hate you," I say into the mic.

"I love you!" she yells.

The DJ starts the song, and I immediately burst into laughter when the piano starts. Of course she chose Journey's "Don't Stop Believin'."

I belt out the first few lyrics and try to hold back a smile. When the buildup to the chorus, Cami stands up and screams the words with me. I wave her toward me, but she shakes her head. "It's your theme song! You're the main character tonight!"

When I look into the crowd, smiling and singing, I spot Ryan watching me in the back. The way his eyes pierce through me makes me almost forget to read the words. I try my best not to look at him, but it's so damn hard knowing he's right there.

Cami comes up on the stage and belts out the chorus that's on repeat at the end. My face is flushed, and my body feels like it's on fire when the music finally fades off. The small crowd of older people goes wild when I walk off the stage. Cami nearly knocks me over when she swings her arms around me.

"You've had a lot to drink, and I've apparently not had enough," I say with a chuckle, leading us back to the table. As soon as I saw Ryan, I sobered up. Once we're seated, Eli offers to get us more drinks, and I see him stop and chat with Ryan.

"There he is," I mutter.

Cami perks up and sees her brother. "Ryan!" She waves him over.

I shake my head and grab her hand. "No. No. Please."

"It's time to rip off the Band-Aid," Cami demands. "Just give him a chance."

When he comes closer, I force a smile, then glare at Cami.

"I'm going to get you back for this," I say between gritted teeth as Eli returns with our drinks.

He looks at me, and a million unspoken words stream between us. Right now, I want to disappear.

"Have a seat," Eli offers to Ryan.

"You can have mine. Excuse me." I walk past him, then hear Cami calling out my name. I know she means well, but as much as I thought I was prepared to be around him, I realized I'm not ready.

Needing to get away, I go back inside and go down the stairs. Considering I have this house memorized, I walk the long hallway that leads to a balcony that oversees the city.

Once I'm outside and alone, I suck in a deep breath, trying to calm down. My heart hammers in my chest, and it doesn't help that Ryan looks sexy as sin. He's wearing a navy button-up shirt, tucked into black slacks with a belt. As I eyed him up and down, undressing him, I remembered what it was like to be with him. I'd be fucking lying if I said I didn't still want him.

As I lean against the railing, I can hear off-key singing in the distance. Looking up at the night sky, I close my eyes and suck in a deep breath, losing myself in my thoughts. Hearing my name being called pulls me back to the present.

At first, I think I'm imagining his deep baritone, but then I glance over my shoulder and meet Ryan's eyes. He shuts the patio doors behind him and moves closer.

We stand inches apart in silence.

"Can we talk?" I hear the brokenness in his tone that Cami was referring to. "Please."

"I have nothing to say to you," I admit, crossing my arms over my chest.

"That's fine because I just need you to listen." Ryan takes a step even closer. I shiver, realizing how cold it is out here. His warm hands touch my arms, and he briefly rubs his palms up and down.

"Just five minutes?" he asks.

There's no way I'll be able to deny him when he's right in front of me. Sucking in a deep breath, I nod. "Okay."

Ryan opens the doors and leads me inside. I follow him into his father's study.

Wood is burning in the giant fireplace, and two loungers are

THE BEST OF US

positioned in front of it. Ryan takes my hand and leads me over, so I take a seat.

For a second, he paces and runs his fingers through his hair. He looks exhausted, like he hasn't been getting much sleep. Immediately, I begin to worry about him and how much he must be working and not sleeping. He finally sits down next to me, leaving hardly any space between us.

His mouth opens and falls as if he's searching for his words before he finally exhales.

"I'm truly sorry, Kendall. Before I explain anything, I owe you an apology. I should've never ever said those things to Eli. It's inexcusable, and I didn't mean them. I panicked and wanted to change the subject, so I thought dismissing us and acting like I would've before you and I ever got together would get him to talk about something else. It wasn't the place or time, and I already knew you weren't happy with me by how awkward things were between us. Please believe me when I say I respect you way more than that, and I don't think you're a spoiled princess. Well, a princess maybe, but not a spoiled one." He grabs my hand and squeezes, but I remain silent as I take in his words.

"I never wanted to hurt you." He still has my hand in his, but I can't find the strength to pull away. "I never want to hurt you, period. Ever. I felt awful the moment I said those words and would do anything to take them back because they're not true. I think you're amazing."

I nod, lowering my eyes. "Thank you for your apology. I appreciate that," I finally say. "For all of my life, people have assumed I'm nothing more than a pretty face with my family's money. After showing you my true self and really getting to know each other, I expected more from you, so it really hurt to hear you say those things about me."

"I completely understand. You had every right to be mad at me, but I just wanted to explain and apologize. I've been trying to reach you. I've left voicemails and texted you a dozen times.

Thinking you probably hated me nearly has destroyed me these past few weeks," he admits.

I lick my lips, trying to find my confidence. "I blocked your number, Ryan. I didn't want to hear from you," I admit. "It was easier for me not to know when you were calling or to read your texts so I could get over you. My heart was breaking, but as much as it hurt, I wanted to move on."

He lowers his gaze and shakes his head. "I don't blame you. My heart's been breaking since the second you said goodbye the day I dropped you off."

"What do you mean?"

"I didn't know where we stood. Those two weeks at the cabin were the best of us, and I thought it was over now that we were home. Instead of just asking you, I froze. Like an idiot." He chuckles.

"I did too," I tell him honestly. "I wasn't sure what to say or if you wanted to even have a discussion, so I just pretended it wasn't an issue." I shrug, feeling flushed and stupid now that I say it aloud to him. "I was nervous and lost the courage to tell you how I really felt."

"How did you really feel?" he asks.

I watch the fire, listening to the wood snap and pop. "I need to know something first...is there anything going on with you and Rachelle?"

Ryan's eyes flick over to me. "What do you mean?"

"I saw she called you the night of the rehearsal dinner when you got up, then she showed up at the wedding like you two were a couple. Did you get back together?" I ask, and it causes a spike of adrenaline to rush through me. Ryan doesn't immediately answer but seems confused.

"No, Kendall. Absolutely not. I didn't invite her. I wouldn't do that to you..." he reassures me.

I almost smile, but somehow hold it back. "Then...why did—"

He places his hand on top of mine again, and just his touch causes goose bumps to trail over my body.

He tucks a loose strand of hair behind my ear as he smiles at me. "She had called me earlier that day to tell me Joey was sick with a fever and coughing. He's not vaccinated, and Rachelle was nervous, so I told her to give him some meds and keep me updated. That evening, she called to tell me he was doing better and to thank me for my help. That's all it was."

My face contorts. "That's it? Then why'd she show up at the reception?"

"She asked if I had a date, and when I said no, she said she'd come, but I indirectly told her not to worry about it. I guess she took that as an invitation, and when she showed up, I didn't want to be rude or cause a scene at my sister's wedding. We're only friends, nothing else," he explains wholeheartedly.

Guilt washes over me. I made him out to be the bad guy and thought the absolute worst of him. "I feel stupid for assuming," I admit. "But I don't have the best track record with men so—"

"Don't," he interrupts. "You're the only woman I want, Kendall. I knew the moment we left the cabin, and then the next day when I woke up and you weren't next to me. Hell, I knew days into our sex-only agreement that I'd want more. I haven't been able to get you off my mind, and it's nearly killed me not having you in my life."

My breathing increases as he says the most amazing things to me—words I've been dying to hear. "I owe you an apology too, and I'm not always good at admitting I was wrong, but I should've given you the chance to explain before I blew you off completely. However, in my defense, I was really hurt by what you said and reacted out of emotion."

"You had every right to. This is my fault, not yours. I should've manned up and told you how I felt, so Eli didn't even have to question it. So, lesson learned," he says with a chuckle.

"I think we both learned something here," I admit. "I should've confessed how I felt."

Ryan leans forward and brushes his lips against mine as he

holds me closer. I moan into his mouth as our tongues twist together, and it feels like heaven being back in his arms.

When we break apart, I place my palm against his cheek. "I'm in love with you, Ryan."

He traces his lips with mine before resting his forehead against mine. "Fuck, that feels good to hear." He laughs. "I've never felt this way about anyone, Kendall. It scares the shit outta me, but I'm not gonna run from it. I've fallen for you too, Angel. I'm so deeply in love with you."

Tears well in my eyes, and I can't contain how happy I am to hear those words. "Thank God. I would've been really embarrassed if you hadn't said it back."

He chuckles, then our lips crash together, and I feel as if I'm floating. His warmth sends butterflies in my stomach, and it brings me back to all those moments we had at the cabin.

Ryan's phone vibrates, and when we look down, I realize the countdown to midnight has begun. He unlocks his phone, and we watch the seconds tick by.

I hear party favors and fireworks in the background, but right now, all that matters is being here with him.

"Happy New Year, baby." He stands, then brings me up with him. Ryan wraps an arm around me and pulls me closer until our lips collide. Things quickly become more heated between us, and I don't think I'll be able to stop once we start.

"I need you," he whisper-pants in my ear. "Come home with me and wake up next to me."

His warm breath brushes against my cheek as a shiver runs down my spine.

"You're mine, Kendall. Say it," he demands as he fists my hair.

"Yes," I agree. "All yours."

CHAPTER TWENTY-SIX

RYAN

SOMEHOW, Kendall and I sneak out of my parents' house without being stopped by anyone, which is a small miracle, considering how many people are here. We climb into the Range Rover, and I'm tempted to pull her into the back seat and make love to her right now, but I also don't want to rush being with her again. There are things I need to say to her before this night is over, and it won't be in my parents' driveway.

Over the past week, I've been so damn distracted, worried, and I've told myself that if I didn't run into her tonight, I'd go to her house. I didn't want to come off like a crazy person, but it's hard when I know she's the one. I never expected to fall in love, but it happened, and I can't get over her that easily.

We head down the long driveway and turn onto the street, and I see my parents' house fade into the distance. It takes about forty-five minutes to get to my part of town. When we stop at a red light, I glance over at her and grin. "You're so fucking beautiful," I say, leaning over and stealing a kiss.

"I've missed you," she admits as I place my hand on her thigh. As soon as I turn and park in the private garage, we rush inside, growing more greedy and ravenous for one another.

She looks around as if she's taking it all in, and all I can do is watch her. "I can't believe I'm here with you."

"Why?" I ask, stepping forward.

"Because I've always imagined being at your place," she mutters. "Look! A Christmas tree! Are you no longer a scrooge?"

"You might've rubbed off on me a little." I chuckle. "Want a tour?"

Her eyes light up. "Absolutely."

My apartment isn't huge, but I do have an amazing bird's-eye view of the city from here. Living on this side of the city makes it easier to get to the hospital than if I were downtown. Emergencies happen too often, and time is usually of the essence, so I needed to be close.

I lead her around, showing her the bathroom, kitchen, balcony, and even my bedroom. When we go back to the living room, I light the fireplace. It's gas, so there's no need for wood like at the cabin.

"Are you ready for the main reason I bought this place?" I ask.

She nods with excitement, and I slide open the blinds.

"Though I've lived here all my life, I never tire of seeing the building scape," she admits, moving closer.

I wrap my arm around her shoulder and trail my fingers across her skin. "Me either. I've been offered positions at other hospitals, but I don't think I could ever leave. New York is too special."

When she looks at me, she's chewing on her bottom lip. I smirk then dip my head and kiss her, and she pours herself into me.

"God, I've missed you," she pants as I slide my mouth across the softness of her neck.

"Same," I whisper, then lead her to my bedroom. Once inside, I turn the lights down to a low glow. Kendall wraps her arms around my waist, then looks up into my eyes.

"I've dreamed about this," she admits. "About being with you again."

"Me too, Angel," I mutter, then carefully unzip the dress that fits her like a second skin. When the fabric falls to the floor, she blushes.

"No panties?" I cross my arms over my chest and grin.

She shrugs. "Foxy Fireball, remember?"

I snort. "How could I forget?"

"I was hoping I'd get lucky tonight," she says with confidence in her tone. "With *you*."

"There was no way I was leaving that party without explaining myself. I didn't want to start a new year with that on my shoulders."

She comes to me and hooks her fingers in my pants, then quickly undoes my belt. "Instead, you'll be starting it with me on your face."

"Fuck, I love it when you talk dirty."

Kendall chuckles, then unbuttons and unzips my pants, and moves them down. I'm hard as fuck and have been ever since I kissed her in my father's library. She removes my shirt and slides my boxers down until they're around my ankles. Her eyes go wide when she sees how turned on I am.

"Mmm," she hums, then drops to her knees. With big brown eyes, she looks up at me while teasing my tip. Kendall makes a show of it, licking my shaft, then shoving my length to the back of her throat. Picking up her pace, she reaches behind me and grabs my ass, taking full control.

"Baby," I say in a hushed tone, moving her hair from her face so I can see her. "If you keep this up…" I can't even form a complete sentence when she grabs my shaft and sucks me. My eyes roll in the back of my head, and I don't want to lose myself yet. As my muscles tense, Kendall pulls away and stands up. She seductively strips out of her bra and bends over, showing me her ass as she takes off her strappy high heels.

I lift an eyebrow at her, then move her to the bed. She lies back, her hair cascading around her, and hooks her finger.

"I need you, Ryan. So damn much," she admits.

Giving her a sly grin, I grab her ankles and move her to the edge of the bed. "Not until I taste you, sweetheart."

I bury my head between her legs and don't leave an inch of her perfect pussy untouched. Her ragged pants let me know everything she doesn't say. Reaching forward, Kendall tugs on my hair, and when her back arches, I know she's close.

"Yes, yes," she mutters and moans, riding my face.

"You're such a greedy little thing," I mumble against her clit as she teeters on the edge. Kendall grinds against my tongue, then lets out a guttural groan as her body tenses, then trembles with satisfaction.

"Ryan, Ryan," she whispers, riding out her release. Before she comes back to earth, I hover above her, allowing her to taste her arousal on my lips.

"I can't wait to fuck your little cunt," I whisper, and she smirks. Kendall loves it when I talk like that. Our eyes lock together as I slowly enter her. She gasps, and I keep my pace, pulling all the way out, then slamming back inside. She whispers my name as I meet her eyes.

"I love you," I whisper across her lips. "I love you so damn much," I finally admit, and it feels as if my heart stops beating when she says it back.

"I love you, Ryan. I always have," she tells me, blinking away emotional tears. "I was so scared I was going to lose you."

"I know, Angel. I know." Our kisses deepen, and it seems as if I leave my body as the orgasm threatens to take over. Kendall's pants increase, and I know she's close, and when her pussy nearly squeezes my dick off, I lose myself inside her. Making love to her is like having an out-of-body experience, and I'm blinded by my emotions. Being with her is almost too much for me to handle.

Once we clean up, we lie back on the bed. She snuggles close and lays her head on my chest. "It's almost like being back at the cabin again."

I kiss her hair and smile. "It is."

Kendall pops her head up and brushes her lips against mine,

then plops down on the pillow. I roll onto my side and meet her eyes. "I want to be with you."

"You are," she says.

"No, like be with you, Kendall. Date you."

Her eyes go wide, and I continue talking. "I know I come with a lot of baggage because of my job, but my boss is being strict with my hours. Two required days off per week. I have to take vacations. And no more doubles."

When her mouth falls open, I place my finger under her chin and close it.

"I've never felt this way about anyone but you. If you're willing to take the risk and be mine, I promise I'll do whatever I can to make you happy and give you the attention you deserve."

Kendall wraps her arms around the back of my neck and pulls me close to her mouth. "Yes, Ryan. I guess that means you're my boyfriend?"

I slide my tongue between her lips and deepen the kiss. "For now. Well, until I make you my wife."

She giggles, and when we pull apart, she lets out a long, content sigh. "Didn't think I'd be starting the New Year in a relationship, but I'm sure as hell not complaining. I'm glad you'll be taking more time for yourself. But even if you're at work, I might need you to meet me for a quickie in the parking lot if I miss you," she adds.

"Deal. I'd have you breakfast, lunch, and dinner if you'd allow it."

"Music to my ears," she says with a snort. "Thank you."

"For what?" I ask.

"For not giving up on me. The thought of losing what we had made me feel sick, and I tried so damn hard to forget you, but it was impossible," she admits.

I give her a smirk. "You understand why, right?"

She nods and looks at me with hooded eyes. "Because what we have is the real deal."

"It is," I confirm as she loops her leg over my body and

straddles me. I dig my fingers in her hips as she rocks her pussy against my growing cock.

"I can't get enough of you," she says and takes control, guiding me inside her. The feeling is more than mutual as she rolls her head back and lets out a guttural groan. Dipping down, she meets my mouth, and we kiss as my cock slides in and out. Kendall picks up her pace, sitting straight so I have the perfect view of her beautiful breasts.

I hold her hips, guiding her, giving her more friction as she bounces on my dick. "Yes, yes, like that," she whispers as I rub circles on her clit with my thumb.

"You're so fucking gorgeous," I say as her eyes flutter closed. Her sweet pants drive me crazy. She rides me hard, with more intent, and soon, she scratches her nails down my chest and unravels. When she lightly pinches my nipples and rides out her release, mine comes like an explosion as my muscles tense.

"Fuck," I moan, and it only encourages her to keep going. Kendall smiles and topples onto my chest as she tries to catch her breath while wearing a satisfied smile. I wrap my arms around her and hold her.

"You're mine," she says with a sigh. "I don't like to share."

I laugh. "Don't worry, Angel. I don't either."

"Oh, since I haven't talked to you in a little while, I've got some good news," she tells me, and I can see her excitement bubbling.

"I found a place for my business and signed the lease yesterday! I'll be able to get started sometime soon."

I pull her into my arms. "I'm so fucking proud of you! What did you call it?"

A small grin falls on her lips, and she sucks in a deep breath. "I don't know yet," she admits.

"Aw. I'm sure you'll come up with something. Just have to remember what the mission of your business is," I offer.

Kendall tilts her head. "Hmm."

"You're doing it for the love of people and to help those who need it most, Angel. What about…"

"All for Love." Her eyes go wide. "I can already imagine the logo."

I chuckle. "It's perfect and true. You're doing it all for love."

Eventually, we get up and go to the kitchen for some water. After I grab two bottles, we sit on the couch and stare out the large windows. Kendall leans against me, and I pull her into my arms.

"So when do you want to tell Cami the good news?" she asks, and I watch the blue-colored flames dance and flicker.

"I'm pretty sure she knows," I say, smirking and turning to her.

She tilts her head, confused. "How?"

"Because I told her I wasn't leaving that party until I found you and told you how I felt. I'm sure when the countdown happened, and we were nowhere to be found, she got the memo," I explain. "Cami's been waiting for this to happen for over a decade, and she promised me you'd be there tonight."

Kendall grabs her phone, unlocks it, then lets out a hearty laugh. She shows me texts from my sister, and I snort when I read them.

Cami: You better be banging my brother's brains out. Oh, and HAPPY NEW YEAR!

Cami: Bring in the new year the right way—in a relationship with Ryan.

Cami: Last text, but I expect you two to get married this year. THANK YOU!

I look back at Kendall who's grinning.

"Yeah, she knows," I say.

"Yeah, but I'll confirm in the morning," she admits.

"She might not be too far off," I offer.

"About what?" She furrows her brows.

"Marriage," I say.

Kendall sucks in a deep breath. "A *Distant Diva* would never say that."

I chuckle and pull her into my arms. "I just don't think it's out of the realm of possibilities, Kendall. When you know you've found the one, you don't let them get away."

She grins and smacks her lips against mine. "You just might be right. It'll be the best year I've ever had."

"Same."

Kendall stands and grabs my hand, then leads me back to the bedroom.

"Time for round three," she says, wearing a smirk as she looks over her shoulders.

"I'm so glad I have off tomorrow." I laugh and follow her. At this rate, we'll be making love until the sun comes up, but I'm not complaining.

CHAPTER TWENTY-SEVEN

KENDALL

ONE YEAR LATER

IT'S OFFICIALLY BEEN a year since Ryan and I were snowed in at the cabin. I honestly can't believe so much time has passed, but then again, it also feels like it happened just yesterday. When I think back over the past year, a smile forms on my lips.

After Ryan admitted his true feelings to me on New Year's Eve, we officially became a couple. It was one of the best decisions I've ever made, and I didn't think it was possible to ever love a man as much as I love him. Two months later, he asked me to move in, and I agreed because I wanted to spend every waking second with him. We got a bigger place, but in the same building because it's close to his job, plus the view is to die for. While Ryan doesn't work nearly as much, I still miss him when he's gone.

Over the summer, he took two weeks off, and we went to New Zealand. We hiked the mountains and visited every place on his bucket list. It was an absolute dream vacation and to spend it with Ryan made it a thousand times better.

However, before we left, Cami and Eli announced they were pregnant. Of course, I couldn't have been happier for them and am so excited they're expecting a baby girl next March.

After I signed my new office lease, I went all-in with my company, and it's booming. It's allowed me to donate to the charities I adore and give more to the local food banks and community in an even bigger way.

I've already lived one of the best years of my life, and it's not even over yet.

I don't know how anything else could top it.

"Hey, babe. Are you almost ready?" Ryan asks from the doorway while I look at my empty suitcases.

I bite my bottom lip. "Not exactly. I'm trying to decide what clothes to take."

He moves forward, places his hands firmly on my waist, and pulls me toward him. "You won't be needing them."

Ryan's lips trace the shell of my ear, and I shudder. "Keep it up, and we won't make it to Roxbury before dark," I warn.

"Fine, fine." He looks at both suitcases. "You're taking two?"

"Remember what happened last time? There's no way you can convince me to take less. Also…" I hold up a spare battery that I don't travel without anymore, just in case my phone dies. "I've got this too."

He snorts. "Fine. Pack tons of lingerie. Thanks in advance."

Before leaving the room, he shoots me a wink. My heart still flutters around him. I won't *ever* be letting him go.

I do as he requested and bring tons of panty sets that serve no other purpose than to be seen, then I go in the closet and pull out a tirade of outfits. Once everything is packed, I wheel them into the living room where he's waiting on the couch.

"Ready?" he asks, perking up.

I nod. "Yep. I think I am. Also, do you think we can stop and get a coffee before the drive?"

He narrows his eyes at me before breaking out into a smile. "Whatever you want, Angel."

"That's exactly what I like to hear." I move toward him and pull him in for a kiss.

"But we *should* get going. I've been told we may run into some snow on the way there."

My eyes go wide. "Do you think...?"

He chuckles. "No, there's not a predicted snowstorm, just flurries. We'll be fine."

"Okay," I breathe out. "I don't want to be without electricity that long again."

Ryan loops his small bag over his shoulder and grabs my suitcases, then we make our way down to the Range Rover. On the way out of the city, he stops at a coffee shop and allows me to order the biggest peppermint mocha they offer.

On the way to Roxbury, he keeps his hand placed on my thigh, and we listen to his favorite medical podcast. Most of it goes over my head, but I'm too busy texting Cami to care.

Cami: Hopefully there's not a storm! Be safe!

Kendall: It's supposed to snow, but no arctic blast is in the forecast, thank goodness!

Cami: So while you're there, can you go ahead and get knocked up so we can have kids close to the same age?

Kendall: CAMI!

I snort, and Ryan looks at me.

"She's starting the baby thing again, isn't she?" he asks.

Placing my hand on top of his, I squeeze his fingers. "You know your sister too well."

He arches a brow. "Tell her to stop it. I mean, I love the thought of you carrying my baby, but we'll have kids when we're ready, not because Cami has to have you do everything she does."

My head falls back, and I laugh, though I can't wait for when we do start our own little family and have babies.

"I'll share your sentiment, though just get ready for a plethora of angry pregnant woman text messages."

Just as I pick up my phone to send his message, Ryan pulls it away, then sets it in my lap. "How about we don't piss her off today?"

"Good choice." I give him a smirk. "She's been an utter savage lately."

"I know. She asked me to bring her some red velvet cake from the bakery that's around the corner by the hospital, and I told her I wouldn't get off work until around eight. You know what her response was?"

I shake my head.

"She told me to go fuck myself."

A laugh escapes me because I wasn't expecting that. "Hilarious! She's been as sweet as sugar to me, but then again, I haven't told her no either. She only gets yeses from me."

"Which makes you part of the problem. Don't spoil her."

The three-hour drive passes by in a blink. By the time we arrive at the cabin, my bladder is ready to burst from drinking nearly thirty ounces of coffee. Ryan pulls the Range Rover into the garage, and all those old feelings I had the last time we were here come rushing back. When I get out of the car, I can't stop smiling, and he notices.

"Love you," he says, placing a kiss on my forehead, then opens the back hatch. I grab his small duffel bag, and he sets my suitcases on the concrete.

"I'll come back out for the box of food and booze," he tells me with a wink, then unlocks the door.

When I walk inside, I suck in a deep breath, inhaling the familiar smell. I set Ryan's bag on the couch, then go to the large windows and look at the snowcapped mountains. From behind me, Ryan wraps his arms around my waist and places a soft kiss on my neck.

"Are you hungry?" he asks.

I turn around and smile. "For you."

"Oh, there will be *plenty* of that."

I laugh, then my eyes go wide when I notice the Christmas tree lit and decorated. "How did you…?"

"I've got my ways," he quips. "Now let me make you dinner."

Ryan goes out to the Range Rover and grabs the extra food, then meets me in the kitchen. He pulls out a skillet and a pan, then places them on the stovetop. He moves to the fridge that's somehow full of food. I narrow my eyes at him, but he doesn't notice.

"Wanna open some wine?" he asks over his shoulder as he pulls out two gigantic steaks.

"Sure." I set two glasses on the counter and fill them with the cabernet Ryan brought. "Delicious," I mumble after taking a sip and hand him his.

Considering he lived off shitty sandwiches before I moved in with him, this is super impressive and sexy as hell. I lean against the counter and watch him move around the kitchen like he owns it. I'm convinced he's been practicing for this very moment.

I watch him over the rim of my wineglass, drinking him in. When the food is ready, he leads me to the bar top. I take a bite of steak and let out a moan. "This is so good."

"It's all about the cut," he says. "So what do you wanna do tonight?"

"You," I hum. "Not even kidding."

He licks his lips and arches a brow. "I was thinking we could take a bath after dinner."

My eyes light up. "Yes, I love that idea."

"Then give you a full body massage…"

"You're speaking my love language..." I encourage him to keep going.

"Then fuck you until the sun comes up," he adds.

I scoot my nearly finished plate away. "I'm ready."

Ryan chuckles, and it's so damn contagious, but I hope he wasn't teasing me about any of that. After the kitchen is cleaned and the dishes are done, Ryan takes our things up to the master bathroom. He places lit candles all around and tells me he'll be right back as the water runs. Once the tub is full, I turn it off and wait for him.

Five minutes pass and the power in the cabin goes off. My heart begins to race, and I immediately leave the bathroom with a candle in hand to look for Ryan. Before I can make it to the door of the bedroom, it swings open.

"The power's out," I tell him. "What are we gonna do?"

He's not even fazed as he leads me back to the bathroom where the warm glow from the candles fills the space.

"It'll be fine. I'm sure it will come back on soon," he says and dips down to meet my lips. I get lost in his kiss and don't care about anything else but being with him.

His fingers and kisses trail over my body, light like butterfly wings as he undresses me. It takes no time before I'm standing in front of him completely naked. I tug on his belt and unbutton and unzip his jeans. Ryan takes off his shirt, then kicks off his shoes and socks.

I moan as he kisses me, then leads me to the tub. Carefully, he helps me in, and once I'm settled, he climbs in too. Instead of slipping in behind me this time, he sits in front of me. He moves closer, and I loop my legs over his.

"I think we should upgrade the tub in the condo," I whisper right before our lips crash together.

"I agree," he says, then slides his tongue against mine. Things grow more heated between us, and water splashes on the floor. We laugh and decide to get out before we make a mess.

No matter how much time I spend with him, I can't get

enough. I'm greedy when it comes to him and am not ashamed to admit it. Ryan wraps me in a robe and grabs one too, then he leads me downstairs with the flashlight from his phone.

"I seriously can't believe we lost power!" I say as he goes to the fireplace.

I stand behind him, watching how he gracefully stacks the wood, then uses a quick start log to get it going. Soon, the heat brushes against my skin, and I smile down at him.

A second later, Ryan crawls to me and grabs my hand, and I can't help but laugh.

"Need me to help you up?"

He shakes his head, then pulls a velvet box from his robe pocket, and I nearly lose my balance when he opens it.

"Kendall." He clears his throat. "It's been exactly one year since I fell madly in love with you. Actually, right here in this very place. I know without a doubt you're the one for me and my forever."

My emotions take over, and happy tears stream down my face as he continues.

"The day you decided to give me a chance was the day I felt whole again. Angel, I know it's not been that long since we started dating, but I can't imagine my life without you. You're my everything. You're the reason my heart beats. You're the love of my life, and I want to spend eternity with you."

My breath hitches as I wait for his final question.

"Kendall Montgomery, baby...will you marry me and be my wife?"

Wife. My heart soars. He looks at me with so much love, I don't even need a second to think about it.

"Oh my God," I whisper. "Yes, yes of course."

CHAPTER TWENTY-EIGHT

RYAN

AFTER SHE SAYS YES, Kendall falls toward me with her arms open, and I catch her. We kiss as tears stream down her cheeks. "I love you so much," I tell her.

"I love you more," she taunts.

I never imagined I could feel so strongly about another person. It should be illegal, but knowing that she wants to spend forever with me makes me the happiest man alive. We're so lost in the moment, holding each other and laughing, that I realize I never gave her the ring.

As if she read my mind, she giggles, and I reach for the black box that's toppled on the floor a few feet away. I take it out and slip it on her finger. She gasps, and her face lights up.

"Ryan," she whispers, studying it on her hand. "This is so... beautiful."

"After I asked your dad—"

"Wait, you actually asked my parents for permission?"

I squeeze her hand and kiss her knuckles with a smirk. "Absolutely. It's the proper thing to do considering who our folks are. Sure, it's a little old-fashioned and traditional, but I was raised right." I flash her a wink.

With her hand over her heart, she waves me on with the other one. "So what did they say? Were you scared?"

"Your dad is a little intimidating, but overall, your parents were incredibly supportive. Your mom cried, and your dad wanted me to smoke cigars with him, but I declined the offer."

"He knows you're a doctor, and health is your top priority." She rolls her eyes but still smiles.

"Apparently, our wedding is going to be like royalty or something. I don't know, your mom started talking about our families finally being connected and all sorts of things I didn't understand. I explained I wanted to marry you because I love you. I told your parents how I'd spend the rest of my life trying to make sure you were happy and well taken care of."

"Pretty sure your mother is busy planning the whole ceremony right now." I snort.

"I'm sure she is. Thanks for the warning. I bet she's been dying inside not being able to say anything until after this weekend."

"I'm sure she has," I agree. "I've asked everyone to keep it a secret. I don't want the media to find out. I don't want paparazzi following us around."

"Does my sister know?" she asks.

"Oh yeah, she knows, but she swore on all things holy she wouldn't slip and tell you," I say.

She leans forward and kisses me. "Thank you for everything. It means a lot for you to ask for their blessing. They've kept me in a protective bubble for so long, and never really trusted anyone I brought home, but they've always loved you, Ryan. And Cami. Your whole family. I didn't know it was possible for me to be this incredibly happy. I have no idea how you pulled all this off without me knowing."

"Trust me, you're very hard to surprise," I admit. "While I was there, your dad insisted I take your grandmother's diamond ring. He told me he had promised her that when the time came for you to get married, it'd be used for your engagement ring. So I took it to a jeweler and had it put in this setting. It's one of a kind, just like you, baby," I tell her. "I know how much your grandma meant to you. Now, she'll always be with you, especially during this special time."

Tears stream down Kendall's face as she looks at it on her finger, admiring it even more than before. "Seriously?"

I nod, letting her fully take in the moment.

"Thank you, Ryan. I love you so much. You have no idea how much this means to me. I can't even express how I'm feeling right now. Overwhelmed with emotion."

I wipe the tears from her cheeks and lift her chin up so I can kiss her easier. "I love you too, baby." I don't dare tell her I have earrings too that she'll get before the wedding ceremony. Honestly, I don't think I would've been able to get any of this done without the help of my sister. She kept Kendall occupied when I needed her to be busy so I could arrange everything. I'm just kinda surprised Cami didn't slip because she's not always the best at keeping secrets plus her hormones are out of whack because of the pregnancy. I owe her a lot, and of course she was so damn happy about the wedding.

While we're still on the floor, Kendall moves to me and straddles my lap. We're naked under our robes, which is great for easy access. I lift my hand and palm her breast as our tongues tangle together. She lifts her hips, and I feel her wetness on the tip of my cock before she slides down on me. I wrap my arms around her body and hold her as she rides me.

We make love in front of the fire, not rushing, and I soak in every second of being with her like this. Kendall's already my everything, but now she's going to be my wife.

Her hair surrounds my face as I kiss her, and she smiles against my lips. "This feels right."

"It does. Like it was always meant to be, just me and you, sweetheart, together forever," I admit.

She throws her head back and bounces on my dick with more vigor. "When I was a teenager, I used to imagine marrying you."

I pull back, but she keeps gently rocking her hips.

"Really?" I ask, tugging one of her perky nipples into my mouth, nibbling slightly. She groans, allowing the pleasure to shoot through her as she runs her fingers through my hair.

"I've masturbated thinking about you," she admits. When I slightly sit up, she forces me back down, steadying herself even more.

"I'm guilty of the same thing. There was a summer when you wore nothing but a bathing suit. My dick nearly broke off thinking about you."

She giggles. "The hot pink bikini?"

"That's the one," I tell her, reaching up to grab her other breast.

"Fuck," she says, rolling and rocking her body, fucking me so goddamn good. My moans and breathing increases, as Kendall's face moves inches from mine.

"I'm so close, baby," she whispers against my lips, slamming my dick inside her. "So close," she groans one more time before she completely unravels. Gently, I flip her on her back and lay her down. The glow from the fireplace casts shadows on the wall, but lights her face perfectly.

"Ryan, yes. Please," she says, digging her heels in my ass, forcing me forward. "Harder."

I give her exactly what she demands, and the only sound that can be heard is our bodies slapping together. She reaches up and cups my face, pulling my mouth down to hers. As we kiss, it becomes too much for me to handle. When I finally give myself permission to let go, I moan into her neck and fill her full.

My heart races, and my brain can't form comprehensive thoughts. I roll over on my back and lie next to her as we stare up at the ceiling, trying to catch our breaths. My mind and body are reeling, but I can't stop grinning.

"Being with you like that will never get old," she says with a laugh.

"I'll try to make sure it never does," I promise and notice Kendall shivering. "I should probably turn the power back on," I admit, sitting up, knowing the power has been off for a little over an hour. The ceilings are so high, the temperature drops quickly.

"Wait, you're responsible for this?" she asks with wide eyes, perking up and glaring at me.

"I wanted it to be like old times. No power or outside distractions, just me and you, and this fire." I shoot her a wink.

After I stand, I hold out my hand to help her up. She takes it, and I give her a chaste kiss before walking away. When I turn around, she slaps my ass with a giggle. "Mmm," she says as I grab my robe and slip it on my body.

I go to the utility room and flip the breaker. The lights buzz on, and I return to the living room where she's waiting for me. Kendall hooks her finger, gesturing me toward her.

"Damn," I say, studying her naked body and how her dark hair falls around her face as she looks at me with hooded eyes. I hold out my hand and interlock our fingers, then lead her upstairs where I lay her on the bed and worship her body with my mouth. My only goal is to make this a night to remember for her, and while I'm pretty sure I accomplished that, I want her to feel where I've been in the morning. It doesn't take long before she writhes beneath my tongue. Kendall pants and grabs the sheets with her fists.

"Yes, baby," she says, lifting her head and watching me ravage her clit.

Right as her body explodes, I tongue fuck her, tasting her sweetness as she lets out a guttural groan. Her breathing is heavy and rough as she rides my face.

Once she returns to reality, she opens her arms. "Come here, baby."

I lay beside her, kissing her like tomorrow will never come. All I want to do this weekend is live in the moment with Kendall and give her my undivided attention. I imagine we won't be leaving this bed unless we need to eat, or at least that's the goal. Kendall's eyes flutter closed, and her breathing slows.

"I'm so comfortable." She sighs, and I laugh, already feeling hungover from the amazing sex.

"This weekend, we're christening every fucking room in this cabin," I say, holding her in my arms as my eyes grow heavy.

"Cami already has." She snickers, then smiles. "Love you," she says as I run my fingers through her hair.

"Love you." I return the sentiment, my heart swelling at the words. Staring up at the ceiling while holding the woman of my dreams, I feel so damn lucky to be alive. Too many people weren't allowed this opportunity, so I promised myself that I wouldn't take things like this for granted after living through the pandemic.

I had to force myself not to pass up life-changing opportunities because I was too busy dealing with my personal demons. That time we spent together at the cabin changed my life. Kendall showed me I was worthy of *being* loved and worthy enough *to* love. She has my whole heart and means so damn much to me.

Eventually, I fall into a deep sleep, and the only thing that wakes me is the sunshine leaking through the window. Last night, we were so enamored with one another that I forgot to close the curtain.

I hold Kendall, and her ass presses against my morning wood. She rustles and lets out a hum, and I can't stop smiling. Her eyes flutter open, and she looks at me over her shoulder. I press my lips to her cheek.

"It wasn't a dream, was it?" she whispers, then lifts her hand and looks at the diamond on her finger.

"No, Angel. It wasn't."

"Good," she says. Laying her head back down, she immediately drifts back to sleep.

It's incredible how much life can change in just one year.

CHAPTER TWENTY-NINE

KENDALL

FOUR MONTHS LATER

Waking up next to Ryan each morning is a dream come true. While we've been living together for a while, I now get to call him fiancé. Our parents are thrilled we're getting married and so are Cami and Eli. Piper's really excited about it too.

"Almost ready?" Ryan asks as I slip a scarf around my neck. It's the middle of March, and it's still a little chilly outside. I'm excited for summer, mainly because we're getting married in June.

"Yep," I tell him, grabbing my phone. Today, we have a cake tasting appointment. I've been so busy building my business that I kept putting it off. Since I hired Stephanie, Cami's planner, to help me, she's been on my ass about choosing my cake. It's the last thing on my wedding to-do list, then everything's complete.

We've already secured a private venue in Manhattan, and I've been fitted for my custom designer wedding dress. Even though Cami's ready to burst, she's been a tremendous help and has insisted on being a part of everything. I honestly wouldn't have it any other way.

After I grab my purse, Ryan and I hop in the Range Rover and drive out of the city. There's a small bakery located on the outskirts that's been around for nearly one hundred years. They're known for making expensive luxury cakes, but I don't care. I plan to only get married once.

Ryan interlocks his fingers with mine. "So not to give you a scare, but Cami's water could break at any moment."

I let out a laugh. "I know. I already texted her this morning and told her she's not allowed to go into labor until after I've left the cake shop."

Ryan snorts. "Okay, I'm sure she can help that."

"My niece and I have made a very special deal. If she waits until I've chosen my favorite flavors, I'll buy her a Lamborghini on her eighteenth birthday."

His eyes go wide. "You're kidding."

"Maybe." I shrug. "Maybe not."

"Do you want to get a coffee?" he asks, changing the subject. I love teasing him about things like that.

I give him a grin. "The answer to that question is *always* yes."

When he pulls off the highway and turns, I know exactly where we're going. When he parks, he turns to me. "Remember this place?"

"How could I forget it? They had the best gingerbread coffee ever," I say, and we step out of the SUV and walk inside.

It looks different without all the Christmas decorations, but it still brings me back to the day we left the cabin. Neither of us knew where this would lead, but here we are. I feel as if life has gone full circle as I order my white mocha with sugar cookie crumble whip cream. Ryan gets his black.

We thank the woman, then leave. By the time we arrive at the bakery, I've already finished my drink, and I'm more than ready for dessert.

He parks and looks at the giant building. "So this is the place?"

"Oh yeah. This is it," I say. "They're known for extravagant cakes. Even made a few for the Royal family when they came to New York for holiday."

He chuckles and opens the door for me. "I should really get out more."

As soon as we step inside, I smell the sweet fragrance of vanilla and sugar. My mouth waters with anticipation as a woman approaches us, wearing all black.

"Hi, I'm Jennifer. May I help you?" she asks.

"Yes, my name is Kendall Montgomery. I have an appointment today. This is Ryan, my fiancé. He's the semi-picky one," I say, giving him a wink.

He reaches forward and squeezes my hip with a smile as the woman leads us to a private tasting room.

"I'll let everyone know you've arrived," she says, leaving us alone. The ceilings are high, and the large windows give the perfect view of the river down below.

"You look so goddamn gorgeous," Ryan whispers. He walks over, tucks long strands behind my ear, and kisses me. "If we weren't in public right now…"

"You are such a tease," I say, brushing my lips across his. A second later, several people enter and deliver at least fifteen cakes on platters.

Jennifer returns with serving plates and a gigantic binder. Ryan and I exchange looks, and I laugh.

"So, we've created several cakes based on the survey you took before your arrival. We've got strawberry buttercream, chocolate almond, raspberry vanilla, and more."

"Mmm," Ryan says when she hands us forks, then cuts slivers of each one.

We work from left to right, and it takes everything I have not to eat more than one bite of each.

"This one's my favorite," Ryan says, taking another bite.

I try it, and my eyes go wide.

"Ahh, that's white chocolate amaretto."

"So, how much would it be for us to get these eight?" I point them out.

"It depends on the tier level of each cake and the design." She opens the book that's full of photos. "We can make all your dreams come true."

I flip through the pictures until I land on the one I adore. It's ten layers with flowers trailing up the side. It's elegant but extravagant.

"I love this one," I admit, pointing at it.

She smiles. "Oh yes. That was created for the Luxury Bridal Show in Beverly Hills. It's very special. These are actual gold flakes, and diamonds stud the flowers on the cake from top to bottom."

Ryan nearly chokes. "Diamonds and gold flakes?"

I grin, and so does Jennifer. "Yes, that's why it cost twenty."

"Twenty?" he asks.

She nods, but her tone stays serious. "Yes, twenty million."

I chuckle when he looks like he might faint. I continue flipping through the photos and see a cake that looks like a castle. One that's at least six feet tall with twelve layers, and another that's built upside down with the large layer on top. These cakes are incredible and look like displays, not something that should ever be eaten.

"I'll leave you two to discuss what you'd like." She smiles and excuses herself.

"Kendall," Ryan mutters and comes close. I kiss him and taste the sweet sugar on his lips.

"Hmm?" I ask.

"You're not about to buy a million-dollar cake."

I snort. "A million? Could be five."

His eyes are huge. "That's too much."

Grabbing his hand, I kiss his knuckles. "I'm the first of my parents' kids to get married. My father has insisted *only* the best."

With a lifted eyebrow, he tilts his head. "I should've asked Cami how much her cake cost."

"You'd shit your pants if you knew. You're so adorable," I admit, kissing him again.

He hums against my lips. "Should we have discussed a budget?"

I pull away and playfully smack him. "Is there a budget for the most important day of our lives?"

He rolls his eyes. "Choose whatever you want. It's why you're my spoiled little princess," he teases, which has me reaching forward to tickle the shit out of him. It's become an inside joke between us. I lean forward, nibbling on his earlobe before I whisper. "The only thing I'm spoiled with is your cock inside me."

"Fuck," he groans and grabs my ass. "You play so dirty."

"Just wait until we get home," I warn with a smirk. Minutes later, Jennifer returns, and Ryan lets me make the final decision.

I choose the flavors and give them permission to stack them so the flavors complement one another. Instead of having the diamond gold flake cake, I choose the twelve layered one with flowers that light up. After we sign the paperwork, I snap a picture of the cake so I can show Cami and Piper.

When we climb into the Range Rover, Ryan grins before our mouths crash together. We're so damn greedy for one another, there's no way I can wait until we get home. With a snap, I undo his jeans. Just as things start to grow more heated, my phone buzzes.

Ryan's hand slips into my jeans, and I'm so goddamn wet as he circles my clit.

"I should probably get that," he whispers against my mouth as his phone vibrates. "Fuck."

He pulls his phone from his pocket and sees it's Cami. When he answers it, his eyebrows lift. "Right now?"

I watch him as he starts the engine. "Okay, we'll be right there."

He ends the call. "Cami's water broke, and they're heading to the hospital now."

"Oh my God, really?" I ask, excited that I'll meet my niece today.

He nods. "Yeah, but we've got time to finish what we started."

"You're sure? I swear to God if I'm not there..."

"Yep," he tells me, his hand returning inside my panties. I slide my jeans down, giving him more access. My eye rolls in the back of my head when he inserts two fingers. I'm so worked up, it takes zero time before I'm losing myself.

On the way to the hospital, I'm giddy as hell. Eli has been keeping us updated.

"Your parents are there already," I tell him.

"We should probably wait until the baby has arrived before we show up. I'm sure Cami's overwhelmed enough already," he suggests.

I give him a pouty face, but I know he's right.

Instead of rushing there, we decide to stop and grab turkey wraps from a little deli down the street from the hospital.

"This is really good," I say around a mouthful.

Ryan chuckles. "I know. I've eaten here probably a thousand times. It's an enjoyable walk from the hospital. Gives me time to clear my head if something goes wrong."

I give him a smile. "Hopefully that doesn't happen too much."

He reaches across the table. "Not too much. You keep me grounded, Kendall. You give me something to look forward to and live for each day."

My heart melts. "I love you so much."

"I love you too, Angel."

After we finish eating, we get a message from Eli that Cami's fully dilated and starting to push. We walk over there as fast as we can.

The waiting room is bare other than Mr. and Mrs. St. James

and Eli's parents. Of course we say our hellos, then Clara starts in on Ryan and me.

"So as soon as the wedding is over, I expect another grandchild."

Ryan groans as I loop my arm with his and lean into him.

"Don't worry," I offer. "Cami and I always talked about our kids growing up together. Trust me when I say we'll try right away." I shoot her a wink, and it seems to appease her for now. She excuses herself and gets up to grab some coffee.

Ryan laughs. "Well, if there's any woman in the world that I want to give children to, it's you."

"I'm looking forward to it," I admit, leaning in and giving him a kiss on the cheek.

"You two are perfect together," his mom says, returning with a Styrofoam cup. "Happy you found each other."

After another hour of making small talk with everyone, Eli bursts in and announces the baby is here.

"Oh my gosh, congratulations!" I wrap my arms around him and ask how Cami and the baby are.

"They're doing great. I have to go back to them, but I just wanted to tell you guys. You'll be able to come in shortly."

Eli gives his mother a kiss on the cheek before walking back through the doors. We sit and wait until we're told she's ready for visitors.

"Did you mean it?" Ryan asks. "About kids?"

"Absolutely. I can't wait to start a family with you, baby. You're going to make such an amazing father. And I'm convinced we're going to have gorgeous children."

He leans over and presses his lips against mine.

"Only a few more months until the wedding!" I remind him. "Then we can get to baby-making."

A half an hour passes before Eli sends us a message with Cami's room number and says we're allowed to come in. We tell Cami's parents and let them go in first to meet their first grandchild. They return after twenty minutes and say their goodbyes on their way out.

When we enter, I immediately rush over to Cami and give her a gentle hug.

"How are you feeling, mama?" I ask as I gaze down at the precious bundle in her arms.

"Well…like I just pushed a ten-pound bowling ball out of my vagina." She laughs.

"Ouch," Ryan mutters.

Eli laughs. "Imagine witnessing it."

"Oh my God, stop…don't make me laugh, it hurts!" Cami scolds him.

"Wanna hold her?" Cami looks at Ryan. "Come meet your niece."

Ryan comes over and carefully takes her, then holds her against his chest. My heart and ovaries nearly explode.

"What's her name?" I ask.

"Laney Grace," Cami responds.

"Oh, I love that so much!"

"Hey, Laney," Ryan says so sweetly, looking at her with so much adoration. "She's beautiful," he says.

Cami and Eli talk while I watch Ryan with Laney. "Wanna hold her?" he asks me.

"Yes, of course."

I smile as Ryan passes her to me. She's so tiny and precious. "Hello, sweet baby girl. It's nice to finally meet you. I'm your aunt Kendall. Guess you're getting that lambo after all."

Ryan chuckles beside me. After a few more minutes, I hand her off to Eli.

"Fatherhood looks good on you," I taunt.

Cami pipes in. "Right? So sexy!"

I go over to her and notice how tired she looks. "So on a scale from one to ten, how painful was it?"

"Right now, I'd say a four, but ask me tomorrow. The meds

they gave me worked pretty great," she says with a smile. "The aftercare, that's a different story."

"So you're saying adoption is the way to go?" I chuckle, already nervous about the stages of pregnancy and giving birth.

"Don't worry, the pain could be a ten and still worth it in the end," Cami says.

"I have no doubt." I smile, gazing over at Eli and Laney.

"I'm so happy you came." Cami takes my hand and squeezes.

"I wouldn't miss this moment for the world." I squeeze hers back.

Ryan notices how exhausted Cami is and immediately switches into doctor mode. "You need to get plenty of rest and walk around a little when you're able to so—"

I cut in when Cami's eyes start to roll. "—and we'll let you get some sleep and visit you tomorrow. I'm going to drag him out of here before he starts ordering you around." I give her a wink. "Eli can handle this."

"That's right," he tells Ryan with a pat on the back.

"If you need anything at all, call us," Ryan offers. "My shift starts at five, and I'll be here within minutes. I mean it, anything at all."

"Thanks, man," Eli says with a grin I don't think has faded since we entered.

We say our goodbyes and walk back to the Range Rover.

"Laney is already so loved. She has the best parents in the world. Cami's gonna be an incredible mom," I say as I buckle in. "I mean, she already is. And Eli. Oh my God, that kid won the parent lottery."

Ryan squeezes my thigh. "That's going to be us one day."

"It will, and I know our kids are going to get the very best of us. They'll be smart and generous like you."

"And talented and beautiful like you," he finishes.

As he turns on to the street, I daydream about our future and can't wait to start our forever.

Only three months until we say I Do.

EPILOGUE

RYAN

THREE MONTHS LATER

MY FACE HURTS from smiling so damn much. The ceremony seemed to pass by in a blink, and the only thing I remember is being able to finally kiss my *wife*. Though the chapel was full of people, at that moment, it was only Kendall and me in the room. My heart overflows with love to everyone who's made this day special for us.

After we finish taking photos, the wedding party enters the reception hall. Before we make our grand entrance as husband and wife, I move closer to Kendall. She smiles up at me with bright eyes. I brush my thumb across her cheek. "You're finally mine, Kendall St. James."

"I've been yours. Always," she reminds me.

I take the opportunity to kiss her. She lets out a light moan as the doors open, and Stephanie tells us we can now enter.

"I can't wait until we leave," I say with a wink as we walk forward.

"Same," she replies as we're escorted inside. Our guests applaud and scream as we make our way to the middle of the dance floor. As soon as the notes to "Consider Me" by Allen Stone play, I pull Kendall close, and we sway to the beat of the music. I can't stop staring at this gorgeous woman who I'm going to spend the rest of my life with. When I spin her around and dip her, the moment grows more magical. The lights dim, and the dance floor casts a soft glow. I place my forehead against hers.

"I love you so much," I whisper. "You've made me the happiest man in the world."

"Love you more." She smirks.

The music fades out, and then I hand Kendall off to her father just as my mom walks up. I pull her into my arms and smile. A tear spills down her cheek, but I can tell she's happy.

"Now both of my kids are married with families of their own."

I chuckle. "Don't worry, when we have kids, we'll let you babysit as much as you want."

"Good! I'm so happy for you and Kendall. I can tell how much she means to you and the vows you wrote to one another...I wish I would've had a warning. I cried through the entire ceremony." She grins, and I spin her around. When I do, I catch a glimpse of Kendall, and she immediately meets my gaze. I shoot her a wink, and she gives me a smirk.

The song ends, and as soon as it does, Cami and Eli force Kendall and me to eat. It's some fancy chicken Florentine dish, and I didn't realize how hungry I was until I cleared my plate. I feel like a ping pong ball being bounced around everywhere. Just as we're done eating and start making our rounds again, Piper walks up to us, giddy as can be, and we exchange hugs.

"Everything has been perfect," Piper says. "Look at you two. Gah, I can't wait to find love like this."

Kendall snorts. "It wasn't butterflies and rainbows, but it was worth it."

A man dressed in black stands behind Piper, watching her. "Who's that?" I ask.

"Oh him? It's my bodyguard, Tristan."

"She's kinda a big deal," Kendall tells me with a laugh. "My famous sister."

"Famous? Pfft. Before I forget, I think we should have a celebration shot! What would you two like?" She quickly changes the subject, but I don't think Kendall notices.

"Anything," Kendall tells her.

"Surprise us," I say.

Piper shakes her head, wearing a sneaky grin. "Shoulda never told me that. I'll be right back."

She walks away, and Kendall turns to me. "I can't believe she still has a personal bodyguard. It's been six months. I'm kinda surprised she brought him to the wedding since we already have security here. Do you think there's something to worry about?" Kendall seems concerned about this, so I try to ease her worry.

I place my hands on her back and graze my hand across her soft skin. "I'm sure it's nothing. Your parents are protective of you both. There's a lot of security here. Did you see them all?"

"Kinda," she says, glancing toward the door. At every entrance stands a man dressed in black. This place is guarded like the White House. Before I can say anything else, Piper returns with our shots.

"So when are we cutting the cake? That thing is gigantic. I don't think I've ever seen one that tall before. It has lights, Kendall. I mean, I saw the picture you texted me, but it literally didn't do it any justice. I'm surprised it's not surrounded by a moat of champagne." She snickers.

"That would've been a good idea, though," Kendall says as Piper hands us the glasses. "I almost thought about getting one with diamonds and gold, but Ryan would've lost his shit on me."

"We don't need to eat a multimillion-dollar cake. It all comes out the same, if you know what I mean."

Piper laughs, and Kendall playfully rolls her eyes. The cake was still expensive, but nothing like what it could've been, and I know it'll still taste amazing.

"What is this?" I smell the shot, and it's scented like rubbing alcohol and cranberry juice.

"It's called Death by Sex," she barely gets out before laughing. "'Cause I'm sure that will be you two later tonight."

"God, I hope so," Kendall tells her, biting her lip when she looks at me.

Piper holds up her glass. "To the happy couple! So excited you're finally getting your happily ever afters."

We shoot them down, and I'm shocked it doesn't burn.

"That was really good," Kendall exclaims.

"So when are we finally cutting that giant-ass cake?" Piper asks again, and Kendall explains the itinerary. I glance at her bodyguard again and notice he's speaking into an earpiece. He grits his teeth, then meets my eyes. I give him a head nod, but he's all business. The man actually looks like he could break bones with his bare hands.

After a few minutes, Kendall and I are interrupted by family, then Piper excuses herself. I watch as she meets up with Tristan, and they make their way through the crowd. He moves closer to her, guiding her around people, constantly scanning the crowd.

Once she's out of sight and we're finally alone, I pull Kendall close and kiss the hell out of her. My entire body is on fire, and I need her more than I need air. The anticipation of tonight is almost too much to handle, but I know it'll be worth it.

"Looking forward to peeling this dress off your body later," I whisper in her ear.

"Can't wait for you to see what I'm wearing underneath."

I lift an eyebrow and bite my lip. "Fuck, you're such a tease." But I love it.

Stephanie comes over and tells us it's time to cut the cake, and Kendall nearly jumps out of her skin with excitement.

We're escorted over to that area, and it's the first time I've gotten a good look at the sugary masterpiece. The photographer snaps pictures of us standing beside it, and I almost feel guilty cutting into it.

We're placed in poses with the knife, and soon, we're placing slices in each other's mouths. Kendall makes sure to suck all the icing off my finger, and I swear to god, she did that shit on purpose. The smirk on her face gives her away. As I watch her laugh, I wonder how I got so damn lucky.

KENDALL

Since I was a little girl, I've dreamed about my wedding day. The ceremony and reception have exceeded my expectations. Ryan has too. Before my father escorted me out, my mother delivered a pair of diamond earrings that Ryan had made from my grandmother's jewelry. I cried, and thankfully, Piper and Cami were there to catch my tears with tissues before I ruined my makeup.

The entire week, I've been full of nervous excitement. To keep up with tradition, I made sure we did the rehearsal dinner two days before and stayed at a hotel last night. The first time Ryan saw me in over twenty-four hours was when I walked out to be his forever. We wrote our own wedding vows, and his words hit me in the heart. Being snowed in with him changed my life, and I owe Mother Nature a big thank you.

After we've cut the cake, Ryan leads me onto the dance floor. His strong hands pull me close, and I wrap my arms around his neck.

"I think I'm going to have to go to the bathroom soon. My bladder is so full," I admit when he spins me around for the second time.

Ryan chuckles and trails kisses across my neck. "I'll find Cami. There's no way you're getting out of that dress on your own."

"No kidding. It's practically glued to my body."

He lifts a brow. "I know, glad I put a ring on it so everyone in the world knows you're *mine*."

"Trust me, everyone knew before that."

Lifting my chin, Ryan looks into my eyes, then kisses me. I melt into him, wishing we didn't have so many people watching us right now. Right as the song ends, I spot Cami as she's handing

Laney over to her mother. Ryan waves her over, and immediately Cami is beside me.

"I have to use the bathroom and need your help," I whisper.

"Of course!" Cami says and escorts me across the large venue to the restrooms.

"I've been holding it for nearly thirty minutes." I let out a relieved breath.

"You should've found me sooner. I would've helped right away," she scolds, then turns me around and undoes the buttons leading down my back because sitting in this thing isn't easy. Once I'm free, I breathe for the first time since I put it on.

"I don't think I could've lived in the olden days. The dress is beautiful, but I can't say it's the most comfortable thing I've ever worn."

"I know, I felt the same way." Cami snickers, then bends over and grabs the extra fabric and holds it in her arms as we walk to the biggest stall. She turns her back as I finally go.

"I'm so damn happy," I tell her with a sigh. "Today has been perfect."

"It truly has! Now you're officially a St. James and my sister for life," she says, then helps me stand.

"It certainly has a ring to it," I sing-song as we walk out of the stall, and she buttons me back into my dress.

"Right! I'm happy to have taken Eli's last name, but St. James just sounds...elegant."

We laugh, then notice the music suddenly stops, and we hear a commotion.

"What is going on?" We rush out of the bathroom and make our way back to the ballroom and see everything's in complete chaos.

I rush around, looking for Ryan as people head toward the exit. Panic streams through me when I see the expression on Ryan's face. He comes to me and pulls me into his arms for a hug.

"What the hell happened?" Cami bursts out.

"It all happened so fast." Ryan shakes his head.

"What did?" I panic.

"Someone got past security and tried to grab your sister. There was a fight, and the next thing I saw was a gun."

"A gun?" Immediately, my emotions get the best of me. "Where's Piper now?"

Ryan opens his mouth, then closes it.

Eli comes over with Laney in his arms and tells Cami they have to go. She gives me a tight hug. "I'm so sorry. Text me as soon as you know anything, okay?"

Once they're gone, I look back at Ryan, and ask again, "Where is she?"

"I don't know, baby. One second she was there, then the next she wasn't," he explains. I look past him and see my parents speaking to the police. My mother is frantic, and my father looks enraged. This definitely can't be good.

I rush over as Ryan follows me.

"What happened?" I interrupt as my father continues his conversation. My mom takes me over to the side. "I'm so sorry this ruined your night, sweetie."

"Someone better tell me what's going on right now!" I demand, growing more frustrated.

"Someone tried to attack Piper. Tristan took her. She's okay."

Relief floods through me. "Thank God he was here."

"He was instructed not to take his eyes off her."

"Why? Did something else happen?"

"She's been getting death threats. Her stalker somehow hacked into her cell phone and was able to track her. The police have been involved, but they haven't been able to track him down to arrest him."

"Jesus," I hiss. "I hadn't realized it'd gotten so much worse."

"No one wanted to worry you. I wanted this day to be so special for you and now look at it." A tear streams down her face, and I wrap her in a hug.

"It was perfect. I'm fine. Seriously, I'm more concerned about my sister than any of that. Do you know where Tristan took her?"

241

Mom shakes her head. "Tristan will let us know when they're in a safe place. For now, it's too risky with the stalker on the loose."

"They didn't get him tonight?" Ryan asks.

"Unfortunately, not." Dad frowns, but I can tell he's heated. "As soon as Tristan drew his weapon, the asshole bailed, and the police couldn't catch up to him."

"How's that possible?" Ryan asks the same question I had. "He can't be that fast."

"He is," Mom clarifies. "Always one step ahead of us and gone before anyone can get him."

That makes me worried even more. "I hope Tristan takes her far from here then, somewhere the little fucker can't find her."

"He will, trust me. He's military trained."

"What's his motive? To kidnap and kill her?" I ask. "For what?"

"I don't know, sweetie. He's been obsessed with Piper for months," Mom explains. "It started with a ton of emails and comments on her videos, then exploded to tracking her down and threatening her life."

A chill runs down my spine, and Ryan rubs his palms down my arms.

"I think it's best if we get this place cleared out," Dad suggests. "For the safety of our family and friends."

Most people are gone by now, but security empties the venue. I look around the reception area that was once full of smiling faces. Empty champagne glasses are scattered around, proof that people were having a good time.

Ryan pulls me tight. "I'm so sorry this happened."

I force a grin and suck in a deep breath. "It's not your fault. At least I know she's with someone who'll protect her. But I guess that means we get to start our honeymoon a little sooner."

"Hell yeah," he says, sliding his lips across mine. Ryan leads me to the limo waiting for us outside. My heart is heavy as we climb in. As excited as I am to spend the night with my husband, I'm worried about my sister's safety.

As we drive off, Ryan hands me my phone from his pocket.

Kendall: Mom and Dad told me what happened. Please tell me you're safe.

She immediately responds, which has me blowing out a breath of relief.

Piper: I'm with Tristan! I have to be careful what I say until I get a burner phone, but we're going into hiding. I'll be safe with him and will text you as soon as I can. I'm so sorry this happened on your special night. I love you guys!

Kendall: It's not your fault. I love you too! Text me and keep me updated when you're able to, please!

Piper: I will. Plus, it might not be so bad being locked up with my hot bodyguard ;)

Kendall: Don't say I didn't warn you before...don't get involved!

Piper: You're no fun!

I laugh, knowing she's going to do the exact opposite of what I tell her anyway.

Kendall: Love you, sis. Please stay safe.

"Well?" Ryan asks when I release a giggle.

"They're going somewhere undisclosed for now. She'll tell me when it's safe."

"Thank God. I hope they find the little bitch and put his ass away." Ryan groans.

"Me too." I sigh.

"Well, Mrs. St. James, hopefully, I can take your mind off all that as soon as we get home."

I laugh and curl into his arms. "I have no doubt you will, Mr. St. James."

This concludes Ryan & Kendall's romance and we hope you enjoyed it! Don't worry, you'll see glimpses of them soon.

Curious about what happens with Tristan and Piper?
Stay tuned for their story in *The End of Us*!

THE END OF US

Next in the Love in Isolation series is
Tristan & Piper's story!

**What happens when a stalker threatens your life and you're
thrown into hiding in the middle of nowhere with your sexy
new bodyguard? You break the rules and hope he falls madly in
love with you.**

*The End of Us is an opposites attract, forbidden, romantic suspense
standalone.*

ABOUT THE AUTHOR

Brooke Cumberland and Lyra Parish are a duo of romance authors who teamed up under the USA Today pseudonym, Kennedy Fox. They share a love of Hallmark movies, overpriced coffee, and making TikToks. When they aren't bonding over romantic comedies, they like to brainstorm new book ideas. One day in 2016, they decided to collaborate under a pseudonym and have some fun creating new characters that'll make you blush and your heart melt. Happily ever afters guaranteed!

CONNECT WITH US

Find us on our website:
kennedyfoxbooks.com

f facebook.com/kennedyfoxbooks

🐦 twitter.com/kennedyfoxbooks

📷 instagram.com/kennedyfoxbooks

a amazon.com/author/kennedyfoxbooks

g goodreads.com/kennedyfox

BB bookbub.com/authors/kennedy-fox

BOOKS BY
KENNEDY FOX

CHECKMATE DUET SERIES

BISHOP BROTHERS SERIES

BEDTIME READS SERIES

ROOMMATE DUET SERIES

CIRCLE B RANCH SERIES

EX-CON DUET SERIES

LOVE IN ISOLATION SERIES

Find the entire Kennedy Fox reading order at
Kennedyfoxbooks.com/reading-order

Find all of our current freebies at
Kennedyfoxbooks.com/freeromance

43596050R00152